Sword Art Online Alternative

# GUN GALE
# ONLINE
# I
## SQUAD JAM

## Keiichi Sigsawa

ILLUSTRATION BY
**Kouhaku Kuroboshi**

SUPERVISED BY
**Reki Kawahara**

SWORD ART ONLINE Alternative Gun Gale Online, Vol. 1
KEIICHI SIGSAWA

Translation by Stephen Paul
Cover art by Kouhaku Kuroboshi

SWORD ART ONLINE Alternative Gun Gale Online Vol. 1
©KEIICHI SIGSAWA 2014
First published in Japan in 2014 by KADOKAWA CORPORATION, Tokyo.
English translation rights arranged with KADOKAWA CORPORATION, Tokyo,
through TUTTLE-MORI AGENCY, INC., Tokyo.

English translation © 2018 by Yen Press, LLC

Yen On
1290 Avenue of the Americas
New York, NY 10104

Visit us at yenpress.com
facebook.com/yenpress
twitter.com/yenpress
yenpress.tumblr.com
instagram.com/yenpress

First Yen On Edition: June 2018

Yen On is an imprint of Yen Press, LLC.
The Yen On name and logo are trademarks of Yen Press, LLC.

Library of Congress Cataloging-in-Publication Data
Names: Sigsawa, Keiichi, 1972– author. | Kuroboshi, Kouhaku, illustrator. |
    Kawahara, Reki, supervisor. | Paul, Stephen (Translator), translator.
Title: Squad jam / Keiichi Sigsawa ; illustration by Kouhaku Kuroboshi ; supervised by
    Reki Kawahara ; translation by Stephen Paul ; cover art by Kouhaku Kuroboshi.
Description: First Yen On edition. | New York : Yen On, June 2018. |
    Series: Sword art online alternative gun gale online ; Volume 1
Identifiers: LCCN 2018009303 | ISBN 9781975327521 (paperback)
Subjects: | CYAC: Fantasy games—Fiction. | Virtual reality—Fiction. | Role
    playing—Fiction. | BISAC: FICTION / Science Fiction / Adventure.
Classification: LCC PZ7.1.S537 Sq 2018 | DDC [Fic]—dc23
LC record available at https://lccn.loc.gov/2018009303

ISBNs: 978-1-9753-2752-1 (paperback)
       978-1-9753-5389-6 (ebook)

10 9 8 7 6 5 4 3 2 1

LSC-C

Printed in the United States of America

Sword Art: Online Alternative
# GUN GALE
## ONLINE

Sword Art: Online Alternative
# Gun Gale Online
## I

### Squad Jam

**Keiichi Sigsawa**

ILLUSTRATION BY
**Kouhaku Kuroboshi**

SUPERVISED BY
**Reki Kawahara**

# CONTENTS

DESIGN: BEE-PEE

# THE 1st SQUAD JAM
# FIELD MAP

AREA 1

AREA 2

AREA 3

AREA 4

AREA 5

AREA 6

AREA 7

AREA 8

N

**AREA 1 :** Grassland

**AREA 2 :** Forest

**AREA 3 :** Marshland / Downed Spacecraft

**AREA 4 :** Residential

**AREA 5 :** City

**AREA 6 :** Lake

**AREA 7 :** Wasteland

**AREA 8 :** Desert

PROLOGUE

# PROLOGUE

"Oh yeah, Llenn."

"What is it, Pito?"

"Did you read that newsletter about a new tournament called Squad Jam? It got sent out this morning."

"……Jam…made of…squids?"

"Ewww! You just made me imagine that!"

"But wouldn't that just be squid *shiokara*? I mean, that's basically salted, blended squid guts, so…"

"Hmm… I suppose you're right about that."

"I actually like that stuff! Especially when you put it over fresh steamed rice!"

"I only eat it as a snack with drinks. But if anything, I prefer *shuto*, the pickled bonito version of this."

"Ooh, I love *shuto*! Did you know that means *sake thief*? I'd rather just steal the *shuto* instead!"

"Hang on… Do I recall correctly that you're still a minor IRL?"

"I don't actually drink alcohol with them, of course. I just like snacks that go with drinks. Whenever my dad or my brothers have drinks at home, they bring that stuff out."

"Oh, I see… So you have multiple brothers. There you go letting personal details slip out again, Llenn."

"Oops…"

"Look, I won't do anything with that knowledge, but you

should watch what you say here—especially girls like us. You'd be surprised how many people collect little bits of information or trick you into revealing something, then search that stuff online to find your identity."

"I'll do my best to be careful... I deeply appreciate the warning."

"There you go getting all formal on me again! None of that! We're all equals in this world! We talk as equals!"

"Got it, Pito!"

"Much better. Now, we were supposed to be discussing a tournament. What is wrong with us? Two girls hanging out in a virtual reality online game and chatting about fermented squid guts?!"

"Yeah, good question."

"While we stand with guns at the ready in a desert, no less."

"It's very odd."


Two women stood in a desert of rocks and sand.

In this world, the clouds choked the sky, turning the sunless atmosphere a yellow gradient. They didn't move, as there was no wind, but occasional flashes of distant lightning led to eerie rumbles in the background.

The earth consisted of brown sand and rocks of various sizes—some as large as boulders—that were steadily crumbling into the former. A cluster of high-rise buildings were barely visible in the distance, jutting askew from the ground in their ruined state.

Amid an environment that could only be described as desolate, the women sat at the foot of a car-sized rock, their legs extended.

"So...what's this squad thing?"

"I'm glad you asked!"

"Well, you brought it up first, Pito."

"Did I? Gosh, I think I've already forgotten about that."

"Ah, I see. So you're an old woman IRL."

"Oh no! I've been exposed!"

They chatted and laughed as though they were killing time on a

weekend at a restaurant—except that here, nobody was around to request they keep their voices down.

One of the two said, "Anyway, I'm not deliberately trying to cover it up—I mean, obviously I'm not going to divulge my exact age—but I'm really not that old, in truth. I'm just not one of those underage honeys like you, Llenn!"

"Um, Pito...nobody actually says the word 'honey' anymore. At least, nobody in college does."

"Boom! So you're in college! I had my suspicions, and now they're confirmed! Another detail uncovered!"

"Oh nooooo!"

Llenn wasn't really a woman as much as she was a girl; practically a child, in fact.

A child wearing all pink. Not the cute, peachy kind of pink, but a deeper one with hints of brown, to cut down on the brightness.

She was well under five feet tall and fragile in stature. Her round face was monopolized by two very large eyes, which only pushed her apparent age further downward.

Her hair was dark brown and cut in a tomboyish bob, atop which she wore a knit cap. Her whole outfit was pink. Both her top and bottom were fairly common combat wear—trousers like cargo pants and a long-sleeve combat shirt. Elongated pouches rested over both thighs, and short laced boots protected her feet.

"I'm serious, you've got to be more careful about this stuff, or I'll have you all figured out!"

"It's your fault for being so clever with your words, Pito! You con artist!"

"Aw, shucks."

"Huh? That wasn't a compliment."

"It wasn't? But you're going to praise me, right?"

"That wasn't my intention, no."

"Aw. But I'm the type who does better once I've been flattered."

"You do know that's the kind of thing other people are supposed to say about you, right?"

The other woman in the pair, Pito, was dressed all in black.

She looked much older, in her late twenties. She had tan skin and sharp features—pretty, to be certain, but the brick-red geometric tattoos on either cheek stretching toward her neck gave her a dangerous vibe.

She was tall, easily over five foot eight, with long hair tied into a simple high ponytail.

Her outfit was a navy-blue so dark, it looked almost black. As the skintight profile made extremely clear, her figure contained none of the stereotypical feminine beauty. It was like a muscle model, the kind of sharply silhouetted body one might assume belonged to an android rather than a human.

On her feet were black boots, on her waist was a military belt, and running from her sides to her back were vertical magazine pouches.

There was one thing both had in common: guns.

The girl in pink was equipped with a P90 from the Belgian manufacturer FN Herstal, a gun about twenty inches long. It was an odd weapon that didn't look like a typical firearm, more like a rectangular box with a grip cut out of the middle to grab.

The bullets were visible from the clear plastic clip, which slotted onto the top of the gun's frame. It held a full fifty rounds, making it one of the largest magazines not made for machine guns.

Like her clothes, the P90 was colored smoky pink, which, combined with the strange shape of the gun, made it look like a toy. She was like a kid on Christmas carrying a present in bright wrapping paper.

The taller woman in black had propped her assault rifle against the rock next to her. It was a Russian AK-47, one of the most recognizable guns in the world, equipped with a curving magazine holding thirty rounds of 7.62 × 39 mm ammo.

"Listen, Llenn. Complimenting others is the very bedrock of flirting techniques."

"I-I'm not trying to become a master flirt!"

"What? Don't you want a girlfriend?"

"Nope. I'm already a girl."

"You really shouldn't get all hung up on the little stuff, like whether someone's a man or a woman."

"I would think that's the *most* important part."

Just before the woman in black and girl in pink could really dig into their latest point of discussion, a muffled explosion burst into the world.

The instant the ground rumbled, they leaped to their feet and yelled "Got 'em!" in unison. The woman opened fire with her AK-47, and the girl did the same with her P90, while they cried "Get 'em!" again in unison, leaping out from either side of the rock they'd been hiding behind.

About fifty yards away, a plume of dust was quietly falling back to the dunes after the underground explosive had blown it sky-high. Without any wind to stir it, the cloud cleared very gradually.

In the middle of the dust was the victim of their trap, an enormous worm monster over a foot thick and nearly five yards long. It was writhing and buffeting the earth as red light spilled out of it from all over.

"I'll back you up! Empty that magazine!" commanded the woman, who was a fifth of the way to the beast already, her AK-47 propped against her right shoulder.

"Roger!" replied the pink girl, who sped even faster.

The AK-47 howled, gunfire rattling the air. A hail of 7.62 × 39 mm rounds sank into the agonized earthworm in semiautomatic rhythm.

The dull-green cartridges that ejected from the right side of her rifle bounced off the sand, then flashed and vanished from the world forever.

To the side of that gunfire and nearly as fast as the bullets whizzing by, the girl hurtled in a forward lean, P90 on her shoulder. She unleashed the weapon on full auto. Its drumroll percussion joined the AK-47's rhythm.

"Yaaah!"

5.7 × 28 mm bullets shot from the P90 and tore holes in the giant earthworm. Little gold cartridges poured out of the bottom of the gun in a torrent. The agonized worm opened its mouth, splitting its head into two, and issued a creepy roar.

"Here comes the tail attack!" the woman in black yelled, halting her AK fire.

"Roger!" said the pink girl, who continued her charge. She took her left hand off the P90 and thrust it into the pouch on her left thigh, pulling out a new clip. The earthworm undulated, whipping its tail toward the approaching girl.

"Haah!" she cried as she leaped, spraying sand behind her. The jump launched her easily over six feet into the air.

The giant earthworm's tail swung through nothing, and above it, the girl switched out the old magazine, boldly discarding the eight shots left in it, and slammed the new one into the slot with robotic efficiency.

"Yah!" She landed light on her feet and made a broom-sweeping motion over the worm just below her reach, unloading the magazine mercilessly into her target.

Three seconds later, the red light stopped pouring from the holes all over the worm monster's body, and it burst into tiny glowing shards that vanished without a trace.

"So, uh…what were we talking about while we were waiting for the trap?" the woman in black asked.

The girl in pink responded, "It was some kind of squid tournament, right? You always forget what you're talking about when you're the one who brought it up in the first place, Pito."

Under the eerie, rolling sky, the two women slung their guns over their shoulders and strolled through the desert. It was almost like watching a mother and daughter going on a walk, if one ignored the deadly environment and guns.

"Oh, right, right. I remember that you admitted you had multiple older brothers and that you're in college now."

"Okay, so forget all that stuff and tell me more about these squids," the girl said, her boots compressing the desert sand.

"I said *squad*, not squid. Do you know the difference? Are you a STEM student? What's your major?"

"Huh? I'm a… I'm not telling you."

"Oh, you didn't fall for it this time. You're learning! I'm so proud of you."

"So anyway, what's this about squads?"

"It's referring to the military definition, of course. You know, companies, platoons, battalions? The squad is the smallest grouping of soldiers, usually around ten."

"Hmm… And what's the jam for?"

"It's not for your toast—it's more in the sense of like a traffic jam. To jam stuff together."

"Yeah, I know. Same definition as when your gun doesn't work because the cartridge or bullet gets stuck. It jams, right?"

"Exactly. Ooh, I should have thought of that one first."

"So…it's a 'big mess of squads'?"

"Indeed. Or in other words…"

"In other words?"

"The Squad Jam is a *Gun Gale Online* tournament where a bunch of squads get together and have a battle royale to determine who's the best."

# CHAPTER 1

## SECT.1

Karen's Melancholy

# CHAPTER 1
## Karen's Melancholy

When Karen Kohiruimaki returned to the real world, the thin digital clock on her wall indicated it was 5:49 PM on Sunday, January 18th, 2026.

Her apartment was devoid of human presence. The compact bedroom connected to a larger living room through a sliding doorway. The windows were dark after the sun had set, so only the LED hanging from the ceiling offered any illumination.

The walls were all painted a soft white. A thick cream-colored rug decorated the living room, the center of which featured a large, low table and cushions. A full-length mirror stood in the corner.

The bookshelf along the wall was packed with texts and reference books, painstakingly ordered by subject. The orderly interior spoke volumes about its resident's personality.

The bedroom, which was currently open to the living room via the sliding door, featured a low wooden bed and a wide dresser on the wall opposite the window.

Karen sat up in her bed and removed the AmuSphere—the device on her head that covered her face and sent all her senses into the virtual world—then laid it carefully on the right side of her pillow.

Wearing pale-yellow pajamas, she spun her legs over the left side of her bed, letting her feet touch the ground, and stretched

her left hand toward the wall. The sensors recognized her movement and slowly powered up the room.

After allowing her eyes a few seconds to adjust to the light,
Karen got to her feet. With two barefoot steps, she reached the living room. A clothing rack was next to the standing mirror—and it
included one object that was definitely not clothing.

Karen grabbed it and faced the mirror.

"…"

There she saw herself, a grumpy-looking reflection.

A girl with long black hair who stood six feet tall.

She held a black plastic air gun, the same P90 she'd clutched
just moments ago—but it appeared much smaller now.

Slowly, Karen's lips moved. "Squad Jam… Should I even
bother? A team PvP battle… I don't know if I feel up to that…"

✳        ✳        ✳

Karen Kohiruimaki grew up without wanting for anything.

Her parents were originally from Aomori Prefecture before
moving across the Tsugaru Strait to Hokkaido, where they started
a successful business. Fertility smiled upon them as well, giving them two sons, two daughters, and then, on April 20th, 2006,
their last child, Karen.

And so, in a large and comfortable home in the north, it was
under the doting eye of her parents and much older siblings that
the precious baby Karen grew. And grew. And grew. And grew.

Her growth spurt started in third grade, and by the time she was
entering middle school, Karen was already five foot seven. She'd
prayed and prayed that her height wouldn't climb any higher, but
God gave no inclination that he was listening.

Instead, she kept growing right through middle school, and
now that she was nineteen, she stood at six feet tall. Maybe that
wouldn't be so rare in other countries, but this was Japan.

Her family and close friends understood how Karen felt, so
they never mentioned her height, but the ordinary people of

society were not so considerate. In middle and high school, she was inundated with requests and invitations from school sports clubs, which she had no real desire to join. She knew when someone was asking her merely because she seemed to have aptitude for the sport, but they didn't care how *she* felt about it. She didn't like that.

When walking in public, she was often described by others as the "giant woman," and there were surprisingly many who insulted her loudly enough that they intended her to hear it.

No matter how much this upset her, there was nothing she could do about it. Her personal complex about her height changed her during puberty. Little Karen was the very picture of innocence and liveliness, such that she could often be confused for a rambunctious little boy. And now she hardly ever spoke a word to anyone she didn't know closely, looking inward for her personal pleasures, like reading and listening to music.

She even grew out her hair, hoping it might somehow make her more girlish, but that only resulted in her losing track of when to cut it, and she ended up with so much hair that managing it all in the morning was a pain.

Being tall took a toll on her wardrobe, too. Karen gave up on the idea of feminine fashion and turned to rougher and simpler outfits.

One year ago, Karen graduated high school and moved to Tokyo. Her original plan was to go to a local college, but she'd taken a flyer for one of the most prestigious women's schools in Japan, which happened to accept her. Her parents had been delighted and arranged for her to stay in a unit at the luxury apartment building where Karen's eldest sister and her husband lived.

In April of 2025, Karen began life on her own in the big city, hoping that a new place might change something for her.

However, once she started at the prestigious women's college, she found more of the same.

Given her age, she at least didn't have to worry about other people teasing her directly anymore, but Karen was otherwise

ill-suited to the traditional benefits of the typical college life: try-ing out new fashions, participating in clubs, going on dates, and so on.

On top of that, this college was an escalator school, meaning most of the students had come up through its attached primary and secondary schools. So she didn't make any new friends she could truly open up to—although some of that blame was on Karen, who was introverted and didn't make efforts to reach out to others.

Her daily schedule consisted of attending class, eating lunch alone, listening to music with her earbuds during her break time, returning to the apartment, and spending her free time alone there. The only people she interacted with were her family and friends back home. The only people she spoke to in person were her sister's family members, when she was invited over for dinner with her niece. Her parents forbade her from taking a part-time job and sent her an ample allowance she couldn't possibly burn through.

She began worrying that if she didn't learn to be more social, she'd start to forget how to interact with other people altogether. Then, when she was back home for summer vacation, a particular news article on the Internet caught her eye:

*Virtual reality (VR) games make a massive comeback—desire from the public to enjoy a different life is still strong.*

VR technology allowed the user to experience total sensory immersion by placing a special device on one's head that deliv-ered electronic signals to and from the brain. Thus, a VR game used this full-dive technology to bring together multiple players into the same perceived space over the Internet.

Karen was familiar with the concept; nearly everyone in Japan was. The technology had been at the center of an incident that had shocked the entire nation, perhaps the world, when she was in her first year of high school, in November 2022.

*Sword Art Online*, often known as *SAO*.

The world's first VRMMORPG (virtual reality massively

multiplayer online role-playing game) had turned into a horrifying nightmare through the malice of its genius developer.

The ten thousand players who first logged in on its launch day found themselves trapped inside the VR world, unable to leave the game of their own accord. Even worse, if their in-game characters died, or if someone attempted to force the device off a player's head, the device would output microwaves that fried the user's brain and killed them. It had become a deadly game—literally.

The incident was constant headline news right after the crisis began, but the days kept passing without a solution. Each time a new victim died, everyone heard the familiar and dispiriting refrain of the news cycle. Eventually, the incident simply faded from memory, except for those poor souls whose loved ones were still trapped inside.

Two years later, in November 2024, while Karen was cramming for her college entrance exams, *SAO* became major news again. This time it was good: The people trapped in the game of death were finally free.

Ultimately, however, four thousand lives had been lost, and *SAO* was forever known as the deadliest video game in history.

But only those who already hated the idea of VR games actually thought this would be the end of those dangerous things. Even while some players were still captive in *SAO*, plans for a new device—"It's safe this time!"—were drawn up and brought to market, along with new games.

The article stated, *As of the summer of 2025, the number of VR games continues to rise. The player population is exploding at such a pace that it almost appears as though the traumatic incident of the recent past never happened.*

*These games provide more real sensory simulations of life than ever before, allowing users to experience a 'different self,' but is this really healthy in a humanistic sense? If you want to feel something with all your senses, get off your computer and do what we used to tell children in the old days: Venture outside.*

*If our children are raised in virtual worlds with no sense of real pain, is it possible that they might go on to commit crimes, the likes of which we adults can never imagine? A much-needed rational debate is waiting to be held.*

The article was openly critical of VR games and dripping with the author's bias and distaste, but it had actually stoked the opposite opinion in Karen.

"A different self…"

*Maybe*, she'd thought, *if I play a different person in a game, I might start conversations with other people more often. Maybe it could work as a kind of therapy or social rehabilitation for real life.*

She'd never had any interest in VR before then, but now she had a purpose. When she learned that one of her few friends from back home had VR experience, she went to go ask her about it.

Miyu had said, "Oh my gosh! I'd love to have another friend to play with!"

She'd enthusiastically taught Karen all about it. Soon it became clear that current VR games had none of the danger of *SAO*. She decided to try it out.

There was no reason to waste any time once she'd made up her mind about it, and her stuffy old parents weren't likely to look kindly upon such activities at home, so Karen ended her vacation early and went back to Tokyo. She'd visited an electronics store immediately after landing at Haneda Airport and procured all the essentials for the activity.

First up was the AmuSphere, which resembled a giant set of silver goggles. The device blocked all organic senses and sent only the artificial ones into the user's brain. In other words, Karen would be in something like a coma while operating it, although the AmuSphere did have several safety measures.

While it shut out her real senses, it also monitored them. If the device detected the user's heart rate rising abnormally, drastic slowness of breathing, or the presence of a headache or stomach

pains, its automatic shutdown features would kick in—and they were impossible to remove or override.

The AmuSphere also connected to real-world home security features like home invasion and fire alarms, as well as emergency services such as earthquake and tsunami alerts, to ensure that it shut down when necessary.

Karen had also bought a game. Out of all the VR games available, she picked *ALfheim Online* (*ALO*), which Miyu already played. It was set in a fantasy world, where players turned into winged fairies and went on adventures together.

"You'll love it, Kohi! Yeah, it gets a little dicey when the various races fight it out, but you don't have to do that stuff if you don't want to. It's super-fun just flying around in this beautiful world and chatting with everybody!" Miyu assured her.

Sure enough, the sample screenshots on the package promised a gorgeous world of dazzling green forests and deep-blue skies and lakes. If it was that pretty to look at in pictures, surely *being there* would feel a million times better. Her heart soared at the thought of being able to fly with her own set of wings.

With Miyu's help over the phone, Karen set up the AmuSphere with her computer and finally made the very first full dive of her life. She'd changed into pajamas, closed the curtains, and turned on her air conditioner, as these made for the most comfortable conditions, apparently.

Then she put the plugged-in AmuSphere on her head, lay down on the bed, and closed her eyes.

"Link Start!"

The vocal command instantly took Karen's mind to another world.

First, there was the sensation of leaving the body, like drifting off to sleep, then suddenly she was standing in darkness and receiving voiced instructions.

She knew it wasn't the real world, but her wits were quite sharp. It was like a waking dream, where she knew it was a dream while it was happening around her.

With her heart racing in excitement, Karen followed the instructions and began to type the required information into the floating keyboard before her.

For her character name, she'd taken the *ren* from her name and tweaked some of the letters to ensure it didn't match the name of any other player, doubling the consonants and putting it in all caps: LLENN.

She had the choice of nine different fairy races, but she wanted to play with Miyu, so she selected sylph, the wind fairy. Since each race started in its own territory, this would make it easy for her to meet up with Miyu right away.

Once Karen had become Llenn, she stepped into the world of *ALO*…

"Wh-whyyy?!"

…and screamed.

"I'm sorry, Kohi! I completely forgot you have that thing about your height," Miyu apologized over the phone. But the fact that the avatar Karen wound up with—which was generated at random by the game system—happened to be noticeably taller than the others of the sylph race wasn't Miyu's fault at all.

The shock of seeing herself in a mirror sent Karen's pulse racing, kicking in the AmuSphere's safety measures and automatically unlinking her from the program barely twenty seconds after she started the game.

"Listen… I know that must've been horrible, but there are races with much smaller avatars on average… The cait siths are cat fairies, for example… Why don't you try rolling a fresh character? It's a charged micro-transaction, unfortunately…"

Karen declined Miyu's offer. It wasn't an issue of money.

The shock of being very tall, even as the result of a random roll, had immediately soured her on the entire concept of *ALO*. She still wanted to try VR games, but she was not going back to that one. So she apologized to Miyu for the bad news, after all her friend's help.

"I see... Well, that's too bad, but I guess I can't blame you. That stubbornness of yours is one of your strengths, in my opinion," her old friend said. Then she asked, "Kohi, are you familiar with character conversion?"

That referred to the act of moving the Llenn character she had just created to a different VR game. All the VR games in existence were based on the same foundational system: an engine known as The Seed. All a player needed to move characters around was a simple user ID, and the strength of the character would be converted and preserved in the new game.

For example, if a character that had been painstakingly built to have great physical strength was converted to another game, it would start that new game in a powerful form already. The original would be destroyed, and all items and in-game money lost, but that meant nothing to Karen, of course. Best of all, the ID she had created wouldn't go to waste that way.

This was her shot to get the avatar she really wanted.

"Yeah, it'll be a different game, but feel free to ask me for help if you have any questions! The next time I try to get live tickets to an Elza Kanzaki concert in Tokyo, I'm going to stay with you as payment for all this help, okay?" Miyu said, and Karen promised to do her that favor.

Afterward, Karen used that ID to connect to various VR worlds, converting her character each and every time. Of course, that meant buying a whole new game each time, so she started out with choosing those with a trial period so she could first test them for free.

She didn't care about the genre. There were VR games of every kind imaginable.

Racing games that put players in the driver's seat. Flight simulators that allowed anyone to fly an airplane. Sci-fi adventures in which characters cruised around the galaxy. Virtual versions of any sport one wanted to play. Romance games with beautiful women and girls to woo. Even some that just simulated a "normal" day.

Once she started trying out all the different VR games on the market, Karen decided to switch to a new game any time she found the slightest flaw in the avatar she rolled. Miyu found this stubbornness exasperating, but she didn't give Karen a hard time about it.

A few days later...
"I found you!" Llenn exclaimed at the starting area of another new VR game.
She'd screamed it, in fact.
She was in a world with an eerie, apocalyptic sky and jutting ruins of metallic skyscrapers overhead, staring into the mirrored glass exterior of one such building and proclaiming, "I found you... I finally found you!"
She stared at the person in her reflection—not even five feet tall and dressed in green battle fatigues.
"I found you!"
She was a little girl.

At last, Llenn had found the game she would call her home:
*Gun Gale Online.*
As the name suggested, it was a world of guns, where players engaged in shoot-outs amid postapocalyptic wasteland scenery.

\*      \*      \*

November 2025.
Three months had passed since she started playing the game. Winter had come to Tokyo.
Karen had few hobbies, no friends in Tokyo, no school club activities, and no permission to take a job, so she went to class every day, studied and completed her assignments, and had plenty of time for the game in between.

In keeping with her regimented personality, Karen had decided how many hours she'd spend in *GGO* on weekdays and how many she'd spend there on her free days. She limited her time before tests.

Like Miyu had said, VR games were beautifully constructed virtual spaces. They were just like real life in their use of all the bodily senses, but virtual was still virtual. It wasn't possible to match the sheer amount of information in real life, so there was never a moment where she asked herself, *Wait, which side am I on now?*

Or in other words, she never had to question which of the two was reality, which, in Karen's mind, perhaps meant that this game was carefully constructed to avoid such problems.

*GGO* was set on a decrepit, dilapidated Earth after a devastating war—a place without the first hint of beauty. The sky was always some smeared combination of red and yellow paint, no matter the weather or the time of day, like a sunset gone madly awry.

The default terrain consisted of deserts, wastelands, and ruined cities. It had only the bare minimum of greenery—the polar opposite of *ALO*.

The players of *GGO* were all supposed to be people who came back to Earth on spaceships. In this desolate setting, players hunted grotesque mutated monsters, killer machines, and on occasion, other groups of players. That was the game in a nutshell.

Karen would never have picked *GGO* out of the plethora of games if it hadn't been for the avatar she'd wound up with.

If it wasn't obvious from the name, guns were the central weapon.

In *GGO*, they came in two main categories. The first was optical guns.

Blasters, ray guns, beam rifles, laser guns—the names were varied, but the concept was the same. These were guns with science-fiction

names and appearances that shot amplified light energy rather than bullets.

Even with their energy packs, optical guns were light and compact, with long range and considerable accuracy. At the same time, the damage a single shot inflicted was low, and in PvP battles, there were "anti-optical defense fields" that lowered the damage even further.

Those laser guns looked like classic sci-fi weapons with all straight lines. According to the game's background, they were used on the spaceships.

The other kind of weapon was live-ammo guns. These were explained to be the surviving guns still found on Earth, or perhaps new guns built from the plans for such models. They were actual, real-life guns, re-created within the game thanks to the blessing and cooperation of the gun manufacturers.

Unlike the optical guns, these ones rattled off actual bullets with proper mass—well, virtual mass anyway. They benefited from each bullet having great power and from there being no defensive fields to stop them. On the other hand, they were susceptible to wind and other environmental factors, and the ammo was heavy.

The common practice among players was to use optical guns on monsters, and live-ammo guns against other players. But given how many gun fanatics played *GGO*, many people said "To hell with efficiency!" and used their ammo guns on everything, monsters included. Pitohui was one of them.

Anyway, Llenn had wound up with the tiny avatar she was hoping for. Characters under five feet tall were quite rare in this game, apparently. Both players and computer-controlled non-player characters (NPCs) seemed to come from an endless stock of burly and menacing types. She couldn't have stuck out more if she'd tried.

When she walked through the neon-drenched sci-fi city nestled among the high-rise buildings, everyone seemed to notice her.

"Whoa! She's tiny!"

"What is that...? Is that a girl or a boy?"

"Did you see that? There's a kid here..."

"Heh, that's kinda cute."

"I didn't know *GGO* had avatars *that* small."

"Is that an NPC?"

With each comment, it became harder for her to keep her mouth under control, and she didn't like people seeing her grinning like a madman, so she started covering her mouth with a bandanna.

Just being a virtual shrimp was fun on its own, but Llenn was nothing if not principled, and since she had started playing this game, she was going to figure out how to do it right. And what could be cooler than being a tiny *and* deadly fighter?

Most games have a tutorial feature that teaches new players the ropes of its controls and functions. In *GGO*'s case, this was an NPC drill sergeant that offered a variety of lessons on how to fire a gun, how to hide behind cover, how to recognize and exploit various types of monsters, and so on.

Miyu once said, "You don't need to bother with tutorials! You're just wasting your time! Ask a friend, and you'll pick it up naturally! Just learn as you go! It's called on-the-job training!"

But if anything, Karen was better suited to soaking in a lesson on her own. And she had no friends here to ask.

This was how Llenn, who'd never expected to touch a gun in her life, mastered their use in a virtual setting.

She also learned all about *GGO*'s unique "bullet circle" assistance tool. It was an aid to the shooting process that told the player where the bullet would land. Placing a finger against the gun's trigger generated a light-green circle visible to the player. When fired, a bullet would land somewhere within that circle at random, no matter how big or small a space the circle covered.

The bullet circle's size changed depending on the target's distance, the qualities of the gun, and the player's skill. The pulsing of the circle as it grew and shrank was synchronized to the player's heartbeat.

In other words, a nervous player whose heart was jackhammering away would have a wildly fluctuating circle with no stability. That might not be the biggest problem in a close-range shoot-out, but to snipers it meant everything.

One of the tutorial lessons was about learning to snipe, and it was this process of calming her heart in order to aim that Llenn found toughest. She got horrible marks, and the NPC sergeant was all over her for it.

"Yeah, I'm not going to use a sniper rifle," she said. Everyone was suited for certain things and not suited for others. She would move on from this one without regret.

On the other hand, her lesson in snap shooting, where she took quick aim at close-range targets, was a surprising success. The instructor said, "Nice work! You're best suited to using a submachine gun!"

And so she had received her recommendation.


Once she'd dutifully concluded every last part of the tutorial, Llenn headed out on her own to fight some monsters.

Her first battle had been in a hilly region just outside the city, where she settled on a beast that looked like a cross between a plodding swine and an ostrich. She'd felt bad about shooting a largely docile creature, but when it came time to fire, she didn't hesitate to pull the trigger on the optical gun.

The gun had merely produced a red glowing spot, known as a bullet-hole effect, on the target, and upon dying, it burst into little particles of light and vanished. Psychologically, this lessened the effect of "hurting" and "killing" a living creature.

Llenn took the game seriously. She carried out the lessons she'd been taught and stayed away from monsters she knew she couldn't beat, and if she got killed, she thought hard about where she'd gone wrong. When she simply couldn't win against a certain monster, she'd visit a strategy website and look up the best way to kill it.

It's often the simplest efforts that lead to the most solid growth. As Llenn defeated monster after monster, she earned experience points and credits, the name of the in-game currency.

Once she earned enough experience, she could raise her statistics. There were six attributes to choose from: strength, agility, durability (endurance), dexterity, intelligence, and luck. By making choices among the six, she could build her ideal self.

Since she was already small, she'd decided she might as well raise her agility so she could run faster. If she had dexterity, she could use it to craft things. Having good luck never hurt. Don't forget strength—some guns were unusable without enough of it. Durability wasn't a big deal, since she was fine with being fragile. Intelligence? What's that?

So Llenn focused on agility and dexterity, with strength and luck as sub-stats. Her choices were based in no small part on the trauma of always coming in last in footraces due to her huge size in real life.

Once she had more credits to use, she was able to add on more guns and gear. She'd switched out her optical gun for a submachine gun with a high rate of fire. She'd decided to spend the rest of her credits on a new outfit. She was finally cute and petite, and she wanted some clothes that would take advantage of that. This was clearly the wrong choice for the desolate sci-fi wasteland of *GGO*, but she didn't care.

Llenn went to the town tailor—er, combat outfitter—and excitedly looked through the offerings for something cute. This was *GGO*, so there were no frilly dresses. She found no Lolita fashion, which she'd been so terribly excited about after seeing it in magazines in middle school but given up on wearing as long as she continued to have the dimensions of a eucalyptus tree.

Instead, she found a system that allowed her to change the color of the starter combat suit she was still wearing. This was the sort of thing video games were for.

Llenn went for pink.

In the real world, she'd been unable to wear pink, no matter

how much she wanted to. But if Karen wasn't the right look for it, surely Llenn was. Sadly, the one shade of pink available to sample was not the kind of vivid, bright pink she'd always wanted. It was a dull, shaded pink, a tint rarely seen in real life.

Still, pink was pink. She changed both pieces of her current combat gear to the color, then kept going until her boots, bandanna, gloves, equipment belt, and even the knit cap that kept her hair under control during battle were all the same color.

Llenn left the business, silently humming with pleasure in her all-pink outfit, and caught a glimpse of herself reflected in the store window.

"..."

Her eyebrows furrowed. Yes—something was still off.

She raced to a weapons customization shop and asked for paint. She was going to have that dark-gray optical gun painted the same shade of pink.

Now Llenn was properly pink from head to toe, and so was the deadly looking weapon she carried. She was like some kind of TV character.

Some people who'd spotted her looking like this had laughed, and others had said she was very cute at that size. Some had even been mystified about her gender, since her close-cropped hair wasn't a major signifier.

Llenn had chosen the look for fun, and it was all just a game. Nobody knew the real her, so she wasn't bothered by this now.

But it was the first and last time she wore pink in town.

Shortly afterward, Llenn killed another player for the first time.

She was enjoying her monster battling and didn't have the slightest desire to kill other players in a gun battle yet. Her gun was for monsters; she didn't want to go down the path of "murder," even if it was just virtual.

Like any other day, Llenn went into the reddened wastes in search of monster prey. The sun was high above in the haze, but

the sky and earth were as red as ever, like a sunrise or sunset. According to the game's story, the apocalyptic war had even destroyed Earth's atmosphere.

She prowled the rocky desert dotted with the husks of ancient tanks, waiting for monsters to appear. In this environment, creatures like crocodiles with the torso of a cow dug holes under the tanks for shelter.

With her higher dexterity value, Llenn was able to fashion traps of grenades and slender wires around the vehicles. When one of the giant crocs hit the wires, the resulting blast would make it easy for her to spot.

Then she just had to close the gap, avoid the creature's attack, and blast it with her optical gun at close range, where she couldn't miss. That was how Llenn did things.

She had nothing else to do while she waited, so she sat against a boulder a short distance away and listened to music, like always. By using a music player and earphones, which existed in the game world as items, she could call upon the music files saved to her AmuSphere.

There she sat all alone, gun in hand, outfitted all in pink, letting time pass her by in the wasteland.

Llenn enjoyed doing things she could never do in the real world. At times, she would open her menu screen and retrieve a thermos of hot tea from her item storage so she could sit back and sip it.

Her item storage was something like an invisible bag. If she put things in there, she didn't have to carry them around manually. But the maximum space limit depended on the character's strength, so it wasn't like she could put just anything in there. The weight limit on her storage was the same as the weight limit she could physically carry.

In order to retrieve her items, she needed to wave her hand in the air to call up the window. No matter how quick someone was, the process always took a few seconds, which ensured that if they needed to use weapons or ammo immediately, they needed to carry it.

Normally, she ought to have her storage stuffed with backup weapons and healing solutions...

"Ah, that's good tea."

...but Llenn preferred to save space for her thermos and snacks, even if it meant less ammo.

VR games could even simulate the sense of taste. Of course she was going to make use of that. She could drink all she wanted and not gain weight.

When the Mozart piece was finished, she switched over to an Elza Kanzaki album. She was a female singer-songwriter whose renown was rising rapidly. Her melodies were rich and classical, while her voice was clear and lyrics welcoming. Karen had heard about her through a friend and was now a total fan.

It was this pleasant and charming music that played as Llenn sat amid blasted desolation. The album finished, and there were still no explosions—perhaps that day's stakeout was a bust. At any rate, she'd enjoyed a good picnic, so she was ready to return to the real world.

Just then, people showed up.

Three men appeared from around the rocks dead ahead, about two hundred yards away, and began walking straight toward her. She hadn't noticed them at all, because they'd been climbing a slope before that.

All three were big and buff, wearing armor-like protectors, and carried huge optical guns in their slings.

In this particular game, when players met one another in the open, unless someone was particularly close or familiar with the other side, it was more likely that a gunfight would break out instead of a conversation. People often said, "In *GGO*, we let our guns do the talking!"

They came closer and closer, a tough-looking team, while she was all alone and a complete amateur when it came to battling other players. Llenn was racked with fear greater than any she'd felt facing giant monsters. Numerous questions exploded inside her mind.

*Should I run away?*

*Or should I cut my connection and escape back into the real world?*

*No, most important of all—why are they coming straight toward me with their guns raised?!*

Without a firm decision in hand, all Llenn could do was stand there and watch them. Eventually, they were within thirty yards, at which point she could hear them happily chatting about their gun specs.

That was when she realized they weren't aware of her presence. They had no idea she was there.

They came closer, closer—within ten yards at that point…

An unfortunate incident was about to befall them, but it would change Llenn's *GGO* play style forever.

First, a small explosion occurred behind Llenn, who'd been directly facing the men.

At long last, the giant crocodile she'd been waiting for had set off her grenade trap. The men had no idea about this, of course. They panicked at the sudden eruption and were so distracted by the burst of sand beyond the rock, they didn't even notice that Llenn had started moving.

The explosion had driven off Llenn's fear. At this point, it was simple self-abandon driving her actions. She'd do her best and let things happen organically.

She snatched up the pink optical gun from her lap and rushed forward, spraying fire at the closest man. His anti-optical defense field slowed the progress of her shots, but eventually a few hit his face at close range. By then, she was within two or three yards of the other two men. She fired and fired and fired, always tilting her gun upward at the tall targets.

Once that ten-second stretch of madness was over, there was no sight of the three men anymore. They'd all run out of hit points due to the barrage from extreme close range. They were "dead."

The only thing left in the desert was Llenn, heart leaping into her throat with excitement, and the giant crocodile, which was in agony after setting off the trap near the tank.

*     *     *

*Why did those three not notice me at all?*

Once the crocodile had been put out of its misery, Llenn tried to figure out the answer.

"Maybe..."

She had an idea. She placed her pink gun against the shadow of the rock where she'd been sitting, then moved away from it. It was instantly obvious that her hypothesis was correct.

The gun she'd just left behind was invisible now.

Under the reddish sunset light that always shone in the world of *GGO*, Llenn's faded-pink gun blended right into the brown rock and sand so much that it was almost impossible to pick out. With the amount of light in the sky at this particular moment, it was completely invisible.

"This is neat... I think I can make use of this," she muttered.


After that, Llenn never wore her pink outfit in town. She didn't want people coming after her for revenge. Instead, she bought a plain green combat suit and a burnt-brown hooded robe that covered her body and face. She felt like a kid putting a blanket over her head and pretending to be a ghost, but at least it was less attention grabbing than wearing all pink.

Once she was out in the wasteland and desert, she would change into her beloved pink gear when no one was watching and begin laying her ambush. For the most part, she hunted monsters like always, but if she caught a glimpse of another player—she changed targets without mercy.

If they were coming toward her, she'd hide and wait. She wouldn't move a muscle.

Once she knew that her opponents were a number she could beat (usually one—or two at the most), she would leap out when they were very close and down them in a hail of shots.

She couldn't even remember that, when she had started the

game, her thoughts on the matter had been *I don't want to shoot (anything resembling) people.*

Even for successful hiding attempts, she wouldn't pull the trigger if there were too many enemies, if they didn't come close enough, or if their gear looked too powerful. She'd either wait them out in hiding or steadily back away until she could retreat without a sound.

This was how Llenn got hooked on PvP battling.

It reminded her of playing tag, hide-and-seek, and cops and robbers with her older brothers and sisters as a kid. The thrill of hiding, the excitement of finding. And now the superiority of killing the opponent.

*So this is what it means to fight your hardest within a game and enjoy the competition.*

Now that she'd gained a deeper understanding of *GGO*, Llenn silently apologized to the gamers she'd always made fun of in her mind.

With the experience she gained from fighting monsters and people, Llenn pushed her agility even higher, making her quicker to react and her legs even faster than before. Completely unbeknownst to her, at that time, the practice of focusing directly on agility was called the *AGI-superiority model*, as it was considered the most useful statistic in PvP combat.

She had used the credits she earned to buy herself a live-ammo gun for fighting against other players. It took all of her budget and smarts to arrive at the Vz. 61 Skorpion, a submachine gun from the former Czechoslovakia.

It was twenty-seven inches long with the stock folded, making it one of the smallest and lightest SMGs in the world. Although it used small pistol bullets, it could deplete an entire thirty-round magazine in less than two seconds. It had low power but little recoil, thus better accuracy.

Llenn had bought two, removed the stocks, and painted them pink. Like the name suggested, her style was like a sting from a

scorpion's tail: certain death in one shot. When other players passed by her within a range of ten yards, she would rush them with her considerable agility, a Skorpion in each hand. She'd point at their heads and blaze the weapon's full automatic fire, as though stabbing upward with that stinger. With the right-hand Skorpion against a single foe, or perhaps the left as well, if there were two.

*GGO* had another system tool called the *bullet line*. This was a red line that the targeted player could see, except for the first shot from an enemy whose location was unknown, in the case of sniping or ambush. It allowed players to see an incoming bullet's trajectory and take evasive action.

This was a defensive handicap to make the game more fun overall, and obviously not a thing that existed in real life.

One of the basic elements of PvP combat in *GGO* was being able to spot a bullet line and move out of its way with a minimum of movement. But that didn't help when a gun barrel within ten feet essentially hit its target at the same time it fired. The moment they would have spotted the bullet line was the moment the automatic fire would have sprayed them in the face.

Llenn had devised a truly merciless method of killing, making full use of the gun's properties, much like a Communist assassin from the Cold War.

It was in this manner that she learned and grew as a player, from each and every experience. One day she was crushing monsters; the next she might be blasting some pathetic loser.

At last, one day Llenn overheard a rumor while she was in her bulky robe in town: "There's some horrifying unknown player killer ambushing people out in the desert. A bunch of solo players have been ganked before they even see who it is."

A kind of vigilante team was putting plans together to use a player as bait so they could figure out who this PKing bastard was. Before long, they'd be placing a bounty on her head, too.

Llenn saw the effect her activities were having and decided to stop laying ambushes that might be considered foul play. After

that point, she wore her ordinary green camo in the forest region, hunting monsters and exploring ruined buildings.

She'd been playing for over three months. Now, in the final month of 2025, Llenn had played enough to be in the middle skill levels of the game's population. She had no idea that this was the case, though.

That was when she met the woman who called herself Pitohui.

# CHAPTER 2
Llenn and Pitohui

**SECT.2**

# CHAPTER 2
## Llenn and Pitohui

"Hey! You there, the shrimpy one. You're a girl in real life, right? I can tell from how you walk."

Llenn was strolling through a dazzling shopping mall in SBC Glocken, the capital city in *GGO*, window-shopping for the live-ammo gun she would buy next, when she heard a woman's voice behind her.

"Want to get a cup of tea? Big Sister will pay."

*Big Sister?* She was being hit on.

Llenn turned around, hooded robe swaying, and saw a beautiful woman with tan skin, nearly as tall as Karen was in real life, with black hair in a ponytail and brick-red tattoos on her face.

At this first meeting, she was wearing a very revealing and non-battle-worthy outfit, something like a fur bikini. Her body was cyborg-like, all slim and taut curves, and she had no shame in showing it off.

The facial tattoos were a bit of a mystery, and if Llenn had wound up with that avatar, she would have given up on *GGO* within seconds—but faced with a player so obviously female, Llenn let her guard down a bit.

At this point in time, it was impossible to play a character of a different gender, unless there was some slight error in brain-wave recognition. Some male players chatted her up out of curiosity, but this was undoubtedly her first time speaking to a woman in the game.

For one thing, *GGO* was a game with a very small percentage of female players. She'd seen what was obviously a woman from a distance, but she'd never chased her down to speak to her or anything.

The tanned woman grinned at her. "I'm Pitohui. People complain that it's hard to say, so you can call me Pito for short. What's your name, kiddo?"

"Hello... It's...Llenn."

"Llenn! What a cute name! Now, first things first, I don't want any stuffiness between us! We're here to enjoy an alternate world, so let's not drag all the Japanese hierarchical nonsense in with us!"

This had been Llenn's first true conversation with anyone in *GGO*.

Llenn and Pitohui settled down in a private booth within an in-game restaurant and chatted over tea and cake. It was like a VR girls' day.

At this point in time, Karen hadn't been speaking in person to anyone other than her professors and family members, but for some strange reason, this brisk and informal chat with Pitohui went very smoothly. Something about Pitohui's bright and clever wit reminded her of Miyu.

Their first point of bonding was around the troubles of being one of the few girls playing *GGO*. Pitohui noted that having a very attractive avatar resulted in lots of attention, which she'd cut down on considerably by getting the facial tattoos. She recommended the idea to Llenn, who quickly shook her head.

"Don't worry—I don't have them in real life. I'd hate to be shut out of hot springs on account of that!" Pitohui said with a gentle smile.

This was all very easy to do in *GGO*, where applying or removing a tattoo was as simple as the press of a button and could be done as many times as one could afford.

Pitohui's history with VR games was much longer than Llenn's. She claimed she'd been playing them all through the uproar over the deadly *SAO* Incident. She'd started up with *GGO* when it launched eight months earlier. She loved the desolate setting, something she couldn't find in other VR games, and now it was her only game. Unfortunately, her busy personal life had kept her from playing very often lately.

So she was more experienced as a gamer and also considerably more powerful than Llenn in terms of player stats. Since they'd gotten along so well and so quickly, Llenn decided to register Pitohui as a friend. Now they could trade messages, whether they were playing at the same time or not.

After more than three months of playing *GGO*, Llenn had finally found someone she could call an acquaintance. It wasn't until this point that she finally recalled the entire reason she'd gotten interested in VR games, which was to help ease the social anxiety that stemmed from her height.

She had no idea what Pitohui was like in real life, of course. Miyu once told her, "Even in VR games, it's real people who are controlling those characters, so you're going to get a glimpse of who they are in all their conversations and mannerisms. There aren't many people who can totally pull off a separate personality online."

Pitohui's attitude was cheerful; she wasn't rough or violent in the least. In her amateur attempt at profiling—with no idea if she was correct about any it—Llenn suspected that Pitohui was a generous, outgoing woman in her twenties who liked playing the big sister. She worked for a living, and she was single.

Once they'd finished with the tea and cake, Pitohui asked Llenn whether she was logging off for the day. The smaller girl said she was on the lookout for a new live-ammo gun.

"No way! I can tell you where to go! I know all the best spots!"

Pitohui took Llenn to an out-of-the-way little shop. They headed down winding, narrow alleys until they came to a cramped and

cluttered place, like some kind of squalid dive bar. But to her surprise, it was full of rare and powerful secondhand guns looted from ruins and deadly monsters.

"Wow... I've never seen this place before... I've never seen these guns before...," Llenn marveled.

"Llenn, Llenn, check this out! You should get this—they just stocked it yesterday! C'mere and take a look!" chirped Pitohui, beckoning her over as if she were showing off a new cosmetic.

It was a small, high-powered, and fairly rare gun: the P90. The number on the price tag was devastating, well over the initial budget she'd set for herself. If she bought it, she wouldn't have cash for tea for a while.

"I'll buy it!" she said without hesitation. "What is this...? Is it even a gun...? It's so cute...craaazy cuuute..."

"Llenn, did you just slip into a Hokkaido accent for a second?"

She'd gotten a backup clip and a pouch for holding it thrown in as part of the deal, and thus Llenn strolled through town, quite pleased with herself, P90 hidden under her dark-brown robe.

Of course, she could have opened her game window and stashed it in her inventory, saving herself the trouble of lugging it around, but Pitohui said, "I get that feeling. After you buy a gun, you want to feel it in your hands. You've got to get familiar with the sensation."

Llenn was like a child walking home with a plushie she'd just bought clutched in her hands. She wanted it nearby, of course, so she could stroke and pet it.

"What about the name? You're going to name it, right?"

"N-name it? The gun?" Llenn repeated, looking up at Pitohui.

"Of course!"

"I—I think...I will!"

"You know it. So what's her name?"

After several seconds of silence, Llenn firmly announced, "P-chan."

"I like it. Now your job is to feed P-chan plenty of blood from

your enemies. Guns will never betray you. They grow and grow
with every enemy you shoot."

"Yeah! I'll make sure to kill tons of people with it!"

If this conversation had been happening in the real world, the
cops would have been called on them at this point. Speaking of
which, it was about time to head back, so Llenn gave Pitohui a
deep bow. "Thank you so much, Miss Pito. You've helped me out
a lot."

"What did I say? None of that 'miss' stuff. I'm just happy to
have found another girl to chill with. Let's hang out again some-
time. We'll go hunting next time. I haven't seen the giant crocs in
the desert yet."

"Sure."

*Wow, she's really pretty nice*, Llenn thought as she opened her
window to log out.

"Oh, and I forgot one thing."

"Hmm?"

"Make sure you paint that P90 pink like the rest of your outfit
before we go hunting!"

"…"

*Oh. I guess I shouldn't take her for granted after all.*

Llenn called up the log-out window.


After this, Llenn formed a "squadron" with Pitohui. This was
an in-game team of like-minded friends—what would be called
a *guild* in a fantasy-themed game. You fought together, shared
items, wore your own team insignia, and so on.

Naturally, playing with strong teamwork conferred many benefits on the player. Llenn had started the game as a means to meet
more people, but she hadn't really teamed up with anyone before,
so this was her first squadron experience. It had just been the two
of them, Pitohui and Llenn.

For the following month, she always played with Pitohui when
the two were on at the same time. Llenn was usually active at

the same hours of day, while Pitohui's play time was all over the place. Sometimes she was playing on a weekday morning, and sometimes she never logged in over a weekend.

It made Llenn curious about what Pitohui did for a living, but asking personal information like that was a social taboo, so she refrained from giving in to her curiosity.

As Llenn eventually came to understand, Pitohui was an extremely wealthy player. The tip-off was the number of guns she owned. Every time they played together, Pitohui was using a different gun.

"Pito, what's that you've got today?"

"Heh! It's an L86A2. The L85 is a British Army assault rifle, and this is an upgraded fire-team support version with a reinforced and elongated barrel. It only uses the regular magazines, which makes you wonder what the heck the difference is from the ordinary rifle, but the precision's pretty decent. It's heavy, but I like it."

"I...see..."

"My sidearm is a Colt Double Eagle! It's a double-action automatic pistol that Colt designed based on the M1911, but it looks dumb and it works like a piece of shit! People hated it! When I heard they had it in *GGO*, I knew I had to track one down! So I found a collector who had one and ponied up the credits to buy it off him!"

Pitohui's character was very strong, of course, but more remarkable than that was her collection of expensive, exotic, and downright weird guns. One day, while they were waiting for their prey to come by, Llenn couldn't contain her curiosity and asked how she got so many credits.

"Oh, a real money transaction, of course," Pitohui answered.

Real money transactions, or RMTs for short, referred to the practice of using a real credit card or bank account to digitally purchase in-game credits or items. *GGO* was the only VR game that allowed for equal exchange between in-game currency and real money. That meant there were literal professional players

who made a living by earning lucrative, desirable items in the game and selling them for money.

Pitohui was the type of player who got her way in the game by dumping cash into it. This was a strategy widely criticized by the players who believed the game should be "won" only by those who worked hardest at it. But everyone had their own way to play, and more importantly, the game itself didn't forbid you from playing that way. So people like Pitohui were well within their right to disregard those criticisms as the jealousy of the poor and unfortunate.

Pitohui was rich in real life. Rich enough to pour plenty of money into the game, at any rate. That made *one* thing Llenn knew about her, at least. But thanks to that, she'd learned about lots of different guns.

"I'm using a Remington Model 870 today! Yeah, it's the cliché pump-action shotgun, but it's awesome! Wanna shoot it? Go on, try it out!" Pitohui would say one day.

"Yes, I finally got an M16! And look closely: It's not an M16A1—it's the original M16 rifle!" she'd say the next day.

"Today I brought about five automatic pistols that use 9 mm Parabellum rounds. So let me explain: The first one here is…"

Llenn had also gotten the chance to test out the guns she was strong enough to use.

"Well? Well?"

"Hmm. It's fun to shoot, but…"

"You still prefer P-chan, huh?"

"Yeah."

"You're so dedicated! I want to shoot every single live-ammo gun there is in *GGO*!" Pitohui had announced. "Do you know what an antimateriel rifle is, Llenn?"

"I've heard the word before, but that's it.".

"Then allow me to explain! An antimateriel rifle, explained as simply as possible, is a gun that shoots big-ass bullets."

"How big?"

"Normal assault rifles shoot either 5.56 or 7.62 mm rounds, but pretty much anything that's 12.7 or larger is called an antimateriel

rifle. Those are full-size heavy machine-gun bullets, like the same kind that fighter airplanes in World War II would shoot."

"I can't even imagine it. Does it have more power, the bigger the bullet?"

"Of course. A 5.56 mm round can be accurate on a target up to only four hundred meters, and a 7.62 will go about twice that far, but a 12.7 mm bullet can easily hit a target over a thousand meters away."

"Like…a kilometer? Two-thirds of a mile?"

"It's a crazy amount of distance, isn't it? But that means the gun has to be bigger and heavier! The bigger you get, the more strength you need to equip it."

"I guess that'd be impossible for me…"

"Yeah. Some guns are about as tall as *you* are."

"Heh-heh-heh."

"Why did that make you chuckle? Anyway, up until World War II, they called these big guns anti-tank rifles, but then tanks got sturdy enough to withstand the shots, so the name changed. It's used for long-range sniping and attacking enemy supplies. It's big but still sized so that a single person can carry it, which makes it convenient."

"Ohhh. A gun that's big and can shoot long distances. So does having one make you the toughest in the game?"

"Not at all."

"Wha—?"

"Well, they're huge and heavy, and the strength requirement is ridiculous. Plus, it takes major skill to do super-long-range sniping. Basically, it's not practical unless you're really eccentric. And they're ultra-ultra-ultra-rare, so the day that you lose it on a random drop at death, you'd probably be up all night reeling from shock."

"But you still want one…?"

"You bet! I want to display it in the gun locker in my place! Some say there are only about ten of those guns on this server, so they're worth so much, nobody wants to sell them. I actually know one character who has one. And it's another woman."

"Wow! Forget about the gun; I'm just surprised that it's a girl."

"Her name is Sinon. Do you know her? Got light-blue hair?"

"Sadly, no."

"Oh well. Sinon beat a monster in some subterranean dungeon and got an antimateriel rifle called the Hecate II from it. I heard that she was taking really good care of it, so I searched her out and introduced myself by saying, 'Hello! Sell me your Hecate II!'"

"Pito… Did you really think that was going to work…?"

"Well, it didn't! That girl's stubborn!"

"…"

Llenn realized that Pitohui was both extremely rich and obsessed with guns (and had some personality issues), but everything else about her friend was a mystery.

One day, while they were traveling the wasteland to hunt some monsters, Llenn asked, "What sort of hobbies do you have?" on a whim, like they were on a first date or something.

"Hmm? Well…aside from this game, you mean? Nothing," Pitohui replied.

Given that she'd asked the question first, Llenn felt she needed to answer it herself, so she mentioned that she liked listening to music, often classical music and movie soundtracks. She even mentioned that Elza Kanzaki was her favorite singer at the moment, but Pitohui didn't have much of a reaction.

"Music, huh…? I barely listen to any at all."

"Really? I'm surprised," Llenn said honestly.

"You are?" Pitohui replied, looking surprised herself.

"I guess I just always assumed you liked music, Pito."

"Heh. You'd be surprised if you saw me in real life and realized I can't read sheet music."

"…Um, I'm sorry. I didn't mean to talk this much about IRL stuff," Llenn said, trying to put a lid on the conversation, but to her surprise, Pitohui followed it up.

"Listen, you and I get along pretty well, so I've been thinking it might not be the worst idea for us to meet up off-line and show each other who we really are. Just a little off-line hangout. What about you? You got the guts? You got the determination?"

Llenn thought about her towering height. A few seconds later, she said, "I think…you'd be surprised if you saw me…Miss Pito…"

Normally, that would be where Pitohui yelled at her for calling her Miss Pito, but this one time, she was silent. Instead, she grinned down at the cowering Llenn and chuckled.

"How about this, then? One day, you can challenge me to a head-on fight, and if you win, you get to meet up in person! In fact, I'll go and meet *you*, wherever you happen to live in Japan!"

Why she suggested such a thing was a mystery, but Llenn chose not to be snarky about it. "If I beat you in *GGO*…? Th-that could take forever!"

"Then I'll make you a promise! Train yourself well, until the day you get the best of me with your faithful P-chan!"

"G-got it! Yeah! Just you wait! I'll beat you someday!"

"That's what I like to hear. Then let's engage in the ritual toast!"

"With what?"

"You clash metallic objects together in recognition of a promise. It was a big thing back in the Edo period. Don't you remember much about back then?"

"Pito…are you one hundred and seventy years old?"

"That's still a secret. Anyway, a samurai would use his katana blade or hilt, while a woman uses her mirror. Since we don't have those, we'll have to use our guns! Here we go! If we have a true duel one day, and I lose, then I'll meet up with you IRL, Llenn! It's a promise between women!"

They raised their guns, two women in the wilderness. The muzzle of the P90 hit the barrel of Pitohui's SKS Carbine, producing a dry clank.

Llenn didn't know what thoughts were brewing behind Pitohui's smile, but for her part, she felt like it was pointless. That day would never come.

It was one month after that promise—on January 18th, 2026, coming back from a monster hunt—when Llenn heard about the Squad Jam.

# CHAPTER 3
Squad Jam

SECT.3

# CHAPTER 3
## Squad Jam

"Squad Jam is a *Gun Gale Online* tournament where a bunch of squads get together and have a battle royale to determine who's the best."

"Battle royale…? You mean that thing where everybody fights everybody?"

Llenn and Pitohui trekked across the wasteland as they chatted, giant earthworm successfully hunted. Naturally, they were still wary and watching to make sure they'd be ready for a player ambush. Normally Llenn preferred to look at the face of the person she was talking to, but this situation called for her to scan ahead and to the sides as she talked.

"That's right. You know about the Bullet of Bullets, right? Everyone calls it the BoB."

Llenn nodded. "Only the name and the concept, though."

The BoB was the battle royale event that determined the greatest player in *GGO*. It started with one-on-one preliminary brackets, and the thirty champions who arose were then dropped into a vast map to fight until there was just one left.

It was unquestionably the biggest event in *GGO*, and each successive installment seemed to get even more exciting. Many players practically dedicated their lives to appearing in this tournament as a finalist.

The third BoB had recently taken place. Llenn hadn't considered entering at all, of course, so she didn't know what it entailed or how it looked. She had been away from her apartment, having dinner with her sister's family, so she hadn't dived that night, and she hadn't watched any streamed footage.

"They held the third BoB recently. I was in it, too. I just didn't tell anyone about it, because there was a chance that real life might have interfered with its timing."

"Ooh! How did it go?"

"Lost in the prelims. Just the second round, too."

"Aw… That's too bad."

"Yeah, I got sniped, so I was just unlucky. But something funny happened in the final battle royale event. Right at the very end, two players teamed up to fight together."

"I didn't know people did that."

"Well, I'll avoid spoiling the ending, since you might watch the video at some point, but my point is that it was really thrilling and super-entertaining to watch! I got chills!"

"That's neat."

It was a surprise to Llenn to hear Pitohui speaking so passionately about anything that wasn't more guns. It made her want to watch the event's video.

"So here's my main point. Some Japanese person watching that video got all hot and bothered, thinking, 'I wanna see a team battle royale like this next! There's no way a team-on-team version of this wouldn't be just as exciting!'"

"I see."

"So that blessed soul sent a message in machine-translated English to Zaskar, the American company that runs *GGO*. 'Dear Sirs, everybody. I'd like to see a team battle royale, so please to hold it.'"

"Wait, are you saying they actually did this on a single individual's suggestion?"

"That's right. This person told Zaskar that they'd put up all the funds needed to run such an event—in other words, agreed to

sponsor it. I have no idea how much something like that would cost. The sponsor's identity got revealed, and it turned out to be some fifty-something novelist with a pathological obsession with guns, and whose books all involve shooting stuff."

"Wow…talk about an eccentric…"

"I mean, having an obsession with guns makes you a weirdo to begin with, but especially when you're a writer. It's like the worst possible combination, you know? That's the kind of person who needs to be arrested when they go out in public."

"Um, Pito…do you have something against all the writers of the world?"

"Hmm? No, why? Anyway, that writer's passion got through the poor translation, and Zaskar decided, 'We'll hold a special joint-subsidized mini-event on just the Japanese server.' They ended up calling it Squad Jam, or SJ for short. The sponsor made up that name, so I don't know if the English is proper or not."

"I see. So no connection to squid paste."

"You still haven't gotten over that, huh? They're looking for participating teams for SJ, and the sign-up deadline is the twenty-eighth, midday next Wednesday. The event happens the following Sunday, February first."

"That seems very sudden… Are they going to get enough entries?"

"From what it sounds like, they got a decent number of teams to sign up right away, so they're not worried about having to cancel the event due to lack of participants. This is more like a test run than anything else, so as long as they don't get a huge rush of teams, there won't be any preliminaries. It seems like there are a lot of people happy about getting to jump right into the final event—I mean, even the preliminaries of BoB are packed with total aces. And the ones who would be potential BoB finalists are going to pass on this. They usually don't play well with others. They'd rather take a nap than trust their backs to someone else."

"Hmm."

"You don't seem that interested, Llenn."

"It's the same thing I said about the BoB—I'm just not cut out for these PvP tournaments."

"That's a funny thing to hear from a girl who makes for such an effective and ruthless assassin."

"Th-that's not—! Well…okay."

"Yes, exactly! And you do it so well. So this what I wanted to say."

"Uh…"

"You should enter, Llenn!"

"Huh? Me? On a team with you?"

"Sadly, *very* sadly, I have something to do on February first… the wedding of my best friend since middle school. If she ever found out I ditched her wedding to play some in-game event online…even if I actually *won* the dang thing…"

"You'd get killed IRL instead."

"Exactly!"

"In other words, if I searched for every woman who appeared at a wedding in Japan on that day, your real identity would be among that list…"

"Oh no, my cover's gonna get blown! But anyway, I really want you to participate, Llenn! You free that day? No friends' weddings? No wedding of your own?"

"Well, I'd have to check my calendar to be sure, but I'm pretty sure I'm open that day…"

"Then it's settled! Don't worry—I'll handle the paperwork! The whole team gets registered at once, so all I need is your name."

"W-wait, wait! Who said I was playing?"

"Experience is everything, my dear!"

"But this is a team event, right? Who am I going to team up with?"

"Ah-ha-ha, I can see you're getting excited for this. Very good."

"It was a neutral question!"

"There's another player I know who's pretty damn talented. He's a dude, and frankly, he's kind of a weirdo—deep down he's

pretty much a criminal—but he's not a bad guy. Not a good guy, either. That's your partner. Good luck!"

"Huh? Just two of us?"

"Yep. Just you two. Nobody else was available."

"…Pito…did you think I was going to say, 'Yay! I'm all in!' to that?"

"Experience is everything, my dear!"

"Yeah, but…"

"Listen, Llenn. If you ask me, you've got some problems you're dealing with in the real world."

"Huh?"

Surprised, Llenn finally turned to look at Pitohui. Normally, the taller woman would snap, *No looking over here!* while she ought to be keeping watch, but not this time. Pitohui gave her a look like a kindly therapist (albeit one with facial tattoos) and said, "There's something in the real world that's got you down, huh? That's why you came to *GGO*—to blow off steam. Or more cynically, to escape your troubles."

"…"

"You're looking at me like, 'How did you know?' It's obvious. That's how it was for me, too!"

"…"

"There's way too much stuff in the real world that gets me down or pisses me off, so I tear it up in here instead. I get to come in, guns blazing, and kill tons of monsters and people."

"Pito…"

"So if you have the chance to do stuff you can't do in the real world, why not make the most of it? That's all I'm saying! Will you ever get the chance to experience a team battle royale gunfight in the real world? Don't you *want* to join?"

Llenn continued shaking her head in resistance, but Pitohui never removed that gentle smile of a child-persuading parent (albeit one with facial tattoos).

She wrapped it up by announcing, "So let's kick some ass! If I

don't hear back from you by Wednesday morning, I'm going to assume you're all in and sign you up!"

✳    ✳    ✳

"Aw, geez…what am I gonna do about this Squad Jam thing? It's a team-battle event… I just don't know if I'm into this," Karen complained, back in the real world. Then she placed the P90 in her hands on the clothing rack.

She'd spotted the air gun by coincidence two weeks earlier on a very famous Internet shopping site. The thought of having her very own P-chan to hold in her hands was too tempting to pass up.

She had ordered the P90 air gun, as well as a "recommended for people who buy this item" little P90-shaped key chain charm.

When the air gun arrived the next day, Karen was stunned. Was the gun supposed to be this *small*? Oh, silly me. It must be smaller because an air gun is designed to be more compact than the real thing.

But within moments, she realized her mistake. It *was* the same object; it felt so different only because of the size variation between when she was Karen and when she was Llenn. The realization nearly knocked her for a loop.

Still, she liked the gun, and she kept it displayed in her room at all times, even though it was still colored black. She would just be careful to hide it away in her dresser when her sister and niece came over to visit.

As for the key chain charm, she colored it pink with a marker. It looked great, just like P-chan.

She considered attaching it to the bag she always took to school. Then she realized that there were no college-age women who went around with little gun toys dangling from their key chains, so she hung it up on her wall instead.

*GGO* was a fun game. A truly fun time.

So Karen didn't mind paying the 3,000-yen monthly fee, which

was quite high for that type of game. While it wasn't necessarily always fun and games, she'd also made a friend in Pitohui.

But *because* it was so fun, that always made her return to real life that much more dreary. VR games were like a big fun dream, but one couldn't just hang out in their dreams all the time. Dreams were possible only because they stood apart from the real world. If the settings were switched, it would be more like a nightmare.

Karen couldn't help but find this ironic. She'd started playing this VR game to get away from the pain of real life, and the contrast between this and the real world just made it *more* painful now.

But if she had to pick one or the other, she would obviously have to stick with real life. Once things got busier at school, once she started looking for a job, once she was a working adult, once she got married, once she had kids…escaping into the VR world would no longer be an option.

Of course, there were people who gave up on real life to play VR games, but they were known as "online addicts" or "invalids." Not the best role model for all the good little boys and girls.

So Karen had recently been thinking about that particular option—cutting off all ties to the VR world cold turkey while it still wasn't too painful to leave the dreamworld and, more importantly, before she felt like quitting *wasn't* an option. She understood that, in the long run, this was the best thing for her to do.

In all honesty, she wasn't into the idea of trying out the Squad Jam at all.

She could always enjoy being a virtual shrimp just by logging in to *GGO*, and she was having plenty of fun fighting monsters already. She'd gotten into fighting players for a time, and that was certainly fun, too—going up against powerful opponents did make her heart soar—but that didn't mean she was actively seeking it out.

Plus, she wasn't into the idea of entering this tournament with an unfamiliar man *at all*, even if Pitohui vouched for him. She

couldn't imagine being an effective team with him. Obviously, they were going to try to win, but she was just going to drag him down.

On the other hand, she understood Pitohui's message about undertaking the challenge of finding a new side of herself. That was why she'd started playing VR games in the first place. She couldn't give up and run away now.

But if she was going to back out of the Squad Jam, could this also be the best point to just make a clean break from VR games entirely?

Surely she could keep going for a bit. At least while she was a student, before she started applying for jobs. Her family was always bugging her to get more hobbies—wasn't that exactly what this was?

To play or not to play, back and forth. Several minutes of indecisive agony passed without bearing fruit.

*"Haah..."*

When she didn't know what to do, it was time to reach out to a friend. She decided to call her VR mentor and *ALO*-playing friend, Miyu, for advice.

"Wassup, Kohi?"

Fortunately, Miyu wasn't logged in. She was the only one who could actually give her good advice on the topic.

Karen revealed the problems weighing her down and asked, "What do you think I should do? You're my VR gaming mentor—I need your frank opinion."

"Well obviously, if it's fun, you should keep doing it!" she replied. "If you're stuck between two options, you're going to have regrets no matter what you choose, y'know? Human beings are built so that we overrate whatever option we don't take. Basically, you're fine with either option, so you might as well flip a coin if you want to."

"I see... So what if I flip a coin, and I think...I don't want

that? What if I feel some resistance to the choice God made
for me?"

"Then it means that deep down, you secretly wanted the other
option more, right? So choose that one instead. It's simple."

"Oh... Good point..."

"If you'll allow me to be totally selfish, I like things the way
they are now, when I can actually talk to you about games. Yeah,
I know that's self-centered."

Karen was beginning to think that maybe she could turn down
SJ but still play *GGO* for a bit longer.

"Huh? Wait," Miyu said. "But February first is the day of
Elza Kanzaki's big concert. Weren't you going to go if you got
tickets?"

"Oh!" Karen hastily snapped open her planner and saw that she
had indeed written that down. She'd completely forgotten.

Not once had Karen ever succeeded at getting Elza Kanzaki
tickets. She always played smaller venues, so the tickets came at a
premium. Karen wasn't asking for a stadium tour, but it'd be nice
if she performed somewhere a *bit* larger, like a proper concert
hall.

On the other end of the call, Miyu was checking the online auc-
tion sites for any of the sold-out tickets.

"You're right—I totally forgot. Sorry... Well, if I get tickets,
I'm obviously turning down the event. We'll go together, okay?
You can stay at my place."

"Cool. But what if it doesn't work out? Honestly, based on my
experience, our chances of getting these tickets is about fifty-fifty
at this point."

"When will you find out if we won?"

"Four in the afternoon on Tuesday."

What incredible timing. Karen decided to wager her Squad Jam
appearance on that coin toss. She was conveniently ignoring the
greater question of whether she'd keep playing the game or not
for now.

"Okay…let me know then! If you win the tickets, I'll turn down the tournament!"

The January weather in Tokyo was consistently clear. To Karen, who had grown up in chilly Hokkaido, it wasn't the relative warmth that was novel, but the total dryness. On the other hand, her throat hurt, her skin was awful, and it was a pain to keep feeding the humidifier in the apartment, so she didn't like the experience very much.

Her apartment was barely a mile from the college. That was just one station on the subway, but unless the weather was bad, Karen always walked. She preferred that to looking at her reflection in the train window, and the exercise was better for her anyway.

January 27th, just before four o'clock on Tuesday.

Karen's classes were over, and she walked across campus with the early sunset of winter fast approaching. It hardly needed to be said that she was alone.

Around her, she heard people excitedly getting ready to hit the bars or meet up with their school clubs, but none of that meant anything to Karen. It was all happening in a different world.

She headed home, wearing jeans, sneakers, and a thin coat as she passed under decorative trees bare of leaves. Up ahead, she saw a group of six teenage girls approaching. They wore the same uniform, so their presence meant they were students at the affiliated high school on campus.

It wasn't at all uncommon for her to pass this particular group. It happened two or three times a week, ever since last summer. Karen could recognize their faces now.

Based on the large sports bags they carried, she could assume they were in some kind of athletics club. The college's gymnasium was large enough that they could sometimes hold joint practices with the high school teams.

One of the girls was white, with beautiful blond hair, pale skin, and blue eyes—either a foreign transfer student or the daughter of

a foreigner living in Japan. Both cases would not be particularly rare at this school.

They were all short—to Karen at least, though they were probably normal by the standards of their age—and fragile, and so pretty. They talked and laughed and seemed to be having a great time, just perfectly outgoing teenage girls enjoying the company of their friends in the prime of their youth.

Would Karen have experienced her teenage years the same way if she hadn't grown up to be so tall? The thought cast an unavoidable gloom over her mind. None of this was the fault of those girls.

As the group of six approached, Karen picked up her pace, determined to get home. She'd get word from Miyu soon about whether they'd won the Elza Kanzaki tickets.

One quiet person and six noisy ones passed without interaction.

"Hey, did you see her?" Karen heard one say. "She was really tall and—"

She didn't want to hear whatever came next. Karen hid her face and sped up, fleeing the scene. As she did, a certain desire bubbled up within her.

*I want to shoot them. I want to shoot all six.*

Her right hand grasped for P-chan, which would be slung on her front, but her fingers touched nothing.

Karen fled home and slammed the door. Her smartphone buzzed the moment the automatic lock engaged.

Miyu's message said, No LUCK!

Karen walked over to the PC in her living room, booted it up, and started *GGO*.

"Let's kick some ass!" she wrote to Pitohui.

✳        ✳        ✳

It was just past eight PM on Friday, January 30th.

Karen finished an enjoyable dinner with her sister, brother-in-law, and niece, and then left their apartment. Her four-year-old

niece begged her to stick around and watch an animated movie that would be airing on TV soon.

"Sorry, Aunt Karen needs to go do homework," she lied, then went back to her own place on a lower floor of the same high-rise apartment building.

From there, she crossed dimensions into the virtual world.

"Heya, Llenn! I knew I could count on you!"

Pitohui cheered, smacking Llenn on the shoulders in the bar in SBC Glocken, where they agreed to meet up. The way the taller woman pounded on her, Llenn felt her tiny frame compressing even further.

"Ow, Pito, ow! Well, here I am…," she said, looking around the dim and cramped booth. It was just the two of them.

"Oh, you're looking for your partner. Sorry, he'll be here soon. Look, I'll buy you the usual drink."

"Thanks. Is he shopping somewhere?" Llenn asked, sitting across from Pitohui. By "somewhere," she meant a shop in *GGO*.

"Nope, still IRL. I asked him for a favor," she replied. This came as a surprise to Llenn.

If she was able to ask him a favor in real life and knew that he would be late as a result, wouldn't that suggest that this man was personally close to Pitohui? Could he be…a boyfriend? A lover? Her husband? Perhaps even her son or father?

Being careful not to speak her mind or let any hint of surprise cross her face, Llenn reached forward for the iced tea that rose from the center of the table and popped the straw into her mouth. The taste of cold, sweet iced tea saturated her taste buds, though the sensation wasn't as sharp as the real thing. Still, she didn't have to worry about gaining weight or needing to visit the bathroom later.

Pitohui took a huge swig of some citrus concoction colored like a tropical fish. "Did you read the Squad Jam rules? Knowing you, I bet you read every last word, but I'll go over them just in case."

Llenn indicated that she had, secretly marveling at how well

the other woman understood her. After she'd filled out the forms for the event, an e-mail had come in from Zaskar, the company that operated the game. She'd read it very carefully, without skimming any part.

The basic rules of the Squad Jam were the same as the BoB, its free-for-all counterpart. But there were a few very big differences.

As for the similar rules…

*All participants (teams) will be teleported to a location over a kilometer away from one another. The last to survive is the winner.*

*The match takes place on a special map. The details will not be revealed prior to the event, but it will contain a variety of terrain. Some positions will be more advantageous than others, but all starting locations are random and subject to luck.*

*Any weapons the character possesses are eligible during battle. This includes not just guns but explosives, knives, etc. Vehicles located on the map are available to use.*

*Rather than breaking apart and disappearing, bodies will remain on the map for a set period of time with a* DEAD *tag above them.*

*Upon death, there will be no random drops, in which a dead character's items, including guns, have a random chance of being lost.*

*To prevent one-sided running and hiding, there will be a periodic Satellite Scan. The scan will identify the positions of all players and beam the data to each player's portable device for a brief time.*

"Any questions so far?" Pitohui asked, after she had pointed out each of the rules on the floating screen.

"I'm fine. The only thing I'm wondering about is how to operate the Satellite Scan terminal."

"It's not that hard, as long as you know how to use a smartphone. Now, about the important stuff: the specific rules of Squad Jam…"

Obviously, the biggest thing was the number of participants.

*There is no individual participation. Teams must be composed of two to six players.*

*Attacking teammates (by accidental friendly fire or blast damage) will inflict standard damage.*

*Communications items that were forbidden in BoB are allowed between teammates. It is not possible to communicate with external or dead players.*

Pitohui put a finger to her ear and said, "I'll give you an in-ear comm. It's the same one I used earlier."

"Got it."

It was a two-way comm, meaning you could speak and hear through it simultaneously, making it essentially the same as a phone. Ordinary radios were one-sided, so you could speak to the other person only when holding down a button.

On the other hand, two-way communications meant you always heard everyone, so the more people involved, the bigger a mess it became. This was a decision that came down to personal preference, but for a team of just two players, two-way communication was the easiest solution.

The next big difference:

*Bodies disappear after ten minutes, and players can return to the bar.*

"This is probably because it's not as strict an event as BoB. With the amount of money being gambled during BoB, they force the player to stay in their static body until a winner is declared, to prevent any kind of information leak in the meantime."

"Ah, I see. But in the Squad Jam, you don't have to wait all the way to the end if you die?"

"You'd better not be planning to die early."

"No, ma'am! I'll fight to the bitter end!"

"That's better."

The timing of the Satellite Scan was also altered.

*The interval between Satellite Scans has been reduced from fifteen minutes to ten minutes.*

"This is designed to reduce the length of the event itself. The BoB usually wraps up around two hours after it starts, and this is almost guaranteed to be shorter. It'll start at two PM on Sunday… and it could even be done within an hour."

"That quickly?"

"By my keen, insightful estimate."

"Who says that about themselves…?"

"Why can't I? My point is, if you survive over an hour in this tournament, that's very impressive."

"Oh, I get it. Since we're in teams, it might turn into a huge firefight right away…"

"Exactly. Any enemies will be at least a kilometer away at the start, but that gap can be closed in a hurry at a total sprint, so you can't be careless. In a visible spot, you're vulnerable to sniping at eight hundred meters, and they can hit you with machine-gun fire at six hundred. But I'll leave that stuff up to the person you'll actually be playing with," Pitohui said, referencing the stranger who had yet to arrive. "But here's the most important part of the SJ rules! Pay attention, because it'll be on the test!"

She pointed at the screen. In its characteristic abbreviated tone, the rule read:

*The Satellite Scan will only display the position of the squad leader. Tapping a player marker in BoB displayed the player's name, but in SJ, the team name will not be viewable.*

"What does that mean?"

"Well, with up to six players on a team, if it showed everyone at once, the screen would be absolute chaos."

"I see…"

"So instead, it only displays the leader. Now, can anyone tell me what this means? You, Llenn!" Miss Pitohui commanded.

Ever the dutiful student, Llenn thought it over for a few seconds. "You can't see the other members on the map, so they could be hiding…and the location of the leader could be used as a trap…"

"Exactly! Spoken like the devious antlion trapmeister that you are, Llenn! You're so quick to learn!"

"Please don't bring that up…"

"But that was a compliment! Geez, the brutally dehumanizing way you used to attack your victims! What a thrill!"

"Can we get back on topic? You were pointing out that Satellite Scans have a different meaning in the Squad Jam than in the Bullet of Bullets."

"Indeed. But on the other hand, splitting your team up too much has its own disadvantages."

"Got it… Question, teacher!"

"Yes, Llenn."

"What happens if the team leader dies? Does the team automatically lose?"

"No, because that wouldn't be fun for everyone, would it? And the leader's the only one whose location gets revealed, so they could get picked off by a sniper. No, it just continues like it would in a real battle."

"What do you mean?"

"If the commander of a military group dies, the person in the next rank down—or the senior member, if there are more than one—takes command. So in SJ, the team is ranked in order when you sign up, and thus, leadership passes downward to second, then third, and so on."

"Okay. Well, since there are only two of us, that saves us the trouble of deciding all that, huh? And we're really set on competing with just two…?"

"Yup. Good luck with that. Wouldn't it be cool if you won, just as a duo?"

"I guess."

"There's also a rule that only the leader can surrender, and in that case, the entire team is out. That doesn't mean much to you, either. Basically, it's there in case you lose too many members and feel like there's no chance you can win anymore."

"Ah, uh-huh."

Llenn popped her straw into her mouth to suck down the last of the iced tea.

"And that's all for the rules, Captain Llenn."

She nearly spat out all the liquid. "Wha—? Huh? Eh?"

"Doing some vocal exercises?"

"No! What do you mean, *I'm* the leader? Why? Is the person I'm teaming up with worse than me?"

"C'mon, keep it together. And no, of course the other guy is very tough."

"Then…why?" Llenn asked again, her entire face one giant question mark.

The tattooed Pitohui replied, "It's a secret! Consider it part of the plan."

"…"

Llenn couldn't think of anything to say. The booth fell silent.

Just then, a deep male voice said, "Sorry I'm late," and a huge man entered the space.

# CHAPTER 4

## The Man Named M

SECT.4

# CHAPTER 4
## The Man Named M

When the man opened the curtains and stepped into their private booth, Llenn at first thought he was a bear.

"..."

He was enormous, towering over them at six foot four. He wore camo pants in a venomous green, brown, and black pattern, and a brown T-shirt.

There wasn't a single piece of combat gear on him, which only served to underscore his innate physical menace. Not only was he tall; his chest was wide and stout. In fact, it almost looked like he was equipped with bulletproof plating under the skin of his pecs. The arms bulging from his shirtsleeves were like logs and probably as wide as Llenn's waist.

What made him even more bearlike was his head. His wavy, dark-brown hair grazed his shoulders and covered his skull in a mop. His shaved countenance was as craggy as a rock face. His eyes were on the larger side, but they didn't make him look any nicer.

He appeared to be quite old, at least forty. The avatar's visible age and the player's age had no connection, of course, so he could have been a teenager for all she knew, or he might have been a grandpa in his eighties.

In a reflection of *GGO*'s American origins, massive body-builder avatars like this one weren't uncommon. She'd seen them

around the city before, but it was quite frightening for her to be this close to one.

The funny thing was, if he were a newbie player with low strength, even a giant like him might be unable to carry guns that Llenn was able to equip. But Pitohui did vouch for his toughness, so that was unlikely. He was probably at least as good as she was, if not even more of a veteran player.

"Hey, you're late, jackass."

"Sorry, Pito. But I took care of all the errands," the man said.

Even this simple statement terrified Llenn. She'd never met such a large human being in her life. It was giving her flashbacks to the time she went to the zoo as a toddler and saw a bear through the glass of the exhibit.

She was ready to bow out, to claim that she couldn't perform with such a terrifying partner. But that would be rude to both of them, and she'd already made the decision to play. Besides, he was going to be her partner, not her opponent.

"Fine, fine. Sit over here," Pitohui said, getting up and showing him to her empty seat. The large man switched places with her and squished uncomfortably into the bench seat across from Llenn.

"Here we go, Llenn! This pointlessly and idiotically large fellow here—"

Llenn felt a stab of pain in her heart. That was exactly what people thought of her in real life. But Pitohui didn't know that and couldn't be blamed for it. The whole point of VR games was to hide your real self.

"—is your partner in this event. Go on and introduce yourselves."

Pitohui's attitude toward the man was extremely overbearing. Whatever their relationship was, Llenn got the sense that she had a considerably higher status than him in real life.

The man bowed. "It's nice to meet you. My name is M."

That was it. He looked scary, but his mannerisms were polite and proper. Out of a lifetime of social habit, Llenn bowed in return and said, "Nice to meet you, too. I'm Llenn."

They fell silent. Clearly the man named M was not as sociable as Pitohui.

*Wow, this is awkward. It's a good thing Pito's here to break the ice between us*, Llenn thought.

"Well, I've got an errand to run now. The rest is up to you two youngsters!" Pitohui said abruptly, like the go-between for a meeting between two parties in an arranged marriage.

"Huh? Wait—," Llenn started to say, but the other woman was already gone.

All that remained was an unbearable discomfort.

It wasn't because she was alone with a man. Physical contact with the opposite sex in a VR game activated a harassment warning. If such contact continued, the offender would be penalized and possibly lose their account.

Since puberty, Karen had hardly had any one-on-one interactions with men. And that "hardly" was thanks to her two older brothers and her sister's husband. So at the very least, she wasn't completely terrified into silence around the opposite sex. And yet...

"..."

She wasn't in any type of mood to lead the conversation. Not when her conversation partner looked like he was liable to bite her head off and swallow it whole. At the same time, her reaction registered in her mind as the same thing people felt about her in real life, which only increased her self-loathing.

Llenn stared down at the table, suddenly wishing she could log out and get away from there.

"L-listen," M said in an anxious, stammering voice, "let's t-try not to be too n-nervous about this, shall we? Er, I mean...let's be frank. If we act too polite and stuffy...Pito will...beat me up later."

*Oh, he's scared, too*, Llenn realized with some relief. Although violence was not a good thing by any means, the mental image of

Pitohui beating up this massive specimen of a man was a little bit funny to her.

"Uh, g-good point. Let's be casual, then."

It was a rule in the Kohiruimaki house that one must look the other person in the eyes while speaking. Her parents ran a business, so this was of utmost importance to them. Llenn looked into the eyes of that craggy face and said, "I agreed to take part in this event, so I intend to do my best. It's a pleasure to work with you, M."

"Sounds good. If we want to win, we've got to work together. Let's do our best, Llenn. Uh…is it okay to call you that? I'm not so good with…cutesy nicknames."

Llenn nodded. M was turning out to be much less frightening than he looked. Again she wondered what kind of person was controlling this frightening fellow, and had to summon her self-control to drop that train of thought. If she thought too much about it, she'd blurt it out.

"What did Pito tell you about this? What were you talking about before I showed up?" M asked, a bit more comfortable now that he had received his iced coffee from the hole in the table.

Llenn decided she would treat him like a friendly uncle, someone older she could speak to in a familiar manner.

"She went over the rules for the Squad Jam, explained about the radio comm, and for some reason, she said that I was the squad leader."

"Ah, okay. And did she tell you the reason she put you and me together today?"

"Nope." Llenn shook her head.

It was a good question. Why *had* Pitohui put the two of them together? She'd never said why; she had just asked whether Llenn was available for about three hours starting at nine o'clock on Friday night. It was nice that she wanted to introduce Llenn to M before the event, since Pitohui would be busy with that wedding on the big day, but who needed three hours for a couple of introductions? It would be one thing if the three ventured out to do

some monster battling as a little meet and greet, but Pitohui just scampered off as soon as they were both there.

"Good grief," he said, sighing with a weak smile. The sight of that menacing face smiling put a strange thought into Llenn's mind. *Oh, he really can smile. They do have graphics for a smiling face like that.*

"Well, neither of us knows what the other is capable of. Pito gave me a brief rundown of your abilities, but I'd like to go to the practice grounds and see for myself."

The practice grounds were just what they sounded like. There was a selection of different terrain and building samples to move around in, and unlike an indoor shooting range, you could practice actual mobility on battlefield terrain and long-range sniping. If you set each player to no damage, you could even run combat practice. Best of all, you didn't have to worry about monsters or other players ambushing you. On the other hand, you did have to reserve the time, and the cost was considerable.

"Ah, I see. Still, there's just one thing I can't help but wonder…"

"What's that?"

"Why am I the leader? I mean, you don't have to see me in action to know I'm not good enough to lead," Llenn protested.

M looked down at her and smiled. "Don't worry. We decided on that for a reason. I'll be the one calling the shots."


Karen returned to the real world just before Friday turned into Saturday.

She stretched her larger body, regaining the more familiar sensations, then got to her feet and switched on the light.

She looked over at the black P90 hanging on her wardrobe. "I guess that was…a tryout to join the team?" she mumbled to herself.


For about two and a half hours, M had made Llenn do all sorts of things.

First, they'd gone to the practice grounds they had already reserved. This one was a wasteland of rocks and abandoned vehicles, all set under that oddly colored sky. In the distance were tilted buildings and a mountain with a crater in it. It didn't look any different from the usual environs, but there was a distance limit of a bit over a mile in any direction. At that point, an invisible wall would appear with a NO FURTHER PROGRESS warning.

"Put on all of your gear. I'll give you the comm, too," M had said.

Llenn had gone into her game window and materialized the equipment she had in her item storage: the pink combat suit and her P90. Changing outfits required briefly stripping down to underwear, but since she had the hooded cloak on, she could perform the command in an instant without any trouble.

From that point on, she'd gone through a gauntlet of commands.

"There's a barrel forty yards ahead. Face it and shoot from a standing position. Ten slow shots on semi-auto, then ten more as fast as possible. The last thirty on full auto.

"It's two hundred yards to that burned-out truck. Hard rock underfoot. Sprint for it with your P90 in your hand. Touch the truck, then sprint back here.

"Now, fire while running. Sprint toward the barrel, and on my command, shoot your entire magazine, full auto, at a run. When you have under eight rounds left, switch it out at once.

"How many yards to that pointy rock there, by your estimate? How far to the hole behind that?"

All of these made sense to her. He was testing her capability in battle. But then...

"There's nothing ahead of you. Close your eyes and walk. Just a normal walk at a normal pace. When I give the command, turn at the angle I say.

"Walk slow, walk normal, trot, run. Switch between them on my command.

"Lie facedown on the ground. After a minute has passed, I

will give a signal without warning. I want you to get to your feet and run in the direction I say. Then lie down again until the next command.

"Walk backward as fast as you can. There are rocks, so if and when you trip, flip backward and get down on your stomach.

"Crouch down into a ball, as small as you can go. Then roll down a slope."

By that point, Llenn had no idea what he was getting out of these exercises. There was no physical exhaustion in a VR game, no matter how much activity you did. If your brain gave the order to "run at a full sprint," your body would keep going as easily as if you were holding down the sprint button on a controller.

On the other hand, Llenn certainly felt *mental* fatigue from all the baffling orders, but she eagerly performed them all.

"Okay, got it. Thanks," he said. She figured that was the end of it, but then M went into his inventory and called forth his own gun.

It was a freakish rifle, large and long, with many jutting protrusions. Llenn thought it looked like some kind of power tool at a construction site. It also had a sturdy bipod and scope.

The gun was painted in a brown-and-green camo pattern. Between the chipped paint and the worn spots here and there, it had clearly seen a lot of use.

"Is that your main gun, M? I've never seen one before; what's it called?" she'd asked, thinking that it looked strong and heavy and was probably beyond her ability to use.

"It's an M14 EBR," he'd explained once he was done checking it over. He'd set it down at his feet and continued pulling out more pieces of gear. "EBR stands for Enhanced Battle Rifle. In other words, it's an advanced version of the old M14 rifle. 7.62 mm rounds."

She recalled what Pitohui had taught her about bullet sizes. "So your battle style is...midrange shooting at semi-auto?" she'd asked.

Llenn now knew many different facts about guns that she hadn't

a clue about before she started playing *GGO*. What she learned from the tutorial and from Pitohui's lessons was that a gun's effective range differed by the caliber and by the type of gun within a single caliber. So it was always worth paying attention to the type and caliber of one's own gun versus the opponent's.

A rough description of effective range would be "the maximum distance that one can aim and inflict damage." The maximum range, which was the longest physical distance a gun could fire a bullet, was a different term with a completely different meaning.

When it came to 7.62 mm bullets, they were powerful and best suited to midrange shooting.

"That's true. I prefer to fight out in the open, keeping some distance from the enemy. Of course, I'll still use the EBR up close, but for combat indoors, I switch to this." A reinforced plastic holster had appeared on M's right thigh.

A large black automatic pistol was inside. M had put the M14 EBR into his sling and pulled the pistol out of the holster. Guns extracted from inventory didn't come preloaded, so he'd pulled the slide with his left hand to load the first bullet into the chamber. Then he had pushed his thumb upward to engage the safety mechanism and displayed the side of the gun to Llenn.

"This is a German HK45 from Heckler & Koch. It's a forty-five-caliber automatic. Capacity: ten rounds. If you raise this lever on the right, that's the safety. Set it flat, and you can fire. It's good to know how it works, because you might end up needing to use it."

M's explanation was much more in-depth than what he'd said about the M14 EBR, but Llenn didn't think it was going to be necessary. Still, she had committed the operation to memory. Put the little lever up, and the safety was on.

*GGO* players hardly ever used the safety. Unlike in the real world, where such a feature was absolutely necessary, this was just a game. The benefit of instant use far outweighed the danger of it going off without warning.

That was what Llenn always did. When she left the safety

of town, she loaded her P90 and had the selector/safety set to "full auto." While on the move, she would have her index finger extended off the trigger, and when it came time to shoot, she used the fine control of the trigger to fire in bursts of three to five shots.

M had put the HK45 back in the holster, then brought out some more equipment. In addition to his considerable muscle, he had a vest lined with bulletproof plates and a backpack large enough for mountain climbing, which only increased his world-class bulk. On his head was a boonie hat in the same camo pattern as his clothes.

Pouches on his vest bulged with magazines for the M14 EBR. Given his size, there was room for plenty, at least eight. Limited ammo wasn't something he needed to worry about.

The backpack was bulging, and she didn't know what was inside of it, but she had to assume it was more battle equipment—not picnic baskets.

When he was done gearing up, he said, "Now I'm going to have you take distances of twenty-five, fifty, and a hundred yards."

"Uh-huh. And then what?"

"I'm going to fire the EBR in a variety of directions. Before I fire, I'll tell you the direction."

"Okay…? And…what am I supposed to do? Just run away?" Llenn asked, afraid she was going to be target practice.

"I want you to listen carefully and remember the sounds," he said, to her surprise.

"The sound? Of the gun?"

"That's right. You might already be aware that the close-range gunfire in *GGO* is significantly quieter than the real thing."

Llenn nodded—Pitohui had told her that already. *GGO* was famous for its realistic depiction of guns, but the volume was one thing that wasn't treated as utterly realistic. Otherwise, it'd be impossible for anyone to have a conversation in a gunfight, and you'd wind up with an outbreak of players with hearing difficulties.

"But even though the volume of the gunfire has been lowered to

the point that it won't cause hearing loss, the changes to the sound in terms of direction and distance are realistic. So if you get used to it, you can start to tell how far away an opponent is when they shoot at you, just from the sound."

"Ohhh, I see."

"You're going to learn the difference in sound at various distances, until you get the hang of what direction and how far-off a gun is shooting. Once I've shot enough times, then I'll make you close your eyes. I'll move around and fire without giving you a heads-up. Then I want you to guess the distance and direction, as accurately as you can."

Llenn thought this sounded tough, but she didn't have much choice in the matter. It was better than getting shot. If the last set was a gym test, this one was music class.

"Got it…"

"When we're done with that, we'll repeat the process with obstacles like rocks and cars and structures in between. You need to remember the difference in the sound between them all."

*Aaargh, this sounds impossible.* She screamed in her mind.

\*         \*         \*

On Saturday, the day after her tryout, Karen had nothing on her schedule aside from some studying for class, which she finished up in the morning. Without anything else to do, she wound up glancing at the AmuSphere hanging on the side of her bed.

"Hmm… Maybe not today," she said, opting out of *GGO*.

She could go hunting monsters on her own, but if she got attacked by another player, there was a possibility she might fail to get away and end up dead. Llenn was confident in her ability to run, but there could be even faster foes out there.

When a character died, all that happened was a "death penalty" loss of experience points, after which you were returned to town. However, on rare occasions the player suffered a random drop, leaving their gun or other gear behind on the spot.

In that case, you'd need a friend to pick it up, or else you'd lose it forever. Llenn had no teammates, so the consequences were obvious. With an important event coming up in just another day, she would be letting Pitohui and M down if she lost her crucial P90.

In the end, she did nothing that afternoon. She'd be getting all the action she wanted the next day.

"Ah, there's nothing like Elza Kanzaki..." Llenn sighed, relaxing to the sound of the singer she was missing out on tomorrow.

Elza Kanzaki was a singer-songwriter, so she had her own originals, but many of her songs were arrangements of classical pieces of music. Karen was a fan of the classical genre, so this was one of the reasons she liked Elza.

As she listened, she wondered why Elza Kanzaki wouldn't put on concerts at a bigger venue. Then she had an idea.

*Dear Ms. Elza Kanzaki...*

She would write a fan letter. She had some cute stationery and envelopes from when her niece had come over to hang out.

It was the first time she had ever written a fan letter, but the words mysteriously flowed out of her pen. The next thing she knew, she was writing about how she had a complex about her height, and that in order to cope with it, she was playing VR games with a tiny player avatar.

She followed it up by saying that she loved Elza's singing voice and was hoping to hear it in person, so would she please consider performing a concert in a larger place?

When Karen was done, she ate dinner, then read over what she had written. Even she had to admit she'd overshared a bit, and she felt embarrassed about it.

"..."

But then she realized that Elza would probably never read it anyway, so she decided to send it.

It was made out to Elza Kanzaki's agency. In the hopes that she might one day actually receive a reply, Karen wrote her own name and address on the back of the envelope.

✳         ✳         ✳

While Llenn was sealing her fan letter to Elza Kanzaki with a cute little sticker, people from all over Japan were eagerly looking forward to tomorrow's tournament.

In one case, there were five guys on an Internet call together.

"The time's finally come for us to shine! It's happening tomorrow!"

"Yeah! We're gonna kick some ass!"

"That's right! We may not have been born on the same day, but we sure as hell are gonna die together!"

"No thanks, man. You die first. I'll leave your body, but I'll keep your gear."

"You suck!"

"Bwa-ha-ha! Sorry to ruin your fun, but SJ's just like BoB—there are no random drops."

"Aw. Lame."

"You didn't even know that? You're the worst!"

"Uh, it's called a joke. I'm lightening the mood."

"One day I'm gonna shoot you in the back."

"Look, let's just have fun with this thing, like we're doing right now! They set up this weird tournament to try out, and given that we've all failed to pass the preliminary round of the BoB three times running, maybe it's finally our time to be stars!"

"Yeah! Maybe we'll actually be successful in a team competition!"

"Yes! Let's do this! We can last fifteen minutes!"

"Yeah!" "Yeah!" "Yeah!" "No!"

Elsewhere, a man spoke to a group of six other men.

"Tomorrow's the big day, but since this is just an experiment, it doesn't particularly matter if you do well or not. Given your skill level, I expect you'll get pretty far. But if it looks like you're going to win, resign and quit the game as we discussed. I look forward to seeing your results."

＊　　＊　　＊

Meanwhile, another online voice chat was happening, this time with a group of women.

"It's coming up tomorrow. Don't forget to log in. Especially—"

"I know, I know! Boss is gonna call me tomorrow!"

"Yeah, because you're always late. But at least now we get to shoot some people!"

"We've come this far—there's no way we'll stop at anything less than the championship! We want that prize! Nothing less, right?"

"Of course!"

"Got it!"

"Let's do this! I know we can win!"


In yet another place, a naked man and woman exchanged words in bed, sharing an embrace.

"Tomorrow's the big day. Good luck, darling!"

"…"

"Don't worry. If you die, you only die."

"…"

"As long as you maintain this level of nerves, everything will work out just fine!"

"I…"

"It's okay! It's fine! Look how early it is. Let's do it again!"

"But won't that have an effect on your work tomor…?"

"I'm not that much of a pushover. And what's your excuse? Are you too old for another round, darling?"


Thus Saturday ran its course.

At the stroke of midnight, it was officially Squad Jam Day.

Let the battle begin.

# CHAPTER 5
## The Tournament Begins

SECT.5

# CHAPTER 5
## The Tournament Begins

Sunday, February 1st, 2026.

Things got particularly raucous in an area of SBC Glocken, capital city of *Gun Gale Online*, starting around noon.

There was a large pub along the wide main street. This particular pub also served as a restaurant and a coffee shop; it was adjacent to a shopping mall, had an arcade and casino section, and even had an indoor shooting range in the back.

It was a popular destination for many players on an average Sunday, but this particular day was especially crowded.

The reason was simple: This was the event space for the first-ever Squad Jam event.

It wasn't a massive, game-spanning tournament like the BoB, so instead of holding it at the Regent's Office, the central administration building, everything was happening at this establishment.

The contestants gathered there, and when it came time, the teams were teleported to cramped little waiting areas to get prepped for combat. A ten-minute countdown started, during which they retrieved their gear from storage and held quick strategy meetings. At two o'clock on the dot, they'd be sent to a battlefield they'd never seen before.

The battle would be aired through a number of cameras. With big events like the BoB, the footage was shown on the popular

Net channel MMO Stream so that anyone on the Internet could watch it, but SJ wasn't that big.

You'd need to either watch with the crowd on the wall and ceiling monitors there in the pub, watch it from elsewhere in *GGO*, or acquire a recording to view another day.

When Llenn entered the pub, hidden under her cloak, the digital wristwatch on her left arm said it was 12:45. The watch was synced to the game system, so it would never be wrong.

The Squad Jam participants were supposed to gather at 1:40, and her arrangement with M was at 1:30, so she had plenty of time. She entered the bustling business and looked for an open booth. She wanted to get away from prying eyes so she didn't give away any information to potential opponents.

A couple of players in the building were showing off their treasured guns, but M had warned her never to do that—it was begging other players to start formulating strategies to beat you. On the other hand, there was the tactic of intentionally showing off a weaker gun, then taking advantage of them with a much better one during the event.

Llenn entered a private booth and closed the curtain. She sent the room number to M in a message, as they'd agreed. Within a few minutes, while she was still working on her first iced tea, M showed up. He was as huge as when she first met him, but she wasn't scared this time.

"Hi. Let's do our best today."

"Agreed."

As they waited for the event time, the sounds of excitement growing in the building reverberated in their ears.

On the in-store monitors, a middle-aged man who was the sponsor of the event was doing a video interview, but in his actual body, not as an avatar. He was a sweaty man with unkempt facial hair, and he excitedly jabbered clichés like "I can't wait" and "I hope you guys shoot each other a whole lot."

"You mean the guy who came up with the idea isn't even gonna compete?!" one of the bar patrons yelled at the screen.

"Well, we know what he looks like IRL, but we don't know his avatar!" another one shouted. "So maybe he'll sneak in to participate after this interview."

"Good point! The reverse of the usual way!"

"That's a weird way of doing it…"

"Think we'll get a bonus if we beat him?"

"How much did he pay to sponsor this event?"

Llenn and M pored over the list of participating teams on a floating game window. There were twenty-three in total. Compared to the BoB, which started off with hundreds, who were then whittled down to thirty finalists, this one-round event with no prelims was noticeably smaller in scale.

Still, if each team had the maximum of six members, that was a theoretical total of 138 players at once, and since this was on a map the same size as the BoB's, it was bound to turn into a big mess.

"Let's hope the bar isn't completely empty after it starts," M remarked. Llenn imagined the sight and couldn't stifle a giggle.

However, the number of people in the pub continued to rise, so that didn't seem to be likely. The first Squad Jam was attracting a healthy amount of attention and excitement.

Back to the list of team names. Llenn and M's team was very straightforward: LM, from Llenn and M. The *L* could've been first because Llenn was the leader, or just because it was alphabetical order.

The other team names also tended toward short and simple, like DDL, ZEMAL, SYOJI, CHBYS, DanG, and SHINC. Most were capitalized like acronyms, which probably meant they were abbreviated during registration. Llenn decided that she was quite happy with the simplicity of LM.

The lack of a team members' list was notable. They'd have to assume the worst and fight like every team had six members. On the other hand, that meant they could use their team of two to lure opponents into false confidence.

Unlike the BoB, there was no bookie setting odds on the winning team. Instead, there was a gambling contest to guess how many bullets would be fired by the end of the event, with each entry costing five hundred credits to enter. People seemed to be really excited about that.

Since it was a video game, the system accurately recorded all kinds of statistics, including the number of times any character fired. So it would be quite easy to add up the sum of the shots fired by all participants at the end of the event and compare it to the contest entries.

If a participant guessed the number down to the last digit, they'd win a supply of their favorite ammo in the exact same amount (but only up to 7.62 mm in size).

Ammo in *GGO* had to be bought by the player (or crafted using in-game materials), so an influx of a ton of bullets meant you didn't have to worry about the cost for a while. You could also share it with your squadron or sell it to a shop for cash.

If nobody guessed the exact amount, there would be prizes for the five closest guesses, but the prize rank lowered the more digits the estimation was off—whether it was the tens digit, hundreds digit, etc.

There were plenty of submachine guns and grenades by the dozen involved in this battle. Excitement would abound. But as for the number of bullets fired? You couldn't begin to guess. Contestants typed in random numbers from a few thousand to tens of thousands on the submission machines, covering their guesses with their palms as they submitted them.

"I wonder if Pito's in her dress right about now," Llenn blurted out, remembering that she was supposed to be in the wedding party today.

"I'd guess so. She's probably grinding her teeth with frustration that she doesn't get to play in the SJ. I bet there will be people at the wedding wondering, 'Why is one of the bridesmaids looking so furious right now? Wait, could it be—?!'" M said, prompting a loud laugh from Llenn.

She squeezed her knees together and stretched. "Let's give it a shot, M. I wasn't sure if I wanted to go through with this, but maybe I need to show *GGO* I've got what it takes," she said somewhat stiffly.

"All right. That's enough of the speeches."

"Uh, aye, aye."

"Before this, Pito told me, 'You have to win!'" M said, his voice soft for such a menacing man.

"That sounds like something Pito would say."

"I told her I'd do my best. I mean, it's just the two of us. We're at a major disadvantage right out of the gate. I told her that if you died, and I was outnumbered, I might just resign. She agreed that there wouldn't be much else I could do."

"Yeah. What's wrong with that? Like I just said, I'll give it my best shot, but a game's just a game. Even in a real war, you can surrender when you know you don't have a chance. If I end up alone, that's probably what I'll do, too."

"Still, we'll try to get as far as we can. Let's have fun seeing what the two of us can do together," he said, trying to convince himself.

"Roger that!" Llenn piped.

Just then, a female voice came over the pub's sound system.

*"Thanks for waiting, all you Squad Jammers! We will be teleporting you to the standby area in just one minute. Is your team all in one place?"*

At 1:50, Llenn and M appeared in a dark, cramped room.

In front of them was a countdown timer displaying PREP TIME REMAINING: 09:59 and dropping each second. When it reached zero, every competitor would be dropped into an unfamiliar map and thrust into battle.

"All right!" shouted Llenn, pumped up.

Laugh or cry, there was no escape from the competition now. She was going to kick some ass and burn off stress from her everyday life.

But first, they needed to prepare.

A screen popped up, indicating that their Satellite Scanners had been distributed. Llenn touched the screen, and a tool the size of a large smartphone appeared. There was another display with instructions on it. If you pressed one of the two main buttons, it would display a map either on the screen or projected before your eyes. If you wanted to be secretive, you'd choose the screen button, and if you had the space and wanted to confer with your squad mates, you could project it. Like a smartphone, the map size could be adjusted by pinching and expanding it.

The actual map wasn't available to display, so for the moment, it had a map with SAMPLE written on it so they could test out the functions.

Every ten minutes, when the Satellite Scan happened, white dots would appear on the map, indicating the location of each team leader. Gray dots indicated the final coordinates of a defeated or resigned team. It was all quite simple to use, to Llenn's relief.

She set down the device and changed into her pink combat fatigues underneath her robe. The pink knit cap went on her head. The pink bandanna went around her neck. She moved the robe into her item storage, no longer needed.

Next came her gear. Her little P-chan, the pink P90, appeared in her hands. The pouches that held three backup clips each were along either thigh.

Llenn loved the system of changing her look instantaneously by pressing buttons on a game window—it reminded her of the transformation scenes from the old magical-girl anime shows she liked to watch. Her final form just happened to look a *little* more deadly than theirs.

It was unlikely that anyone would use an optical gun in a PvP contest like SJ, but there were weirdos everywhere. Llenn equipped a defensive field generator, which looked like a large brooch, just in case.

There was space on her belt, so she stuffed another pouch with the tube-shaped emergency medical kits next to one of her

magazine pouches. The medical kits healed about 30 percent of a player's lost hit points after being attached to the skin. However, that process took a full 180 seconds, so its usefulness in the midst of combat was low.

The Satellite Scanner fit perfectly in the large chest pocket of her combat suit.

"There we go."

Llenn was ready to rock. Then M set down his M14 EBR and handed Llenn something. "Here."

"Huh?"

She took it suspiciously. It was a sheath containing a combat knife.

The green plastic sheath had a black nylon cover, with the black knife grip sticking out of it. The whole thing was about a foot long, with the blade itself just short of eight inches.

Timidly, Llenn undid the flap and removed the knife. It looked like absolute evil, a black blade with a matte finish that reflected no light.

She'd used a kitchen knife to cook before, but she'd never held a knife this big. In Llenn's tiny hands, it felt more like she was holding a machete. It wasn't much different than your ordinary knife, but that was a weapon much more familiar and close to home than a gun. She was overcome with fear.

"…"

She put it right back into the sheath, closed the flap, and turned to M.

"Um…what am I supposed to do with this, M?"

"You've got plenty of strength for it, so keep it around as a side weapon. Without one, you'll be helpless if you run out of P90 ammo."

"But I've got seven magazines. That's three hundred and fifty bullets," she argued. There were three magazines in either thigh pouch, plus the one attached to the P90 already. It was a ton of ammo for a single person to carry—a bonus from the P90's high-capacity magazines.

On the other hand, its special design made exchanging clips more difficult than other guns of its type, but with Llenn's excellent agility and dexterity, she could complete the process in midair during a single jump.

She even had another three stashed in her inventory, so she could load up more clips if she had time between battles.

So far, Llenn had never run out of bullets for her P90. It was why she'd never carried a sub-weapon with her.

But M was insistent. "*GGO* is based on gunfights, but when you're in cramped interiors or fighting very close, it can turn to hand-to-hand combat. Especially in the Squad Jam. Additionally, I might need to give you orders to use your knife, so that you don't make any sound."

Llenn couldn't deny that logic. When hunting monsters, there were times that she got too close and was shooting down at her feet. If she'd had a knife, she could've stabbed and slashed them at that point—and without making a racket.

"There are times when a knife is better than a gun in close combat. Especially when the person is as nimble as you, Llenn. Stash it level, behind your lower back. You'll pull it out backhanded with your right hand…"

He whipped his right hand around to show her the motion.

"Your enemy is very likely to be bigger than you—"

It was hard for her to imagine anyone being smaller.

"—so when facing them, charge forward and duck through their legs, slashing at the interior of either thigh. That's the location of the femoral artery, so you'll do massive damage, perhaps even more than a bullet could."

"…"

This lesson was a bit more realistic than anything Llenn wanted to hear.

*GGO* was quite true to life in the ways that it modeled the human vital areas, for the purpose of identifying and reflecting bodily damage. Even a small-caliber bullet to the center of the skull or the spine could be an instant kill. Damage to areas

susceptible to major bleeding, or that impeded proper movement, caused much higher HP loss.

It seemed to Llenn that she had less mental resistance to guns but significantly more desire not to use the knife. It was a bit of a relief that no matter how much she might shoot people in *GGO*, the physical, kinetic act of directly attacking and killing a person wasn't going to come naturally to her.

On the other hand, that *ALO* game that Miyu wanted to play with her was a world where any fighting not using magic was physical sword combat.

M's lesson on how to kill a man continued. "If they point their gun at you, slice upward at the inside of their upper arm. That will inflict devastating damage, and it might cause them to drop the gun out of pain and numbness."

In VR games, taking damage of any kind, whether getting punched or slashed or hit or blasted with magic or bitten by a monster, caused the player to feel pain.

How much it hurt—or simulated the brain signal of being hurt—depended on the game, and *GGO* was definitely on the harsher end of the scale. Getting shot felt like being prodded in a weak spot. It was very similar to the sensation in shiatsu when a pain center was pressed, inflicting a numbness and lack of strength. The pain also went away immediately and didn't cause enough damage to harm one's skin.

Gunshots to the arms and hands were especially painful, the effect acute enough that it was quite easy to accidentally drop your gun.

"If they drop their gun, don't bother going after it. Keep up the attacks against their thighs and inner arms. People who only fight with guns are surprisingly brittle when it comes to hand-to-hand combat," he continued.

The matter-of-fact way he was saying these things only made them more frightening.

"If you're able to attack an unsuspecting enemy from behind, stay low and slice the back of the leg just above the boot. This

will sever the Achilles tendon. If they topple, don't go for the stomach or chest, where they'll have bulletproof armor. Aim for the neck and slice as long a gash as you can. Like you're caressing the whole front half of the neck with the knife blade."

"......Okay...," Llenn said.

But on the inside, she was thinking, *Who is this guy?!*

He knew too much. All she could do was pray that this knowledge came from video games and not real life.

"When attacking the head, go for the eyes. Human bones are surprisingly tough, so the blade won't go through them. The exception to that is the eye socket. Stab the eye, and you can do direct damage to the brain. The only places where you can score an instant kill with a knife in *GGO* are the neck and the eye."

Llenn filed this information away in her mind, as distasteful as it was to her. Being diligent and studious had its downsides at times like this. She was learning all kinds of things that no girl in college needed to know.

"That's all," he concluded.

M wouldn't take the knife from her, so she had no choice but to equip it behind her back. The convenience of a video game was that she could just press a button in her menu screen, and it attached itself right to her belt.

Llenn slung the P90 under her left shoulder and reached for the knife with her right hand. A little pressure from her thumb released the strap without a sound, and the blade slid free. She tried swiping it forward with the backhand grip. It didn't feel that heavy in her hand.

Given her high agility stat, if she tried to whip it around as fast as she could, the speed would be deadly.

"Good," M said, satisfied.

But as Llenn returned the knife to its sheath, she assumed that she would never use the thing.

By the time the countdown reached three minutes, M had finished his extravagant preparations. Like the other day, he wore

venomous-green camo. He had on the same boonie hat again, but this time there were little dangling pieces of camo fabric all over it to help disguise the distinct shape of his head.

Over his torso, he wore a vest with thick bulletproof armor inside and a number of magazine pouches. This time, plasma grenades dangled from his back, not his side. These grenades were actually much stronger than the traditional kind that exploded with gunpowder and shrapnel.

When a plasma grenade burst, it created a spherical blast of pale energy nearly fifteen feet wide that would eradicate any but the heaviest objects within its radius. Depending on defensive power, any person with at least 60 to 80 percent of their body in the blast radius would instantly die. Anything less than that meant major damage in proportion to weight.

Plasma grenades were light and cheap for the damage they did, making them one of the more popular offensive items in *GGO*. In a close-range battle between players with cover in between, it was often the case that both sides would throw one, like a very violent and dangerous snowball fight.

M still wore the huge, bulging backpack, stuffed with contents unknown. On his right leg was the HK45 holster, and on the left, pouches for both M14 EBR and HK45 clips.

With his formidable size, bulked up with extra gear, and carrying the sizable EBR, he looked like a robot soldier from a sci-fi movie.

*It'd be easier to get around if he just let me ride on his shoulder*, Llenn thought. She decided not to ask.

The countdown timer was under one minute now. Only the part of the clock indicating seconds was active, speedily descending to 43, 42, 41, 40, 39…

"All right…here goes," M said, his voice relaxed. Llenn heard it directly in her left ear, thanks to the comm. She wouldn't need to switch it off until the game was over.

"Let's raise some hell!" Llenn pulled the loading handle of the

P90 and released it, loading the first round into the chamber with a dry click.

M did the same with his M14 EBR, which produced a much deeper version of the same sound.

Nothing got Llenn more pumped up for battle than that loading sound.

The countdown dwindled. Her anticipation rose.

When the line of numbers all read zero, light engulfed the players.


Color and shapes returned to her blank vision.

*Where am I?* The most important and immediate task was to identify her surroundings.

But no sooner had she visually registered it than she heard M say, "Forest. This isn't good."

"Aw, a forest…," Llenn murmured.

They were in the midst of a forest of very tall, extremely straight trees. It reminded her not of the thick, overgrown forests of Japan but of the North American terrain she'd seen on TV before.

The trees were a good ten feet wide, and with so many there, visibility was terrible. You couldn't see a hundred yards ahead. The ground was damp and littered with knee-high ferns, and there was a defined but subtle slope to it.

Llenn looked up and saw a dark canopy of branches overhead, with only hints of the red sky visible through them.

The reason M said it wasn't good became immediately apparent to her. "There are two reasons, right? One, you can't snipe in here. And two, I stick out like a sore thumb."

With so many massive trees around, the range for open shooting with an enemy was a few dozen yards at best. That was within the P90's effective range, but M would not be able to provide long-distance support.

And Llenn's pink camo was most useful in the desert and

wasteland, when the red sun shone down on her. This place was dank and gloomy, and her color was guaranteed to stand out. M, on the other hand, was almost eerily well blended with his green-based pattern. If he stood still, he could practically melt into the forest.

"Exactly. This place is bad for us," M said, reaching behind his back to rummage in one of the backpack pockets. Whatever she was expecting him to pull out, it was not a large poncho. It had the same green camo pattern as his clothes.

He threw it over Llenn's head. "Put that on until we're out of the woods. You can ditch it in an emergency. Shoot the P90 through the poncho if you need to."

This would certainly help her blend in better than the pink. She felt like she'd just learned the nature of one of M's secret tools. He probably had different-colored ponchos for each type of terrain.

She put it on. It covered her hands and weapon, but she could just shoot through the material if they met enemies. It'd probably be a messy process in real life, but here in *GGO*, she'd have that helpful bullet circle for aiming. And it would appear just by putting her finger on the trigger, so she didn't have to worry about holding the sight up to her eye. If she wanted to aim precisely, she'd have to steady herself like usual, however.

Placing the circle over an enemy and firing at close range without stopping to aim was one type of shooting technique in *GGO*, and it was the one Llenn was best at. This was also the reason that dot sights, which displayed the bullet destination with a red dot through a nonmagnifying lens, and laser sights, which cast a laser beam for aiming purposes, weren't popular in *GGO*. Both forms overlapped with the bullet circle feature, which actually made it harder to aim.

"We'll check the map, then move," M said. Given their disadvantage, he probably wanted to get out of the forest as soon as possible.

"Got it! Where to?" Llenn asked. The poncho was so big on her that she looked more like a green ghost now. M pressed some

buttons on the Satellite Scanner and brought up a projection of the map, which made it easier for them to view it together.

The map was justified north and displayed in color and three dimensions, which made it very easy to read. Like any smartphone or tablet, it responded to zooming and rotating motions.

For the first time, Llenn was looking at the setting in which she would be fighting. Deep canyons bordered the sides of the map, meaning the east and west edges. Mountains were to the north, and cliffs bordered the south.

The canyons to the east and west were a common feature meant to limit the map's area and keep players within the proper space. The sheer cliffs towered hundreds of feet high, so any drop meant certain death.

Perhaps sensing that players would snark about it being too artificial of a limitation, they had actually come up with a decent in-world explanation of the feature: "When the giant spacecraft crash-landed, the safety wings on the underside tore these huge rivulets into the earth."

The north end of the map was an abrupt mountain range, while the southern end was a cliff so sudden, it looked like an open fault line. Naturally, both of these were also impregnable obstacles that couldn't be crossed with any action or combination of skills.

Like in the BoB, the accessible area of the map ran about ten kilometers north to south. There were eleven evenly spaced lines displayed vertically and horizontally, which created blocks of one square kilometer each.

The terrain of the map, separated into areas, was as follows:

The bottom portion, about three kilometers wide, was a wide-open area of rocks and sandy wasteland. There were multiple rocky outcroppings and ruins big enough to provide cover.

In the middle of the eastern side lay what remained of a major city. The map showed large streets and high-rise buildings that were still standing. Apparently, the players were supposed to believe the story about the spaceship tearing those canyons into

the earth, yet the city was right next to the eastern edge and the buildings there were still standing.

In the center of the map was a former residential area with simple suburban-type homes. With all the roads and buildings carefully represented on the map, it looked like a maze. A large portion of this part was colored blue, a sign that the ground was underwater there.

Nearby, there was a river flowing from the upper right section to the lower left, so that was likely the water source. It could be walked across if shallow enough, but at a certain depth anyone would be forced to swim. Then they'd have to put their guns and other heavy gear into storage to avoid sinking, unless they were extremely good at swimming. HP steadily dropped in water, so it wasn't where anyone wanted to stay.

Green forests covered the northeast sector, where a tiny marker blinked to indicate their current coordinates. According to the SJ rules, everyone's locations were visible only for the first minute of the event as a handicap. After that, they would be updated only by Satellite Scans.

This view of the map made it clear that they were basically in the upper right corner. The rule was that any potential opponents were at least a kilometer away, so that meant no enemies could be to the north or east.

In the northwest quadrant, west of the forest, it was all fields: wide open with nowhere to hide.

Below that, along the western edge, was a circular marshland area. A massive, spaceship-like structure stuck nearly straight up out of the swamp there. Like a building, it should be available to enter and climb. Most likely, the marsh formed after the ship had crash-landed.

Llenn looked up after about ten seconds, but M still stared at it for another fifteen. He was utterly still, and there was an unfamiliar look of intense concentration on his face—not that she knew him that well—so Llenn waited for him to finish.

"Okay." M pressed a button on the Satellite Scanner to close the map. "First things first, we get out of the forest. I want to make use of the city as much as possible, though we won't get there by the first scan. Let's head straight south. Follow behind me by about thirty feet."

His actual voice was barely audible, but thanks to the modulation of the comm unit, it was crystal clear in her ear. It was so effective that they could communicate in practical silence in the presence of enemies without resorting to hand signals.

"Copy that. I'm following," she said.

M immediately started running south. There was nothing but crisp efficiency in his motion. The direction took him down the gentle slope toward the city.

There wouldn't be any enemies nearby yet, but M was totally alert, with the EBR held in front of him and ready to fire at an instant's notice as he ran.

Llenn wrapped the camouflage poncho around herself and let him get the requisite distance ahead before she followed. The gap between them was to ensure that if they fell into an enemy trap, the automatic fire or grenade blasts wouldn't wipe them both out at once.

She had to be careful not to run too fast, or her superior agility would cause her to catch up, so Llenn reminded herself to run a bit slower than usual.

Once they had passed through several hundred feet of forest, they heard a sound like distant drumming.

"Stop. Get down," M snapped, dropping low—his reactions really were that quick. Llenn followed his lead and crouched down about thirty feet behind him as quickly as she could.

The gunfire was a series of overlapping light bursts, *ta-ta-ta-tan*, carving out a chaotic and irregular rhythm. It sounded like an amateur banging on some hand drums for fun. Clearly, two teams were having a firefight nearby.

The sound would continue for a long period, then a shorter one,

but never stopped for more than two seconds. They were expend-
ing an impressive amount of ammunition.

"Those are 5.56 mm assault rifles. Someone's shooting an
SMG, too," M observed.

"You can tell, M?"

"I can."

The developers of *GGO* had recorded actual gunfire for their
live-ammo guns, so the accuracy of their sound effects was
impressive. But the idea of identifying the type of gun, whether
through some in-game skill or just player knowledge, left Llenn
a bit stunned.

"Huh? Oh…" Then she thought of another question. "So they're
already fighting? Isn't it a bit too soon for that?"

"They probably wanted a better position and took off running
at top speed, then ran into each other. Sounds like it's farther to
the west of us in the forest. Not that far-off."

"I see…"

As M said, seven minutes remained until the first Satellite Scan,
so it must have been a coincidence that they'd encountered each
other. That was a very unlucky stroke for the two teams. They
were locked in a chaotic battle before either side could get a better position. Most likely, some characters had already died, three
minutes into the Squad Jam.

As the gunfire rattled on, M swung his left hand in a different
direction. "We'll take it slowly from here. You go first, Llenn. In
this direction. I'll correct you if you start to drift. If we run across
any others in the forest, duck. I'll give you orders after that."

"R-roger…"

In all honesty, not knowing when they might run across enemies and dealing with the supremely poor visibility of the forest made her very nervous to take the lead, but she couldn't just
refuse an order from a teammate who was likely a much better
player.

Llenn proceeded forward, weaving around the thick trees,

trying to maintain as straight a bearing as she could, at a brisk walking pace. On and on she walked, but the forest didn't change one bit. It was enough to make her wonder whether she was actually making any progress.

*Please don't let me run into any enemies, please don't let me run into any enemies*, she prayed, fighting the urge to place her finger on the trigger of the P90. It would be very poor form to move in that state, in case she tripped and misfired the gun.

Eventually, the distant gunfire came to a total stop. She couldn't tell whether one team had won or whether both had survived and disengaged.

*Please don't let there be any enemies, please, please, please, pleasepleaseplease—*

She headed down the forest slope, nerves strained with fear. *Someone might be hiding* right on the other side *of that tree there. They might shoot me from the side as soon as I pass by.*

Of course, there was no end to the ways she could imagine an attack, so eventually her mind-set turned to: *Ugh, if you're going to come, then do it already! I'll gladly feed your blood to P-chan, even if I go down in the attempt!*

But the goddess of good luck smiled upon her. Nine minutes had passed from the start of the game, and they hadn't made contact with any foes.

"Okay, halt. Crouch. Stay on alert," M commanded, while he got ready for the Satellite Scan.

"Phew…," she exhaled, squatting.

If he had been a bit later to give the order, she would have stopped on her own. The forest came to an end about thirty feet beyond Llenn's position. The slope continued from there, bare of anything but grass, and then there was the ruined city.

Just before her was a six-lane road, probably a highway. It was level with the adjacent ground, not elevated. Based on the position, she guessed that the river was running in a drain system beneath the highway.

At least the road surface looked sturdy and easy to run on.

Overturned and burned-out cars dotted the road. Compared to the forest, there was far more visibility, but at the cost of less cover to hide behind.

Beyond that were a few little hills of rubble, then a number of abandoned buildings between ten and thirty floors tall.

Llenn looked around very carefully. She couldn't see anyone from their current position. They'd definitely crossed at least one kilometer going south, so if any enemies started to the south, they'd have moved even farther south, or west.

"Phew…" She turned around to see where M was.

"I'm three hundred meters behind you," came his voice into her ear.

"Huh? That far?" she blurted out.

"The scan's about to begin," he said calmly. "Your location will be revealed. So I put some distance between us."

"…"

"If we're unlucky, and there are enemies nearby, they're going to come bearing down on you right after the satellite passes."

Llenn knew that already. But that would mean she'd be facing up to six combatants alone. There was no way she could win.

"A-and…? What should I do then?" she had to ask, as she couldn't tell what M was thinking.

"Just fire like crazy—you don't have to aim—and retreat from tree to tree. I'll swing around to the left and pick off anyone who comes chasing after you."

So she was going to be a decoy, and because they were so close to the edge, M knew that he could move around her that way without running into anyone.

It made sense to Llenn, but it was also rather infuriating. *How can he use the team leader as bait?!*

At 2:09:30 PM, the watch on Llenn's left wrist started vibrating. She'd set the alarm to go off thirty seconds before each Satellite Scan.

"Don't worry about watching the scan come in, Llenn. Just keep an eye out."

"Roger."

She didn't need an order to remind her not to get distracted while enemies might be bearing down on her; she was quite capable of doing that on her own. Underneath the poncho, she felt for the P90's safety to make sure that it was off and ready to fire.

The very next moment, she saw a human figure on the move.

"Huh?"

# CHAPTER 6

## The Battle Begins

**SECT.6**

# CHAPTER 6
## The Battle Begins

"Huh?"

Llenn had definitely caught a glimpse of a human being.

In the city across the wide highway from the forest where she was standing, there was a line of men walking down a street, hiding as they moved from mound to mound of rubble. From what she could make out at this considerable distance, they carried round black sticks with them. There was no likely answer other than firearms.

She ducked behind a stout tree nearby and leaned so only her right eye was visible.

"Uh, M...? Enemies spotted..."

"We've got thirty seconds to the scan. Describe as much as you can."

"Huh? Um, uh, they're across the highway! In the town! At least two hundred yards, I think! Um, um..."

"Calm down. How many are there? What are their guns?"

"At least five! Can't tell what guns! But they're not small—I can tell that much! They're hiding near rubble, and— Oh! They just stopped!"

"They're going to watch the scan. Then they'll see you."

"Wh-wh-wh-what should I do? Fire? Sh-should I open fire?" she stammered.

"Like I said, calm down. There's no point shooting with the

P90 from that distance. They'll spot you either way. The scan's about to start. Just stay put."

"*Eeep!*" she shrieked, glancing at her wrist. It was 2:10. "Darn, right when I spotted them first!" It was just her bad luck.

Llenn couldn't see the results of the scan, as she didn't have her device active at the moment. Instead, she waited a very long ten seconds for M to speak.

"Got it. There's one team in the city, across the highway from us. A bit over two hundred yards away."

"A-anyone else?" Llenn asked.

"We're fine. None that are within range of imminent combat," he replied.

She exhaled in relief at the good news at the exact same moment that a number of translucent red lines silently appeared in the forest with her. They looked like aiming laser sights, but in fact, they were bullet lines.

It was a friendly *GGO* warning: *Bullets are about to fly here.* And over a hundred of them.

Day or night, rain or shine or fog, they would be clear as could be. The way the red lines danced and pierced through the forest looked like some kind of concert.

"Aaaaaaaaaahhh! M, they're aiming at me!" she screamed, ducking back right at the moment that something cracked like a whip past her. All around was the sound of wooden trunks splitting and splintering.

A moment later, she heard a low *du-du-du-du-du-du-dum* and a higher-pitched *ta-ta-ta-ta-ta-ta-ta-ta-ta-tak*, but much louder than before.

They couldn't see her, but they knew where she was, thanks to the scan. They all trained their guns on her general location, and a hail of gunfire blasted through the area within a hundred feet of her.

Soil shot up from the ground, and fern leaves danced. Occasionally, a bright-orange projectile, not the bullet lines, would shoot

past. That would be a tracer bullet, a special flared round that helped the shooter see where their gunfire was going.

Her sight was full of red lines and pieces of the ground and tree trunks bursting like popcorn kernels. The air was heavy with the twang of bullets rocketing past, the heavy pummeling of the trees, and the distant gunfire.

"Eek! They're shooting at me like crazy, M! I'm scared! Help me!" she yelped, trapped in place.

M's helpful response was "Ah, good. They've got machine guns."

"Whaaaat?"

"Standard 7.62 mm machine guns. Based on the sound, I'd guess there's an FN MAG there, probably at least two. There's a lighter, faster report mixed in, too, which means a 5.56 mm. That's got to be a Minimi, also from FN Herstal."

"Hello?! Are you gonna rescue me?"

"You're fine for now. Just stay hidden where you are and don't move."

"Blast 'em!"

In front of a mound of rubble in the city, about two hundred meters away from Llenn, a group of men let loose with their machine guns, smiles plastered on their faces.

"Hya-haaa!"

There were five in total.

All were large and gruff types, though none were as impressive as M. The weapons they carried were just as menacing.

"This ruuuuuules!" bellowed one as he sprayed full auto gunfire from his FN MAG, one of the most famous machine guns in the world. There was a bipod set up on the rubble so he could aim into the distant forest beyond the highway.

It spat a deep rumble, *du-du-du-du-du-du-du-du-du-du-du-du-du-du-dum*, the muzzle ejecting with such force that little shock waves of dust were kicked up around it. The 7.62 mm ammo belt hanging from the left side of the gun was feeding it over ten

rounds a second, the empty cartridges ejected below the gun, while the metallic links that held the belt together flew apart to the right.

The muzzle spat red flame, with every fifth bullet being a tracer that left a bright-orange trail to see.

*"Rrrraaaaaaaaahhh!"*

Several feet to the side of him was another bellowing man, holding an M240B, an American military version of the MAG with only subtle visual differences. This person was standing up, with the carrying handle in his left hand and the gunstock wedged against his side as he fired.

The other three also used machine guns.

One was another 7.62 mm, the M60E3.

One was the Minimi, a 5.56 mm light machine gun.

The last man had another light machine gun, the Negev, which was an Israel Weapon Industries gun modeled after the Minimi. He had it set up in a prone position atop the rubble pile.

Battle scenes were always displayed on the live stream, so there was a light-blue circle that represented the camera's location circling around the group, searching for the most striking angle.

This particular group, the one being beamed to the roaring audience in the pub, was the very group that had sworn a particularly uninspiring oath the night before: "Let's last fifteen minutes!"

On the screen, they were identified as Team ZEMAL. Though Llenn and M and any other player in the event couldn't have known this, it was an abbreviation of Zen-Nippon (All-Japan) Machine-Gun Lovers. And yes, they really did love their machine guns.

The group was made up of players located all over Japan who had bonded within the game over their shared interest. The only reason they called themselves All-Japan, despite having only five members, was because one was in Hokkaido to the north, while another was in Okinawa to the far south. That was it.

They had one very particular interest in common, and that interest was *Holy shit, I love machine guns.* One guess as to why they were all using them.

If any one of them even suggested using a different weapon, he'd be kicked off the team. They didn't even have sidearms. Optical guns? What are those, a new kind of candy?

Heavy guns required a high strength stat, so obviously, all their characters were built in that manner. Machine guns were expensive in the game, so they either had to chip away at the cost by playing or sink real money in to buy the ones they wanted. In either case, the enthusiasm required to scrape together those guns was considerable.

But while they all enjoyed playing *GGO* together, there was another feature they shared as a team: They were all extremely bad at PvP combat.

Machine guns are powerful guns that can inundate a target with a hail of bullets. Their ammo loads on a belt, which means that over a hundred rounds can be fired consecutively before a reload. If used to hold down an enemy for the duration of that belt, with assault rifles or SMGs to pick up the slack in between while reloading, they can be quite effective weapons.

"Raaaaah!"

"Hell yeaaaaaah!"

"Whoo-hooooo!"

"Eat this!"

"Die, bitches!"

However, these five were focused on nothing but their own excitement and didn't have a single thought about teamwork. As long as they could shoot their machine guns, they were happy. All it took to satisfy them was the sound and vibration of that rapid gunfire.

Who wanted to study tactics, put together a plan to fool the opponent, and then work in close coordination? They subscribed to a simpler philosophy: "I point, I shoot."

So they never truly attempted to tackle PvP battle. They'd only

ever blasted monsters for experience and credits. Sometimes they would run across another team while coming back from a good loot run.

But the other team would always think, *They've all got live-ammo machine guns—no way they're coming back from a hunt. Let's steer clear.* Everyone always assumed they knew exactly what they were doing, so other teams never tried to lay an ambush.

The members of Team ZEMAL had attempted the Bullet of Bullets individually, but at best, they'd won their first matches with pure firepower and had never gotten much further. None had ever reached the final round.

Along came the Squad Jam.

They applied to the event with delight, feeling that this was something designed just for them: the chance to blaze their machine guns as a team. And when the game started, blaze them they did.

"Look how close someone is, right at the first scan!"

"Yeah, we're so lucky!"

"Thank you, god of machine guns!"


The actual level of their player skill aside, it didn't change the fact that Llenn was in serious trouble under fire.

"Hyaaaa!" she shrieked. Five machine guns were unloading on her position all at once, so the damage to her vicinity was tremendous. Within a minute, the trees around Llenn were riddled with holes. It was ecological destruction.

She couldn't see it from her position, but Llenn began to imagine that the thick tree trunk she was hiding against was already half-torn to shreds and ready to topple onto her head at any moment. "Brrr…" She felt a chill run down her back.

"M! M, help!" she pleaded as the merciless hail of fire continued. The Satellite Scan must have been over by then, so he should have been coming to her aid or at least trying to do *something* by now.

"Just stay there. Don't move." He was calculated, cold even.

"Ugh…" Llenn just wanted to get away from the downpour of lead, but anywhere she looked to move, she saw glimmering bullet lines. She'd be shot up before she even reached the nearest adjacent tree.

"Shit!" she swore in unladylike fashion, shrinking even smaller.

At that point, M had approached Llenn's position from behind, at a distance of about a hundred yards. Using a particularly wide tree as cover, he carefully peered out to catch a glimpse of the bullet lines laying assault to Llenn's spot. It was hard to miss the red lines shining and waving through the woods.

At times, one would leap and land close to his location, but not close enough that he needed to move. He stayed put, focusing on the western side, where the enemy was more likely to come from, as the bullets shot down their indicated paths, erasing the bullet lines as they went.

M glanced at the watch on the inside of his left wrist. Three minutes had passed since the 2:10 Satellite Scan. "Should be just about time…"

Llenn picked up his voice over the comm and said, "Time for what?" as she hoped that he would give her orders.

"Nothing. Just stay there."

"Switch out!"

The man on his feet with the M240B shouted to the rest of the All-Japan Machine-Gun Lovers, then crouched. He lowered the elongated backpack from his shoulders and pulled out a bag with a spare ammunition belt and a backup gun barrel.

Machine guns could handle a lot of consecutive fire, but not endlessly. A huge burst of concentrated gunfire heated up the barrel until its performance suffered noticeably. At some point, changing the barrel was absolutely necessary, a feature that *GGO* faithfully replicated.

Each gun's parts had different durability settings, and none

were as true to life as the effect of consecutive firing on a gun barrel. Ignore it at your own peril—eventually, accuracy would take a major hit, until ultimately the gun just stopped working.

"Copy that!"

"You got it!"

"No problem!"

"Loud and clear!"

They might not have had a single clue how to operate as a team, but as aficionados of machine guns, they at least understood this much. The first man pulled the bolt back and opened the cover to check for any remaining ammunition. Then he pressed a button on the left side of the gun and yanked the carrying handle on the gun barrel to the left. That unlocked the barrel, which could now be removed from the front.

He put on a new barrel using the same mechanism and loaded a fresh belt of ammo, and within a few seconds, the exchange was complete.

"Hell yeah! Time to get back at it!" he shouted, turning to the woods where Llenn was hiding, a smile on his face.

He crumpled on the spot without firing another shot.

When he hit the ground face-first, there was a shining red spot on the back of his neck along his spine. An icon reading DEAD appeared over his body. He was gone, just like that.

"Huh? What the—?" noticed the teammate who'd been happily firing the Minimi. They'd been blasting away so consistently that nobody had heard the enemy's shot. "Hey! Whoa! Stop firing!" he bellowed.

Thanks to the game's unique sound modeling, they could actually hear him shouting.

"What's wrong?"

"Huh?"

"What's up?"

In the sudden silence that followed, they looked around and spotted their fallen comrade.

"H-hey, what happened?"

"I have no idea, man…"

"Did he blow himself up?"

"He's not *that* stupid!"

"Are they shooting from the forest?"

"Through all of our gunfire?"

The last comment came courtesy of the man with the FN MAG, whose back suddenly glowed with the effect of a bullet wound. He did not die instantly, but it took a devastating chunk out of his HP bar, right out of the safe green zone into the yellow.

"Ngaaaah!"

He arched his back, wincing at the dull pain of being shot, and the next bullet hit him in the back of the head. This critical hit was fatal, instantly obliterating the remaining third of his total HP.

Now that another spinning DEAD tag adorned their teammate, and the sound of two distant shots arrived to echo off the buildings, the remaining members of Team ZEMAL finally understood exactly what was happening.

The man with the M60E3 turned to his remaining friends and shouted, "Sniper! They're shooting at us from behind!"

They were his final words in the Squad Jam.

His teammates saw the bullet strike him right between the eyes as he turned, instantly dead. He should have seen the bright bullet line pointing toward him, but sadly, he did not have the reflexes needed to dodge the incoming shot.

"Hide!"

"Eek!"

The players with the Minimi and Negev leaped toward the other side of the mound of rubble they'd been using for cover.

"Huh? What's going on? What?"

Llenn lifted her head from her squatting position, now that all was suddenly quiet. In fact, it came so abruptly that her first assumption was that she'd been shot in the head and killed already, sent not to Heaven or Hell but to the limbo of the Squad Jam waiting area.

"The team in the city came within their firing range," M explained calmly, and with just a bit of delight. "Did you hear the three other shots? They saved us the trouble. I'm about to come up and join you now. Don't shoot me by mistake."

*Finally!* Llenn thought, waiting. Eventually she saw the shifting shape of a large man in camo pattern coming through the dark woods. In the new quiet, M reached the foot of a tree about ten yards to the left of Llenn's, quickly deployed the bipod of his EBR, and took position lying down.

Once he was in a prone firing position, looking through the M14 EBR's scope, Llenn finally felt relieved enough to ask, "Meaning…what, exactly?"

"I didn't mention earlier that in addition to the machine gunners, there was another team nearby on the scan. They were close enough to take part in the battle, farther south in the heart of the city."

"I see… So they rushed up and attacked the guys shooting at me from behind?"

"That's right. Either the machine gunners thought they had a safe distance based on the scan, or they noticed how close you were and didn't spare a second thought for anything else. Regardless, it was sloppy work."

"W-wait! Are you saying you knew that'd happen, so you used me as bait?" she fumed.

"Yes," he admitted.

She had no words.

He rustled around in his pockets and tossed something toward Llenn. "Take this."

She shrank at first, thinking it was a grenade based on the size, but realized at once that he wouldn't attack his own teammate. The toss was made with perfect control, and she nimbly caught the object with one hand.

It was a simple monocular—like a set of binoculars, but for one eye only. Pitohui had let her use one before. It had a laser-guided distance-estimation function that was very useful, but that made it a hefty item to purchase.

"You didn't have one, right? Use that. We'll stay here and watch for a bit."

"Th-thanks," Llenn said, holding it up to her dominant right eye and leaning carefully around the side of the tree. She couldn't see any bullet lines nearby, so at the very least, she didn't have to worry about those machine gunners.

There was the possibility that the enemies farther south would shoot at her—and she'd be helpless against their first shot, which wouldn't display a bullet line—but they would probably be focused on the nearer enemy instead. They had at least five minutes until the next scan, and it was unlikely that another foe would venture toward them.

"There were five machine gunners. Three are dead now," M said, peering through the scope of the M14 EBR. Llenn herself saw three different shining DEAD markers through the lens. She tried pressing the button just for kicks, and it said *197M*.

Right nearby, in front of the mound of rubble, were the two survivors. They were hiding from the rear shooters, meaning they were in full view of Llenn and M.

"They're not looking this way at all. You could easily finish them off, huh?" Llenn asked. He should be perfectly able to pick off a target at two hundred meters with the EBR. If anything, *she* wanted to waste them with her P90 for terrorizing her the way they did.

"No. We're not going to attack right now. Do not shoot until I give the command."

She wanted to ask why, but she held her curiosity in check.

"Here they come…along the big street to the left. Behind the overturned bus," he pointed out. Llenn moved the monocular left and saw a large, flipped-over bus in a spot about another 150 meters away from the first group, with more figures in motion near it.

"Ooh!" she exclaimed, twisting the wheel to zoom in. It scrolled smoothly, like a video camera, and automatically focused on the targets so she could make them out in better detail.

This new team had four members. They wore matching black-and-dark-brown camouflage uniforms, just like a team would. Their helmets had the same pattern. They also wore black ski caps with the eyes cut out—balaclavas, the kind bank robbers wore—to hide their faces.

They moved in a single-file line, the lead man proceeding smoothly as he walked, slim black rifle point never wavering. The three behind him appeared to have the same gun, held in the same pose, and they maintained a steady distance between one another of about six or seven feet. At times, the rear man would turn back to watch their six.

Llenn couldn't tell what sort of rifle they were all using, but M seemed to sense her question before she asked it. "They're FALs, 7.62 mm. The short-barrel paratrooper version."

FALs were popular among players for their high accuracy in semi-auto fire, and the power of their 7.62 mm rounds. The group of four was carrying the paratrooper version of the FAL. It had a folding stock and a shorter barrel for easier use.

The four men with matching weapons, masks, and outfits moved from cover behind the bus to a mound of rubble, then another burned-out vehicle, their progress smooth and efficient.

Before he ventured around the corner, Llenn noticed the lead man extending something along the ground and zoomed in on the monocular to see that it was a small mirror on the end of a pole.

Realizing that he was doing that to check for information before he moved, Llenn couldn't help but be impressed. Naturally, the group was heading for the two remaining machine gunners, who had been terrified into total stillness after their recent decimation.

"Those guys in the masks are good. They're efficient and coordinated," M admitted.

"Isn't there just four, though?" Llenn asked, not taking her eye off the monocular.

"No. There are more."

"How do you know? Can you see them? Where are they?"

"I can't find them yet, but notice that the guys are moving along the shortest and most efficient route toward the other two, using cover the whole while. Someone must be up above in one of the buildings, giving them directions. I'd bet there are two more watching from a window. They'll have sniper rifles for sure. They're the ones who shot the machine gunners first."

Llenn gasped, zooming out. If you didn't know where the other player was, there would be no bullet line. Snipers who could kill you instantly without warning were as hated and feared in *GGO* as they were in real life.

There were a number of buildings in various sizes beyond the mountain of rubble, meaning there were many potential sniping locations. Llenn looked around closely, but she didn't see any people or guns.

"There's no one up there."

"They're not going to be anywhere you can spot them. Only a failure of a sniper would shoot by sticking their gun or body out where you can see," M lectured. "It takes guts to split up a team of only six. And a team that will do that without hesitation means business. Those two are dead meat."

Llenn stopped searching for snipers and looked back to the two gunners.

The four masked men were about fifty meters from the machine gunners now, weaving their way through rubble as they approached. The gunners had no idea, and they appeared to be talking to each other in a panic, but Llenn couldn't hear them, of course.

*Let's get outta here!*

*But if we move, they'll shoot us, too!* she imagined them saying.

As she watched, the group made it to the nearest mound of debris, just twenty meters from their targets, and finished prepping for an attack. With quick little signals, they spread out.

The point man tossed a grenade. It landed not too close to the machine gunners and exploded out of major damage range, but it was enough.

The gunners launched to their feet and started to run. The other three masked men popped off rhythmical gunfire, painting their backs. The range was close enough that there was no escape, and bright-red bullet-hole effects shone from back to head. They toppled and suffered the same fate as their teammates.

"Oh well…"

It was unclear whether Llenn's lament was for their characters' deaths or their early exit from the Squad Jam tournament, or because she didn't get to kill them herself.

The time was 2:14.

Llenn was stunned to realize that only four minutes had passed. They had six minutes to go until the next scan. The four members of the team were totally visible, and they had no idea Llenn and M were watching them. This was their chance.

"Let's kill 'em, M!" she suggested with a bloodthirsty smile.

"No," he said. "I could take out one, but the rest would hide. Then we'd have to flee back into the woods for safety. We'll ride this one out. They're probably assuming that we've already sunk back deeper through the trees anyway."

*Hmph*, she thought with dissatisfaction. They'd come this far, and she didn't want to go back into the woods, where they were at a disadvantage, no thank you.

"I'd rather stay put and observe them," M said. At least they could safely hunker down in position and watch for the next five-plus minutes without worrying too much.

Llenn looked through the monocular again, but the four were gone. She couldn't find them anywhere. They must've already withdrawn.

"There," M said, thirty seconds later. "Look at the building with the curved exterior, Llenn. Mid-level."

She zoomed in on the building in question. "Aha! There they are!"

It was the people she'd been looking for, at about the tenth story of a building designed to look like a yacht sail. There were figures

standing at the edge of a group of blown-out windows, carrying long and slender rifles.

The measurement on the monocular indicated they were 503 meters away, which would put them at about 300 meters from the machine gunners, an easy distance for a skilled sniper to pick off a target.

Just as she was wondering what they would do, they answered her question by tossing a long rope out of the window toward the ground. One straddled it, facing the building, then kicked the surface with both legs and slid down the rope. He'd been a good hundred feet up the building, but it took just moments for him to descend out of sight behind the debris that covered the ground. The second man followed him and disappeared just as quickly. All that was left was the swaying rope, which soon disappeared as well when one of the men returned it to his inventory.

"Wow, what was that? Amazing!" she exclaimed.

"They were rappelling. It's a vertical drop down a rope."

"Ohhh. So it's good for vertical maneuvering. That's way faster than stairs. I didn't know that skill was in the game. I should try to get it."

"In their case, it's not the same thing."

"Huh?"

"You can't descend as quickly as they did with the in-game rappelling skill. I can tell, because I've done it before," M explained.

"Then how did they do it?" she wondered.

"That's the actual player's ability at work."

"Player ability? What do you mean?" she asked, turning back to look at him.

Without taking his eye off the M14 EBR's scope, M said, "I mean, the people playing those characters in *GGO* are able to do that in real life."

"Oh, I get it! I remember Pito telling me something about that!"

In all VR games, not just *GGO*, the players' capabilities fell into two categories.

One included things the character could do: in other words, abilities automatically available to anyone who spent their experience points on an in-game skill. In *GGO*, that might mean crafting powerful explosives or gun parts and blades, raising your accuracy, gaining incredible eyesight to see distant details, and so on. Skills had their own levels, so you could pump them up for more accuracy, more quality, more strength.

The other category comprised things the player could do in real life, regardless of in-game skills. You didn't need to unlock something to achieve what your body could already do. The AmuSphere simply translated your nerve signals into action.

Take calligraphy, for example. If *GGO* had a skill for writing beautiful kanji characters—it didn't—a character could simply make them by moving their hand in the normal fashion, and the results would be pristine.

But a player who already had real experience with the brush could do the same thing without needing the skill. They would simply move their hand the same way they would in real life, thus faithfully reproducing the real thing, but no better than that.

Naturally, any skill programmed into the game pertained solely to the game. Putting points into a hypothetical calligraphy skill would not carry back into real life.

"So they can just swoosh down those ropes because they know how to do r…rapping?"

"Rappelling."

"Yeah, that. They know how to do that in real life? That's amazing. Are they mountain climbers, do you suppose?" she wondered.

"Don't I wish," M commented darkly.

Llenn watched through the monocular as the group of four headed back to regroup with their sniper comrades, moving as cautiously as ever. "I'm guessing that you know what they do in real life, based on the way you said that."

"I have an idea."

"Which is?" she prodded. She had no clue what his idea was.

From her left, he answered, "Based on how coordinated and precise they are, and the speed of their rappelling, I have to assume that those guys are combat professionals."

"Pros? How?" she asked. They were out of sight now, so she looked back at M and met his gaze. Something in his imposing features seemed a bit weak, concerned.

"I mean, they literally get paid to fight," he said. "Those six are either police, maritime safety special forces, or Self-Defense Force personnel."

# CHAPTER 7

## Battle Against Pros

**SECT.7**

# CHAPTER 7
## Battle Against Pros

2:17 PM.

Three minutes to go until the second Satellite Scan passed overhead. Llenn and M were going to wait in the forest until then.

"What? That can't be fair! Pros can't compete in an amateur contest!" Llenn protested, upset about the possibility that they were up against six trained soldiers.

M thought it over for several seconds. "There wasn't any rule that forbid it. Whether by official partnership or just by individual choice, I wouldn't be surprised if they were using *GGO* as a training method and entered the Squad Jam as a little test of skill. That's been one of the intended uses of full-dive technology since its inception."

When it was laid out like that, Llenn had to agree that it made a bit more sense. She needed to focus solely on the competition—why let outside stuff interfere with her engagement in the game?

"What now? That was the closest team to us, right? We can't set up base in the city unless we beat them. Can we actually take them on and win?"

"Nope," M said instantly.

"Wow, not even an argument!"

"I don't know if we could beat them even if we had a full team of six. So the two of us alone is out of the question. Even if we'd

taken one out with the first strike...I don't think it'd make a difference."

"What's our plan, then? I know! Why don't we fortify ourselves? That way, if any team tries to cross over the highway, we can shoot them from here!"

"I considered that, but we're still at a disadvantage. They have snipers; as soon as we show ourselves, they shoot us. And another team could come toward us through the woods to the west in the meantime."

He was shooting down her ideas left and right, but the reasons made sense, so she didn't get angry. In the meantime, her watch now read 2:19. Less than a minute until the next scan.

"What will we do? Right now, I mean." Llenn was feeling a bit panicked that they had been playing for twenty minutes and had no obvious plan yet.

"Are you the lucky type? Have you been blessed with good fortune in your life?" M asked, out of nowhere.

"What? I dunno..."

Obviously, her luck with regards to height was close to zero, but as for the rest... She'd been born into a wealthy household, with a loving family, and had no restrictions growing up.

"Well...yeah. I'd have to say I've been pretty lucky. I'm a lucky girl!" she said, putting on a braver face than she felt.

"All right. We're going to bet on your luck, then. We'll check the next scan here, and if we're lucky, we'll jump out onto the highway. Get ready now."

"O-okay. Do I have time to ask why?"

Forty seconds left.

"Yeah. My expectation is that after all the sounds of battle, a lot of attention from the surrounding teams has gone toward the city. There's a good chance that another team is pretty close to the pro team, and they'll start fighting after the scan. We'll take that chance to race down the road past them all. Forget about hiding in the city; we'll head to the suburbs in the middle of the map. At the following scan, we'll go from there into the wasteland."

"All right… Got it."

Twenty seconds.

"When the scan hits, count the eliminated teams and memorize the locations of the surviving teams. Ignore any that are far away. Only the teams within three kilos that we might run into within the next ten minutes are actual threats," M explained, sitting up and taking out his scanner. Llenn followed suit and activated her screen.

2:20 PM.

The second Satellite Scan of the Squad Jam had begun.

This was the first one that Llenn actually witnessed. She stared at the screen, every nerve at attention. She wanted to know where their opponents were, even if only in a vague sense. She was tired of the fear of not knowing where they might be lurking.

This satellite must have been passing from the northwest, because lights started coming on beginning with the upper left of the screen. It was moving quickly, so the scan wouldn't take long, either.

"Let's see, eliminated teams…"

Contestants knocked out of the Squad Jam were displayed with an understated gray dot. She counted those dots while allowing the glowing dots to permeate her mind.

One dead team in the northwest field. Another one in the marshland below that. The other team that had been in the woods at the start must have made it out, because they weren't there anymore. With the open views of the desert and wasteland, there was considerable evidence of battle—four dots in total were dark.

The scan line reached the southeast corner, ending the process.

She didn't need to touch the glowing dot on the border of the forest and highway to know it was them. There were two other dots in the forest, but fortunately, both were three kilometers away.

The gray dot at the north end of the city was the machine gunner team. That meant that in just twenty minutes, seven teams had been eliminated from the battle royale, leaving sixteen teams still in it.

Of course, due to the way the scan worked, there was no way to know whether a dot represented a team at full strength or with just one surviving member.

As for the intimidating pro team, they were still in the city, about one kilometer away. The dot was located over a building on the map, so they were probably high up. No doubt the two rappelling players had raced up another building to take a vantage point again. Two crack snipers with a commanding and clear view, coordinating with their four teammates on the ground—a nearly unbeatable strategy.

"Ah!" Llenn gasped.

There was another dot in the square directly to the south of the pro team, and two more to the west of that. "M, look!"

"We're lucky. And they're not."

She looked up to see that M was actually *smiling*.

"Then—?"

"Yeah. We'll run and let the pros handle those three unlucky groups. Go ahead and ditch the poncho."

They put away their devices before the scan data actually vanished. Llenn pulled the poncho over her head and tossed it behind her. It was time for the pink to shine. M stood hunched over and folded up the EBR's bipod, ready to leap out of the woods.

They'd be leaving the relative safety of the trees for the danger of the open.

"Go on my command. Wait for it..."

Llenn swallowed and squeezed the P90.

The next moment, there was the sound of gunfire from the city. A mix of light and heavy fire. It was the start of a very loud battle. The three teams had almost certainly just made contact.

"Now! Go, go, go!" M commanded.

Llenn bolted forward. Out of the forest, onto the grassy slope. She raced straight for the highway.

"Should I be careful not to get too far ahead?" she asked M as she ran.

"If you do, I'll command you to stop," he replied.

*Wait... By going first, am I being the bait like back in the forest? Am I going to be the one getting shot at again?* she wondered, but it was too late to turn back now.

Using the team leader as a decoy. This wasn't shady business—it was shady teamwork!

Llenn's tiny body leaped over the guardrail and onto the paved highway.

"I don't see any enemies nearby, M!"

"Good. Wait until I catch up."

They were still dashing along the highway. Llenn was in the lead, thanks to her ability to run like an Olympic sprinter, if not faster.

Once you got your agility high enough, running speed approached that of a bicycle. The sensation of racing along at top speed intoxicated Llenn.

Forest to the right; city to the left. She took care to look for enemies in visible range and waited behind a wrecked car for M to catch up. As she learned when they left the trees, there was no wind on this map at all. That gave snipers a significant advantage.

M was much slower than Llenn, and he finally came up to her, pounding the concrete at top speed. He slid his considerable size behind cover and commanded "Go!" with his M14 EBR held up to provide covering fire.

They were completely visible from the forest and the city while they ran, but no one shot at them.

All the while, the sounds of distant battle raged on.

\*          \*          \*

Rewinding just a bit to 2:20, right before the second scan happened.

As it turned out, M had correctly predicted what would play out in the city.

After hearing the overwhelming gunfire of Team ZEMAL, three nearby teams had all reached the same conclusion: "Whoever they are, after that much gunfire, the surviving team can't be in perfect condition anymore." They had descended upon the city, attracted by the sounds. They'd had no idea that the surviving team was actually in pristine shape and made up of elite players.

Then, when the second scan came around, two teams had been stunned to realize they were in the same map square, barely two hundred meters apart.

"Huh?"

"No way!"

They'd approached from different directions, keeping them from spotting each other, but there they were, right nearby.

The actions each team chose were remarkably different.

One of the teams wore combat fatigues with a hornet logo on the left arm. They were equipped with submachine guns like the H&K MP5 and Walther MPL and focused on speedy, agile play.

"C'mon, let's do this! Get in there and go all out!"

"We got this!"

"Charge!"

"Roger!"

"Yaaaah!"

"Mommyyy!"

The six had happily plunged into battle as though on a suicide mission. They'd raced down the avenue toward the foe just around the corner.

The other team had a variety of outfits. Their "look" was tied together by the green scarf each member wore around his neck. This team had been unable to make a snap decision in the heat of the moment.

"They're close! C'mon, let's run!"

"No, there's another team on the diagonal! And atop a building! There's nowhere to run! We should rush and shoot back—"

"What if we get trapped, moron? We should hide inside for safety—"

"I don't wanna fight indoors!"

"Stop bickering, dammit! Follow the leader's orders."

Just then, the other team had come racing over from the cross street and started firing. Their submachine guns were good at rate of fire, but the pistol rounds they shot didn't do as much damage.

One had died in the surprise attack, hit by two sprays of ammo at once. The other five, who'd suffered hits but hadn't died, realized there was no escape. They stood strong and shot back, their AKM and M16A3 assault rifles barking automatic fire.

It turned into quite a battle, with two sides facing off within a hundred meters of the spacious street, blasting guns and hurling grenades.

Once you knew where the enemy was, turning your back meant defeat. They shot and shot rather than try to take cover, then switched magazines so they could continue firing.

The battle began to claim its victims, as first one soldier died, then another.

All the while, the floating camera symbol watched it from above with only passive interest.

Happiest of all about this development was a different team of men about a kilometer away. All six wore burnt-red camo and lugged around the same AC-556F rifles from Sturm, Ruger & Co. This gun was essentially the Mini-14, a 5.56 mm downsized version of the M14, with a metallic folding stock and fully automatic fire. It was compact and well made, but unpopular in *GGO*, and thus available for cheap.

When the team leader heard the nearby sounds of battle, he said, "All right! They're fighting now! We can swing around and catch them unawares!"

A teammate asked, "What about the guys in the building?"

"They're far-off, too far for sniping. They can't hit us if we run."

"Ah, I see."

"C'mon, let's move!"

They leaped into action, intent on cleaning up after the first two teams.

The quickest route down the street was through the middle, to avoid having to go around the many piles of rubble along the sides.

"Team spotted to the south. Six members, equipped with AC-556Fs. Designating Delta."

They had no idea that they were being watched with binoculars from a building or that they'd been given their own code name.

Delta's leader wasn't wrong in his assessment that a sniper couldn't hit them from that range and at that speed. An ordinary sniper rifle couldn't hit a target a kilometer away. At that range, only a skilled marksman could do it, with an antimateriel rifle that could reach that distance effectively. He was correct to assume the danger of that choice was low.

Where they were unlucky, however, was that there was a split squad of four extremely talented members who did not appear on the Satellite Scan and were down on the ground.

The sniper with his face hidden behind a balaclava gave those four an order over his communication device. "Delta is proceeding west along South Third Street. Let them pass by the theater, then pursue. Wait until Bravo and Charlie's battle is over."

"Aw, goddammit!" swore a man with an AKM, a very similar update to the classic AK-47. He wore the classic militia uniform as seen in various local conflicts around the world: jeans, leather jacket, chest sling with magazines, and around his neck hung a green scarf.

The man was pressed flat against the ground near a car on the street, with his gun held next to him. His view encompassed only

what came through the underside of the car with its flat tires, but at least as far as he could tell, nothing moved.

"Hey! Anyone nearby?" he shouted in desperation but received no answer. All the teammates he'd been with had either died or run out of earshot.

He'd lost a lot of health, too. He must've taken a good five of those submachine shots at close range when the other team charged at them. He'd fired back, of course—he definitely killed the one he got in the head a few times, and there was another guy he hit in the leg.

About five seconds after he asked, he got a response. "Hey! I'm alive!" It wasn't clear where the voice came from.

A smile of relief returned to the man's face. "Great! Where are you? You okay?"

"Yeah, I made it! My hit points are in the red, though!"

The second response was clearer and closer. His teammate must've come out of the building where he was sheltering.

"Great! Let's meet up and get outta here!" the man said, raising his AKM.

"Sorry, that's not happening!"

"Why not?" he asked. But he should've been smarter.

If he had, he would have glanced in the upper left corner of his vision, where the overlay showed him the HP state of his entire team. He would have seen that all his teammates were in black, with an *X* next to each of their names.

"Because! Just look at me!"

The man peered out from behind the car and saw his conversation partner standing about twenty feet away. The man wore black fatigues and held an MP5A3 pointed right at him. The red line extending from the muzzle hit him in the eye, literally making him see red.

"I'm your enemy!"

One shot.

The MP5's 9 mm Parabellum blasted him in the right eye. His

body lost rigidity and fell to the side, his AKM clattering onto the concrete.

"Whew…"

The man with the MP5 sat down where he'd been shooting from earlier. The parts of his body pelted by bullets were glowing, and his HP bar—what remained of it—was bright red.

When he turned back to the street, he saw bodies all over, friend and foe, each with the glowing DEAD marker hovering over it. He checked the info in the upper left corner and saw that he was indeed the last member of his team.

"Aw, damn… How am I going to manage this on my own now? Maybe I should just resign," he mumbled aloud. Then he thought, *Actually, I guess I could see how far I get before I die…*

He took one of the emergency healing tubes out of his breast pocket and pressed it with a *hiss* to his neck. His HP bar started blinking, then slowly began refilling.

His wristwatch said 2:27. He'd hide to let his HP recover for the next three minutes, and from that point on…

"I'll see what happens!" He stood up with a smile, ready to run.

Then a hail of 5.56 mm bullets tore his slowly recovering HP to shreds.

Another silent body on the asphalt.

From the shadows on the other side of the street, the man who'd just fired the burst from his AC-556F exclaimed, "Yes! Operation Pick Up the Pieces is a success!" and pumped his fist.

This was the team that was waiting for the battle to finish. They'd been watching the first frantic fight for the last minute, ready to pick off anyone who tried to flee, but just about all of them had died before it came to that.

The man with the MP5 was the last one, so their leader had poked his head around the corner of the building and shot him.

"We did it! This is what makes a battle royale so much fun. It's

easy if you just take advantage of the other guys!" exulted one of his teammates, who were all hanging back on the other side of the building and watching their rear.

"But if we're not careful, we'll end up just like them," the leader admonished, a moment before four powerful plasma grenades dropped down on them from a fifth-floor window of the building above.

As the bluish-white explosions devastated their virtual bodies, the team instantly learned a very valuable lesson: that caution in the big city extended not just in all horizontal directions but vertically as well.

The masked man who'd dropped the grenades radioed his distant companion. "Bravo, Charlie, Delta confirmed eliminated. No casualties."

The man inside the building replied, "Roger that. We'll take the next scan here. Keep your eyes open and wait for further instruction."

Next to him was another man, with a Remington bolt-action M24 sniper rifle resting on a camera tripod. He was the one who'd dispatched the machine gunners at the start. Without looking up, he asked the leader, "What should we do about the pink one and the big one who went racing down the highway?"

❊          ❊          ❊

2:29 PM, just before the third Satellite Scan arrived.

"Hyaaa! Whoo, what a sprint!"

"We made it."

Llenn and M arrived at the residential sector in the middle of the map without encountering any enemies along the highway.

"We didn't get shot at!"

"Nope."

They'd heard the sounds of furious battle from the city and from the forest as they ran, but not a single bullet was actually aimed

at them. Of course, there was always the possibility that someone had noticed them and simply decided not to waste ammo on a distant, high-speed target.

They ran a good 2 miles at a speed of 11 miles per hour. A marathon runner's average speed was 12.5 miles per hour, so that was a pretty good clip. Llenn had plenty left in the tank thanks to her high agility, but M was theoretically going about as fast as his character could.

The nice thing about VR games was that you could sprint that far without running out of breath, breaking a sweat, or getting thirsty.

They reached an area surrounded by the uninhabited remains of low-lying apartment buildings and homes that were arranged tightly enough to impede visibility of the streets.

The construction of the homes was clearly not Japanese in nature, more like an expensive foreign suburb. The place was a ghost town, of course, so it looked absolutely desolate. There were decaying cars with popped tires, some of which were even upturned, due to the overgrowth of untamed trees. In one yard, a large lawnmower was bright red with rust.

The buildings were all falling apart; many had collapsed out of degradation. The pavements were cracked, and hardy grass sprouted from the gaps. According to the map, a large portion of the area was submerged, but fortunately, this section was dry.

They approached the door of a single-story home whose lawn was dead, the trees withered. They checked the place for any potential traps.

There was always a chance that a team had started at this spot and left a large stock of armed grenades behind. Wired booby traps were simple to set up and easy to set off.

"Looks good. Go in slowly. Watch for traps inside."

"Got it."

They carefully made their way inside, mindful of more traps. Once they were certain that it was safe, they took shelter.

*   *   *

The living room was cluttered just enough that it was still possible to get inside and move around.

One of the unstated rules of *GGO*'s map design was that you never saw the actual human remains of the so-called apocalyptic war that had brought the world to ruin. If they had placed skeletons and bones all over the place, it would truly have been a hellish sight.

But in every other regard, the set and the graphic design were extremely detailed. In this one random home that Llenn and M chose to barge into, the interior design spoke to the lifestyle of the residents before that war.

Above the fireplace, which was now home to some fine little grasses, silver-framed photos of a smiling family lined the mantel. Some of the plates in the sink were cracked, and some were not. Scattered next to the sofa was a pile of aging magazines and newspapers.

You could even read those publications to get a view into the foolishness that led to the utter disaster of a war that engulfed the planet, if you wanted. Unfortunately, they were all in English.

Llenn recalled a story Pitohui had told her once. Pitohui killed a doglike monster in a ruined church, then went into a smaller back room. A beautiful wedding dress and a crisp tuxedo were hanging on a rack, sparkling with the light coming through the skylight.

"That actually got me a little misty-eyed," Pitohui had said with an uncharacteristically soft smile. "You felt the love between them, the idea that an extinction-level war might be imminent, but they wanted to get married anyway. And it was like the doggy was doing his best to protect them."

"That's a nice story," Llenn agreed.

"So I blasted both those outfits with my shotgun."

"No longer a nice story!"

"Don't worry. The next time someone comes across them, they'll be back to their old condition, for whatever reason."

The attention to detail by *GGO*'s graphic design team was admirable, even if Pitohui's sentimentality was not.

Mere seconds remained until the third scan, at two thirty. Llenn's wristwatch had already finished its warning vibration.

They took out their scan devices and displayed the map between them so they could watch together. There had been seven disqualified teams last time, and sixteen surviving teams. How much had changed in the last ten minutes?

The third scan started from the south-southeast, moving north-northwest, or clockwise, from about five o'clock to eleven. This satellite must've been orbiting much higher, as its pace was far slower than the previous one. Given the extra time, Llenn decided she would count the surviving teams this time, too.

Dots sprang into being along the southern desert and wasteland stretches. The number of gray dots that signified defeated teams grew and grew. It was a large, wide-open area to begin with, but to her surprise, the number of gray dots had doubled since the last scan, from four to eight.

Three adjacent new dots shone in the ruins in the center of this region. Even Llenn could tell that this meant they had each gathered there, trying to seize control of advantageous terrain.

Only two teams were still alive in this area. They were over five kilometers apart from east to west, and neither was particularly close to any defeated dots.

Without knowing how many members remained, there was no way to tell whether either team posed a significant threat. They could have demolished their competition and headed off with smooth precision or emerged as the sole survivor of a devastating fight, limping to safety.

In both cases, the dots were far from their current position, so they could ignore them until the next scan.

On its way north up the map, the scan hit the city center. It produced three gray dots, almost in the exact same location. Nearby

was the glowing dot in about the same place as the last scan. M's prediction was exactly on point.

"Wow…" She breathed out, in admiration of both her partner and the professional team.

Llenn steeled herself as the scan approached the residential area in the center of the map. They were on the northeast quadrant of it—the upper right part on the map. If there was another light shining nearby, that was who they would fight next. Perhaps, unbeknownst to them, the other team was in the house next door. Perhaps even in *this* house.

The answer was…

"Nothing. Thank goodness!"

There was only one lit dot in the residential area. No dead teams, even. The scan proceeded north and revealed still no freshly disqualified teams in the marsh. There was one surviving team, which looked to be stationed at the downed spacecraft.

In the grasslands to the northwest, there were two dead teams, one more than before. One team still survived, and if they had cleared out the others, then they were worth avoiding.

Lastly, within the forest, like last time, there were two living teams and no dead ones. In fact, the two teams had hardly moved since the previous scan.

That made eight new dropouts, for fifteen in total. Eight teams still survived. At this rate, maybe Pitohui had been right, and the Squad Jam event would be over in less than an hour.

The scan was still visible, but M lifted his craggy face from the map. He was ready to plan.

"We're lucky" was all he said.

Llenn bobbed her head excitedly. "Which one do you think poses the most urgent threat to us now, M?"

In his usual flat tone, he answered, "First of all, the two teams in the forest are close, but we can ignore them. They both seem to be staying put out of wariness of the other. Perhaps they each lost members in an initial fight, and they're raring to finish the other off."

"That sounds likely. They're both laying an ambush and waiting for the other one to fall into it."

"Ignore the grassland team—they're too far away. Let's hope that they come over and hit the forest teams from behind. As for the team on the spaceship in the marsh, they probably beat the other team by sitting back and sniping. They're in an advantageous location, so they're not going to go on the move except in extreme circumstances."

"Uh-huh."

"When it comes to the two teams in the desert and wasteland, I have no idea. They could be deadly, or they could be stragglers. I'm having an especially hard time figuring out the actions of the one closer to the ruins. They could be setting up base *inside* the ruins, so why don't they?"

"I was wondering that, too."

"Still, we can probably ignore them until the next scan. The problem is…"

"…The pro team? The one in the city?"

"Yeah. There's no way we can win this event without beating them. Now that a lot of the competition is gone, they'll probably strike out of the city. I suspect their purpose here is training rather than winning, which makes it unlikely that they'll just lie in wait the whole time."

"But they're tough, right? Too tough for us to beat them?" Llenn asked.

"True," he admitted. Then he smirked. "But after this most recent scan, I can see a possibility for us. Maybe, if everything goes right, we can actually win."

"Ooh!"

"And I'll need your help for that, Llenn. You'll be doing lots of shooting, getting right into the action."

"Yeah! Sounds good! I'll do whatever it takes! Just tell me the plan!"

"Good. Here's the first step…"

# CHAPTER 8
## Trap

SECT.8

# CHAPTER 8
## Trap

The watch on Llenn's left wrist vibrated.

She couldn't see it in the darkness, but she knew what it meant. The time was 2:39:30, and that was the alarm warning her that only thirty seconds remained until the fourth Satellite Scan.

*Is this plan really going to work...?* she thought, unable to even mutter it out loud, on M's strict orders. *Another cruel plan! I'm supposed to be the team leader!*

This was by far the most common thought she'd had over the last ten minutes. On the other hand, M had been proposing strategies that completely ignored Llenn's safety since the start of the Squad Jam, so it was hard to get indignant about it now.

She didn't mind dying, because it was just a game. But she hadn't had a chance to fight yet. Her beloved P90 hadn't fired a single bullet so far. If she was going to die, she wanted to do it in a blaze of glory.

And yet, Llenn couldn't even watch the fourth Satellite Scan happen. She had to stay in the darkness, clutching her P90 to her chest. If she were claustrophobic, her mind would probably be teetering on the brink of setting off the AmuSphere's safety system, which would automatically disconnect her from the program. Llenn was glad she was the type of person who enjoyed taking a nap in the closet.

"The scan's about to start. Be ready to move as soon as I give the order," M's voice said into her ear.

"…"

She had no reply as she ran her finger along the side of the P90 to confirm that the safety was where she'd left it.

✳    ✳    ✳

Ten minutes earlier, a masked man in the city had watched the scan sweep over the map and murmured, "We'll need to move."

There were only eight teams left, and none were nearby. The closest glowing dot was in the northeast sector of the residential area.

"Attention all units. Designating resident-area enemy Echo and desert-area enemy Foxtrot," the squad leader said, his voice transmitted through the comm to the sniper next to him and the four men on the ground.

For each enemy they discovered, they gave them a phonetic code designation in alphabetical order so that they could easily identify them over audio communication.

The machine-gun lunatics were Alpha, for *A*.

The wasp-logo team that charged in with SMGs was Bravo, for *B*.

The green-scarf team that clashed with Bravo was Charlie, for *C*.

The team in matching reddish-brown camo was Delta, for *D*.

The team with the tiny pink member was Echo, for *E*.

The team in the desert to the south was Foxtrot, for *F*.

"Echo was at the south end of the forest twenty minutes ago, under fire from Alpha. When they ran down the highway, we confirmed only one member in desert-pink and one member in green. The team is down to two members, weapons unknown," the leader announced. It was so unlikely that there would be only two members to start with that he'd made the only sensible deduction.

"Over the next ten minutes, we will proceed toward the resi-

dential area and search. If you encounter them, engage. If not, we'll get the next scan at fourteen hundred fifty hours."

All the while, he was busy folding up the tripod for his M24 and opening his window to place it back in item storage. Once that was done, he dropped the rope and prepared to descend the exterior of the building.

"Meet up at the intersection of S-3 and W-5. Remain on alert."

Once all six of the masked team were together, they ran at the maximum speed their character stats would allow.

The two at the lead held their FALs, ready for an encounter with Echo. If the enemy was coming their way, there was a high possibility they'd meet along the way. Running with your gun up and ready to shoot at a second's notice without swaying was quite difficult—and another skill that a trained player brought into the game from outside.

After them came the leader and the sniper. The two in the rear were constantly checking back for any sign of Foxtrot.

Eight minutes without incident later, they reached the east end of the residential area and started passing by houses, maintaining an extremely vigilant watch. Since all the buildings were low-lying, there was little fear of sniping from above, but they remained utterly cautious. They could have relied on their wireless comms, but instead they used only hand signals. When they crossed a street, they used mirrors first, then had each member sprint alone with two others providing watch.

They proceeded westward bit by bit, combing their search area, as the clock hit 2:39.

"Forty seconds to scan. Halt. Stay on alert."

They positioned themselves at the corner of a large intersection. The leader then set up next to a garbage truck. This way, when the scan displayed his location, the truck would shield him from gunfire from the west. His five squad members would keep an eye on the other three directions. If the scan showed Echo nearby, they would be ready to charge.

The clock hit 2:40.

"Scan initiating."

While the others stayed vigilant, the leader peered at his scan device.

"They're close!" the leader shouted.

This scan was even slower than the previous one, but the details were before his eyes now. It started from the east and revealed that Foxtrot was still stationed in the desert area and heading east from their previous location, indicating no threat at present.

He zoomed in on the map to display the residential area and what was to the upper left, where their location lit up. And as for their target, Echo...

"Straight north! Eighty meters!"

The two dots were nearly touching. He set it to maximum zoom and saw just how close they were. That would be right around the next major intersection of the road.

The member checking the northern direction exclaimed "I don't see anything!" in surprise.

It was less than three hundred feet away on a wide-open street; they should have been plainly visible. Yet, there were no human figures in the intersection.

Other team members swung around to help.

"No visual here, either! Just an empty intersection!"

"I'm not seeing anything. No vehicles in the crossing!"

"Proceed," the leader commanded. If they couldn't see them from there, they'd just have to approach until they did. If it weren't *GGO*, they could have suspected the scanner of malfunctioning, but that wasn't likely.

The four other men snapped their acknowledgment and moved up, FALs at the ready. They split into pairs, one for each side of the street.

"The scan doesn't indicate elevation. It's highly likely they're under a manhole. Be careful," the leader ordered, watching their tail with his own gun at the ready. He checked the glowing map

screen one more time, but the location was certain. He couldn't zoom it in any farther, so the best he could say was that the dot was in the intersection.

He'd once seen an old movie in which the scanner showed enemies approaching but out of sight, who ended up being in the ceiling above the scanner. This time it was a flat intersection, so they couldn't be above. The only answer was below.

He shrank the map down to show a wider view, just in case there were any other teams in notable range. The only survivors were them, Echo, Foxtrot, and two teams in the marshland: five in total.

That there were two teams in the marsh now likely meant that one had come from the meadows to fight the other. The other team in the southwest of the desert and the two stalemated teams in the forest must have either wiped each other out or resigned in the last ten minutes.

It was a relief to know that they could focus solely on Echo for now. But he still didn't hear any gunfire from his teammates. Instead, one said, rather stunned, "Arrived at the intersection. There is…no manhole. None to be seen."

The other three checked in. "Nothing here. Watching the northwest corner. No hostiles."

"Watching the northeast direction. No holes, no hostiles."

"Watching dead north. Nothing here. You don't think…it was a scanning error?"

"The likelihood of a system error is extremely low," the leader said. "Describe everything you see in the intersection. No matter how small."

A bit confused, his soldiers replied, "I see an intersection of cracked asphalt…overgrown weeds…a rusted bicycle on its side…"

"One car tire lying flat on the ground."

"Two withered tree trunks. One suitcase. One—no, three empty cans."

"One supermarket cart on the sidewalk. A big foreign-made one. Nothing inside it…and no holes in the ground!"

"Nothing here, either. I'm not seeing anything leading underground."

*What could this mean?!* The leader left the rear guard to the sniper and removed his binoculars. Through the round sights, he spotted the intersection where his teammates were and where Echo *should* have been.

Then a voice in his mind—

"One..."

—of his subordinate, moments ago—

"...suitcase."

He screamed, "All units, open fire on the suitcase!"

And in response to the order, the suitcase opened fire.

"W-wait! Are you saying you knew that'd happen, so you used me as bait?"

One of the four men saw it happen.

The suitcase, sitting about a dozen feet away from him, suddenly seemed to sprout human legs. Then its zipper burst open to reveal the flash of gunfire.

That was the last thing he saw in the Squad Jam event.

He was sharp, but not sharp enough to see the 5.7 mm bullets flying at his face.

✳        ✳        ✳

About ten minutes earlier, M had been talking to Llenn.

"First, we're going to look for something you can fit inside."

"Excuse me?" she replied, bewildered.

He explained that they needed to find some object that was so small, no one would ever expect a person to be hiding inside it.

And with an avatar that was near the theoretical minimum size in *GGO*, Llenn would be inside. Then the object would be dumped in the middle of a wide-open intersection in the residential area, where it would draw the attention of their foes after the next scan.

When the team of professional soldiers came along, she'd wait...

"Then you jump out and shoot them. Pito says you're good at close-range ambushes."

"Y-yeah, I've done more than a few... But what if they see through our plan? What if they think, 'That cardboard box looks fishy' and shoot me?"

"Then it didn't work. Let's pray."

"Gahhh!" Llenn exhaled at the ceiling. *Again! Again with the decoy thing!*

She looked back at M.

"Fine! I'll do it!"

A quick search of the house turned up a likely container right away. There were two plastic suitcases in the bedroom, one large and one small.

There were clothes scattered in and around them, as though someone had been frantically trying to throw them together to escape an oncoming war. But where had the person or people actually gone? There were no answers.

M emptied the contents of the smaller suitcase and extended his burly arm toward Llenn.

"The knife."

"Huh?"

"Remember the one I gave you?"

"Oh! Right..."

Llenn pulled the combat knife from its spot behind her back. She'd forgotten about it entirely, assuming it wouldn't get used. *But now the situation had presented itself like foreshadowing coming home to roost*, she thought, presenting it to M, handle first.

M took the blade and used it to tear through the partitions inside the suitcase. It carved them up admirably.

"There. You should fit now."

"What? No way!" she protested. She wasn't *that* small. The

bigger one would have to do. In fact, she stepped inside it with her P90 clutched close, certain that this demonstration would prove her point.

"There."

"..."

He closed the lid and locked it.

"I'm...so...*teensy*!" she said, giggling.

M opened it back up to let Llenn out, then cut out one entire side of the suitcase with the knife.

"Now your feet can stick out, and you can take it off in a blink. It'll make it easier to move when the time comes."

"Except that I can't see..."

That still left the matter of the lock on the suitcase.

"Step back." He pulled his HK45 sidearm from his right thigh, pointed it at the suitcase, and fired two shots to destroy it—*bang-bang*.

The first gunshots fired by Team LM in the Squad Jam were to break the lock on a suitcase.

Now, if Llenn just pushed herself upward while inside, she could swing the suitcase open.

"What now, M? Are we going right away? Where do we set the ambush?" she asked.

He shook his head. "We can wait until the last moment. First give me time to check out the map."

When Llenn eventually settled into the suitcase at the spot M picked out—he said that position had the best visibility—it was around 2:36 PM. He'd placed her in a spacious intersection.

Four short minutes later—which felt much longer than that—she heard his voice again. "The scan's about to start. Get ready so you can pop out when I give the signal."

"..."

She said nothing, feeling the side of the P90 to confirm the position of the safety.

"Scan's starting," M said.

Llenn had no idea where he was. She hoped it was somewhere good for sniping so that he could back her up.

"Got it. They're close. About eighty meters to the south."

"…"

She nearly said something. She wanted them to come soon, but in *GGO*'s world of guns, eighty meters might as well have been right next to you.

"They'll be approaching soon. Wait for my signal."

"…"

"I see them. Four in a bunch, like I thought. It's them."

"…"

"They're coming along the south corner. Ten meters away now. They're fanning out."

"…"

This was followed by the worst stretch of time yet, during which it was impossible to tell whether a dozen seconds had passed, or a minute, or two.

"Llenn. There's one guy about five meters in front of the opening of the lid. Send him to hell first. Whenever you're ready."


*Aaaah!*

Llenn summoned her courage with a silent scream and thrust her feet through the base of the suitcase, standing up and bursting the top of the suitcase open.

It was her first view of the outside world in minutes.

Thanks to the red sky of *GGO*, it wasn't blindingly bright. As M had said, there was a masked man with an FAL right in front of her—and she pulled the trigger of the P90 at the exact moment the bullet circle overlapped his head.

In the span of just a second, she fired fifteen shots, the majority of which hit the man's mask.

Once she was fully upright, the suitcase fell to her feet, and she was free to move again.

In her ear, M said, "Next one's forty-five degrees to the right, at seven meters."

The suitcase sprouted feet, then spat fire, and their teammate got shot.

"Whaaaa—?"

Then a tiny pink human emerged from the case—and even those three elite soldiers were late to react to the bizarre reality of what they were seeing.

But they'd also heard their leader's orders, so that meant the mystery was solved. They knew what to do.

She was an enemy. She'd gotten one of them, but now the other three would finish her off, and that was that.

"Fire!" they cried in unison, pulling the triggers of their FALs in Llenn's direction. All of those 7.62 mm rounds passed through empty space.

"What?!" one of the masked men shouted through the gunfire. The target he shouldn't possibly have missed had slipped out of his line of fire and was now approaching him. At a ferocious speed.

And jutting from her pink hand was a pink gun.

It was like a stabbing by firearm. Llenn evaded her foe's bullet line—literally the line of fire—by ducking to the left, then sprinted directly at him.

"Taaa!" she cried, blasting him with the P90. With another burst of dry staccato fire, she deposited multiple bullets into his neck and face. Those were vital areas, so the damage was instantly lethal. His HP gauge dropped from full in a hurry. He would lose all of it before long. He stumbled backward and stopped firing, but Llenn's onslaught continued. She came to a sudden stop right before him.

*If possible, use the enemy's body as a shield,* M had taught her. *In BoB and SJ, the bodies actually stay intact, and even better, they become indestructible objects.*

Llenn dropped to the ground in front of the man's body as he

collapsed, then she went into prone firing position. The other two men were on the other side of the street, about thirty feet away. They pointed their FALs at Llenn.

"Shit!"

One of them thought about firing but held back. If his teammate wasn't dead yet, that would certainly finish him off. He knew that he shouldn't need to worry about that, given that this was a game, but he couldn't help his instincts.

"Shit!" the other one repeated, opening fire. He had concluded that the guy was a goner already.

His bullets hit the ground and his comrade's body across the street, but not a single one landed on the tiny pink body behind it. The teammate's corpse was indestructible now, essentially a solid wall. The extent of the vulnerable target she exposed was the muzzle of her gun and one eye.

"She's too small!" shouted one of the men, right before Llenn's shot hit him in the right flank. Bullet-hole effects tattooed his torso in an upward line, and he toppled backward. As he fell, her last burst of full auto fire caught his head and finished him off.

"Take this!"

The last survivor opened fire and ran straight for Llenn for greater accuracy. The next instant, a small pink object came spinning at a high rate from the side of his partner's body. It might as well have been a spinning top.

Only when it stopped did he actually recognize it as human, but that was also the moment that the bullet line smacked him in the face.

"Ha-ha!" he chuckled to himself, though Llenn couldn't see it under the mask.

The leader watched all this happen through his binoculars.

Pink legs had sprouted from the suitcase, then a child had emerged, gun blazing, and defeated all four of his subordinates.

One look at the team status in his upper left view told him they were all dead.

The entire sequence took less than ten seconds. A wild mix of FAL and P90 gunfire accompanied the sight.

The team leader lowered his binoculars and turned to the sniper watching through his riflescope. "Don't bother shooting. We're done playing."

"Time to wrap it up?" the other said, lowering his M24. With one smooth and practiced motion, he engaged the safety next to the bolt handle.

As they watched, the small pink person raced with incredible speed toward a house and went out of sight.

"That's not human speed. It's not going to be worthwhile practice," the leader grunted, both in annoyance and in admiration. He opened his menu screen.

*Are you sure you want to surrender?*

He hit the YES option.

"M! Hey, M! Is anyone chasing me?" Llenn asked as she sprinted down the street and changed out the magazine that was down to its last three bullets.

"Nope. From what I can see from here, the last two decided it wasn't worth it, so they resigned."

"What?!" She screeched to a halt, turning back to the scene of slaughter she had orchestrated. A few hundred feet away lay a number of collapsed figures and four red, floating DEAD signs.

"Then, we…we b-b-b-b-beat them?"

"It might be most accurate to say we 'didn't lose' to them—but in a sense, yes. You did good," M said.

"Hnng…hrrrr…"

Over several seconds, Llenn's face morphed into a gaping smile.

"I did iiiiiiiiiiiiiiiiiiiiiiiiiiiiiiiiiiiiiiiiiiit!"

She thrust her P90 and her open hand into the red sky and screamed at the heart of the desolate neighborhood.

\*   \*   \*

But the tournament wasn't over.

The first step after this was to regroup with M somehow.

"M, where are you?" she asked.

"I'm moving westward and keeping an eye on the area," he replied.

"I want to meet up with you again before the scan. What should I do?"

It occurred to Llenn that it might be surprisingly difficult for them to rendezvous. M knew where Llenn was. All she'd done was move about a hundred yards north of where he'd left her in the suitcase.

But where was M?

The residential sector all looked the same, and it was a place they'd never been before. Would M be able to accurately assess his precise location and explain it to her? In the city, they could just say "meet in front of the building that looks like such and such." But Llenn was unsure whether she should just come out and ask for details.

"It's fine. I'll guide the way. Start moving west at a trot from where you are now. The sun should be overhead on your left," he told her.

Apparently, she needn't have worried. M wasn't being careless; he'd found a memorable and visible spot to meet her. Maybe he would even be straight in front of her in this direction.

"Rrrroger that," she said, following his command.

It didn't take long for Llenn to realize her assumption that this would be quick and easy was dead wrong. M's orders soon got bizarrely complex.

"Stop right there. You should see a burned-out truck on your left. Turn toward it and proceed slowly. Then turn right on the first small side street."

And then, "You're at the submerged part now. Go to the path

forty-five degrees to the left. It's shallow the whole way. Then go straight until you hit the big road again."

After that, "Left on that street. Walk normally, counting your steps up to twenty. There's an apartment building with a door that's missing the bottom half. Go inside. It's a total mess, but you can get through it. Head down the hallway and go through the fifth room on the left into the courtyard."

At this point, she had to wonder whether he was actually watching her from above or sneaking behind her as a prank. She had turned and moved and turned and moved so often, she had no idea where she was anymore.

"M…are you sure about all of this? Do you really know where I am? Should I wait until the next scan arrives?"

Her wristwatch said 2:47. Three minutes until the next scan. When that happened, he would know where she was, since she was the team leader. But if he didn't make his own location known to her, even that would be pointless.

"No need to worry. Go into the big house in front of you. I'm in there."

"Oh?"

There was a mansion along the water's edge before her. The street ended there, and everything was underwater beyond that. She couldn't go any farther if she wanted to.

The still surface was red, reflecting the sky, and the house rose out of it like an island. The sight was eerily serene and beautiful all at once. In the distance, some large structure was visible in the red haze. The marshland was much closer now, so that was probably the outline of the crashed spacecraft.

The next moment, something shone powerfully at the edge of the outline, then vanished just as quickly. Probably a plasma grenade blast.

Llenn registered the distant sight as a battle in progress and slipped inside the door of the building, where she saw her partner's familiar size in the middle of a very luxurious living room. The moment she saw him, there was a distant boom, probably the

sound of that explosion earlier, as though it were the sound effect of finding M.

"Wow! How? Why? How did you—?" she asked, wide-eyed.

"How did I what?"

"How did you guide me here? How did you lead me down that maze of directions? You don't have some kind of secret tool that lets you watch me from above, do you?"

She recalled something Pitohui had told her. *GGO* was adding new maps, new monsters, and new guns and gear all the time. Now there were rumors that they had added drones or were about to very soon.

A drone would be like a small remote-controlled helicopter that floated overhead and sent back footage. It would be a huge advantage in battle, so many people dismissed the rumors, as it could catastrophically alter the game's competitive balance.

But a drone would certainly explain M's detailed guidance. Could that be what was inside his massive, bulging backpack? If so, it would also mean that the crazy idea of putting a team of two into the Squad Jam event wasn't so crazy after all.

M said, "You mean a drone? I don't have anything like that. Pito sure wants one, though."

"Then how? You didn't…like…cheat or something, did you?"

In this case, she was thinking about some method of tampering with the system so that he could see his own location on the map, for example. If the developers found out about that, he wouldn't just be kicked out of the Squad Jam; he could easily get his account banned—a thought that terrified Llenn.

"It's my own personal skill. If someone else thinks I'm cheating, that's their problem," he said.

Llenn wasn't quite sure what he was implying, so she prompted, "Meaning?"

"Ever since I was a kid, I've had an excellent sense of direction. Whether in real life or in VR, I've never been lost. For example, no matter how far I walk underground, or what directions I've gone, I always know how far I've gone. I remember a place

almost perfectly after one visit. I can even look at a map and envision the terrain of a place I've never been before."

"That's incredible!" Llenn marveled. Like the stereotype about women went, Llenn wasn't great at reading maps. She'd learned a lot about the process by playing *GGO*, where she had no choice but to learn more about the wilderness maps.

Then she recalled something she'd read in a book once. Just like perfect pitch, some people have perfect navigation. Such people can tell exactly where they are, even if driven blindfolded and earplugged in a car.

"Oh! I got it!" shouted Llenn. "The *M* in your name is short for *map* or *mapper* or something!"

"………Huh? Uh…well…sure…," M said, his fearsome features twisted into an uncertain frown. Llenn barely noticed.

"That makes so much sense! Oh my God, that's so cool!"

"You…you think so?"

"Totally. I mean, my avatar's name is just an alteration of my actual name."

"You probably shouldn't reveal information like that. People will track you down."

"Whoops… Forget I said that! But it's still not my *actual* name, even if it's based on it!"

"It's almost time, you know," M warned, right as Llenn's wristwatch vibrated. Apparently, M had a perfect sense of time as well.

It was 2:50. The fifth Satellite Scan was coming.

Llenn didn't know the full results of the last one, so she stared eagerly at the map.

This scan was a quick one. It started from the east and crossed the map rapidly, throwing the little glowing dots up in bunches. But this time, most were gray, indicating defeated or resigned teams.

"I don't believe it… There are only three teams remaining, M!"

Just three bright dots were left to indicate current combatants.

The one on the west end of the central residential area was them, of course. At last, Llenn understood exactly where she was.

Another light shone in the desert/wasteland region, nearly at the very bottom of the map. It was at least three miles away.

It was good to know that they could ignore that dot, but it didn't make sense that they would move to that location. Were they just staying away from all the combat?

The last one, and undoubtedly their next opponent, was close by, in the swamp. There was a single gray dot on the downed spacecraft nearby, so the surviving team must have overcome their ambush. Or perhaps it was the reverse.

On a straight line, they were about two and a half miles from Llenn and M. But that was just the marshland, and there was a mile-plus of submerged land blocking their way. They'd have to circle around, either north or south, so it was probably impossible for them to arrive within the next ten minutes.

When the scan had finished, Llenn turned to M. "Our next opponent is the marsh team. Do you think we can set up the same plan by three o'clock?"

The last time had worked so well, Llenn was raring to try it again. Her spirits were high, and the words came spilling out of her mouth.

It was incredible that they'd started out under a hail of machine-gun fire and survived all the way to the final trio of teams. And they had a chance to do even better, so it was impossible for her to feel down. They already had the bronze medal in the bag; time to shoot for silver or gold.

"But we can't do that plan again here, right? We'd need to go north or south. Then we need them to come to us. We'll lure them in at the three o'clock scan!"

"One hour…"

"What was that, M?"

"…"

That seemed strange to Llenn. It wasn't like M to just ignore a question.

Was he getting bored of the game after an hour? Llenn almost got the sense that this was true, but she couldn't just ask him that.

She got tired of staring at his face in profile and decided to examine the fancy interior instead.

After nearly a minute of silence, he finally said, "Let's leave and head southwest along the water. We can't set a trap by three o'clock. We'll look for a good spot to set it up on the next one."

"Yes, sir!" she said with a smile and a mimicked salute. Then she started humming to herself: "Hmm-hmm-hm, hm-hm-hmm, hm-hm-hm-hm, hmmm, hmmm, hmmm." It was the "Promenade" piece from Mussorgsky's *Pictures at an Exhibition*.

As far as classical music went, this was quite a famous and memorable piece. Elza Kanzaki even sang it in her repertoire, with Japanese lyrics added.

M carefully followed behind.

They left the mansion and headed southwest, with the water to their right. The number of houses nearby continued to dwindle until there were no more, and Llenn and M reached a large lake. There were no waves and no wind—it was like a mirror surface.

Under the usual sky, the lake itself shone red, a sight both eerie and beautiful. In the distance, they could see the faint outline of the jutting spaceship.

Llenn took the lead, turning back now and then as she ran. It all felt so good that she was in danger of just letting the momentum carry her out of M's range.

Just under two minutes after leaving the mansion, at 2:52—

"Enemies! To the right!"

—M hissed.

# CHAPTER 9
## M's Battle

**SECT.9**

# CHAPTER 9
## M's Battle

"Enemies! To the right!"

Llenn's first thought was *Is he getting his directions mixed up?*

Yes, there was a team still alive in the marshland. They'd confirmed that four minutes ago.

But they were over two miles away on the map, on the other side of the marsh and lake.

It would be one thing if the distance were flat ground and a character with extreme agility were running at the inhuman speed of thirty-five miles an hour. But Llenn just assumed that this was incorrect, a mistake. She stopped and turned to the right.

"Huh?"

Then she learned that *she* was mistaken.

There was something on the lake that hadn't been there before.

Black dots. Three—no, four black dots, floating on the red lake, and getting larger by the moment.

"Get down!"

She followed M's command just as multiple bullet lines passed right over her head.

That left no confusion: The black dots were enemies, and they had their guns out and ready to fire. The sound of bullets passing overhead was one she'd heard more times than she could count in this game, and a few more were just added to the total. A split second later came the sound of the distant gunfire.

"What does this mean, M?" she asked with her face pressed to the asphalt.

Out of sight, M replied, "They found convenient vehicles. That's all."

"Vehicles?"

"That's right. They're close enough that you should be able to see them now."

"..."

Llenn carefully raised her head and looked toward the lake. The four black dots were about a thousand feet away now, but even though they were small, she could recognize them. "Oh, I see."

They were small motorboats with people riding them. That would explain how they'd crossed that distance, over water, at such a high speed.

"They have motorboats! That's not fair!"

"It's perfectly fair. Anyone can use any working vehicles on the map. They found them first, so they can use them."

"Aw..."

"Also, those aren't technically motorboats."

"They aren't? What are they?"

"Hovercrafts."

"Huh?"

"Roll to your left and run!"

Llenn performed the action without thinking. With incredible speed, she rolled over a good twenty times in her prone position, which moved her a few dozen feet away. It was quite dizzying, but it helped her survive.

Red bullet lines glimmered over the spot where she'd just been, followed by a hail of bullets. They were firing machine guns. Llenn had enough recent experience to recognize that.

The bullets sprayed wildly, but if she'd stayed where she'd been, at least one would have hit her. And if it had hit the wrong spot, one might have been all it took to kill her.

"Crap!" she spat, her pink fatigues covered with grass and dirt.

One of the hovercrafts was just a hundred yards away, crossing from left to right at high speed.

She saw it quite clearly. It was about ten feet long. At first glance, it looked like a Jet Ski. But unlike a Jet Ski, there was bulging black rubber beneath the green body, and in the rear was a large propeller, like an airplane's.

The hovercraft was so named because it propelled air downward to lift the body up, which was then pushed along by the propeller. She could hear the whine of the engine mixed with the buzzing of the propeller blades.

There were two men riding the vehicle. The one sitting in front held a control handle horizontally, while the man in the back had a machine gun propped on the flank of the craft to aim to the sides.

Llenn pointed the P90 back at them, but she stopped herself before she could place her finger against the trigger and summon a bullet circle into view. The hovercraft was already snaking away, well out of accurate distance. It would be a waste of ammo.

The other three were farther off. It seemed they sent one up first to do a strafing run along the shore.

"Are you okay, M?"

"Yeah. I didn't take any shots," he said, to her relief. He'd been located about fifty yards behind her, but it was hard for her to see him when she was lying down.

The attacking craft returned to its companions. Now all four were doing little zigzag motions at a distance of about a thousand feet, to make themselves difficult targets.

"Wh-what should we do? They spotted us, so we'll have to get away from them first, or we can't set up our trap at the next scan!"

"That's right."

"Let's go back! To the neighborhood!"

"No. They'll chase us down."

"How come? We'll be on land!"

"Hovercrafts are amphibious on flat surfaces. They can chase

us down on the road. And the waterside here is paved, so it's actually the perfect place for them to ride up onto land."

"What? That's not fair!" Llenn fumed, but that was just the way the vehicles worked.

"If you turn your back and run, they'll speed after you. Once they've caught you, you're done for. They've noticed that there's only two of us, I'm sure. That's a good team over there."

Even in a dire situation, M's calming voice was a source of strength. But it didn't change the fact that they were in major trouble. "So what should we do...? Will I be the decoy and run around while you hide? I mean, I can be really fast on my own. Just not as fast as a machine..."

"That's a good idea."

"I—I mean, right?" Llenn was a bit tickled. He'd never complimented one of her suggestions before.

"But I'm not going to run. I'll shoot from here."

"Pardon? You shouldn't choose the blaze-of-glory option just yet, M," Llenn said, feeling like a suicide counselor.

"I'm not that desperate. Do I look like the type to you? They're still far-off. You can look up."

"Hmm?" She lifted her head a bit.

There weren't any bullet lines in the vicinity, so at least she didn't have to worry about being shot in the next moment. It was scary to imagine a sniper being out there, but on the bobbing and shaking hovercraft, it had to be nearly impossible to aim. So she couldn't hit them, and they couldn't hit her. She raised herself up and turned back in M's direction.

There he was. A large body was prone on the asphalt at the edge of the lake. And resting on a bipod in front of that body was an M14 EBR.

*Huh? What's different?*

She examined the image until she realized what had changed. That giant backpack that seemed more suited for a middle-of-the-night escape or an apartment move was no longer resting on his

back. He had taken it off and placed it before him so he could open it.

"I'll use this," he said, pulling something out of the pack with both hands.

"Wh-what is that? Some kind of super-weapon?" she asked, her voice hopeful.

At last, the secret tool was going to be revealed. Could it be some kind of incredibly destructive anti-tank rocket? A grenade launcher that could hurl someone hundreds of feet away? Either one would be a rare and valuable weapon. It could be just the thing to turn the tables on their attackers.

But M said, "No, it's armor."

"What? Armor?"

"Watch."

He pulled out something that looked like a combination of steel plates.

They were green slabs about half an inch thick, a foot and a half tall, and a foot wide, in a pile of about eight. It looked like one of those stacks of bricks that a karate master smashes.

"Hrmph!" M pulled them apart. It had to be an extremely taxing process if he needed to shout to get through it.

When it was fully extended, it turned into a fan-shaped wall, a foot and a half tall and curving nearly eight feet from end to end, standing at a diagonal angle.

"What is it? What is that, M?"

"I'm a big coward—and this is my coward armor."

He pointed the barrel of the M14 EBR through a slot in the center of the wall. In this position, he had his body completely covered from the front, with an opening in the middle for his gun to shoot out of, like a turret in a tank.

"Another one's coming, Llenn."

"What?!" She turned back to the lake. One of the four crafts was winding along the shore from the right, headed toward M.

"They're coming for me. That's perfect—check this out."

Llenn flattened herself against the ground and turned her face to watch. On the right side of her field of view, the hovercraft plunged forward and banked on a level with the shore. It was the special kind of hovercraft turn where the back slides sideways; in a car with tires, it would be called drifting.

The moment that the left side of the vehicle pointed to shore, the German HK21 machine gun in the rear part of the craft spat 7.62 mm fire. The vehicle passed right in front of M at a distance of just a hundred yards.

Llenn couldn't see the bullet lines aimed at M, but she *did* see the actual bullets. They were tracers. The gunner was using a high ratio of them so that their shining trails left an afterimage as they sank right into M's fortified position.

"Huh?"

Then they shot upward, deflected.

Llenn saw it distinctly. The fan-shaped shield propped up right in front of M diverted the bullets up. A number of shots struck true, but they all vanished into the sky. Others struck around his vicinity, tearing up the asphalt and shredding grass.

She heard the metallic sound of the bullets clanging against the shield clearer than she did the actual gunfire from the hovercraft.

"Shoot your P90 at them while they get away, Llenn. You don't have to hit them. Just empty all fifty bullets."

"C-copy that!" The sound of his voice made it clear that he was just fine.

"Here we go!" She turned the P90 sideways to the left and pressed it firmly against her shoulder, then aimed at the hovercraft, which turned farther right to retreat back into open water. When her finger touched the trigger, she waited a beat to allow the bullet circle to appear. She'd never measured it, but the interval was probably about half a second. A large circle appeared in her view, and once it was at least mostly over the hovercraft, she yanked the trigger.

*Brrrrrrrrrrrrrrrr.* The P90 shot fully automatic fire that sounded like a drumroll. Little golden cartridges shot out of the exhaust to the right.

The P90 expelled empty bullets directly below with tremendous force, but since tiny Llenn was flattened against the ground as she shot, she had no room for the cartridges to build up underneath. Thus, Pitohui had taught her the sideways angled trick as a solution to that puzzle.

The little bullets shot toward the hovercraft, a good one hundred fifty meters away by then, but naturally, at that distance their trajectory scattered far and wide. Little spouts of water kicked up around the fleeing hovercraft where her bullets landed. She wasn't lucky enough to hit either of the riders with an instant-kill headshot or pierce the fuel tank and blow it up.

But the point was to drive them away. Once she was done emptying the fifty-round magazine, she pulled a fresh clip from her thigh pouch and exchanged them. "That shield is amazing, M! I had no idea that's what you were carrying… And none of those shots did anything to you?"

"It can deflect a 7.62 mm round at nearly point-blank range."

"No way! That's amazing!" she marveled.

A while ago, Pitohui had taught her about the concept of piercing power.

"If you hide in a weakly defended spot, the bullet will pass right through your cover to hit you. So be careful of that," she had said.

Grass, for example, might hide you from the enemy's sight, but it would not protect you from their guns. A bullet would instantly pierce through grass.

The penetration of a rifle bullet was far more powerful than the average person could imagine. The popular 5.56 mm and larger rifles of *GGO* pierced even sturdy-looking defenses. A wall of concrete blocks wouldn't be much good to you if it crumbled after one or two shots from a rifle.

Likewise, the walls of wooden housing were vulnerable, meaning that being inside was no guarantee against getting shot. The same for the doors of passenger automobiles.

"The only safe places in a car are behind the engine block

and behind the wheels. Don't hide anywhere else," Pitohui had warned her.

"What the heck is it made of?" Llenn asked M, keeping her eyes straight ahead. The four hovercrafts were in formation again.

"It's some kind of spaceship armor plating that doesn't exist in the real world. The strongest material in *GGO*, apparently. They sell it at some hidden materials shop for a ridiculous price."

*Better not ask the price for eight of those plates, then*, Llenn decided. She was afraid that if she did, she was going to learn they were stuffed with 10,000-yen bills.

"They've seen how tough the shield is. They'll probably come as a group this time. One machine gun for covering fire, while the others bear down on me."

"Uh-oh! Are you gonna survive that?"

"I'll tell you the plan. I want you to stand up and run around, back and forth. As fast as you can. If the bullet lines come toward you, drop to the ground or roll around or whatever it takes to get away. Feel free to fire more warning shots again."

*Another decoy job!* she thought. At this point, she was no longer frustrated; she felt something closer to pride. "And you're going to snipe at them while I do that?"

"Yeah."

"But then, won't you be at a disadvantage with your bullet line?" she asked, more worried about M than herself for once. Since both sides were staring each other down, his bullet line would appear to the enemy before he shot.

Like bullet circles, bullet lines appeared as soon as you put your finger on the trigger. Therefore, the enemy would know he was being targeted before the shots came.

"Couldn't they just dodge out of the way with a little twitch of the hovercraft rudder?"

"That's right."

"Then how will you—?"

"We'll talk later. I'll try to manage. Here they come. Run around."

"Eep!"

Llenn could see that all the hovercrafts were taking action, spreading wide and running serpentines as they approached. Like laser pointers at a concert, bullet lines bounced all over the place from the vehicles. They'd be kind of beautiful, actually, if they weren't indicating the imminent hail of deadly gunfire.

"Ahhh, geez!" If she was supposed to be running back and forth, that meant drawing the attention of the enemy's guns upon herself. "Fine, I'll do it!"

Llenn shot to her feet. When your agility was high enough, standing up quickly was like a grasshopper bouncing off the ground.

She waited for a second, then shouted, "Here I am! Come shoot me!"

When the bullet lines began to congregate in her vicinity, she took off at full speed.

＊　　　　＊　　　　＊

The team with the hovercrafts was a collection of high-level players with significant *GGO* experience. Their leader was one of the finalists in the third Bullet of Bullets tournament. Sadly, he'd been dispatched by an even better player early in that fight.

All six were men. Their main choice of weapon was the HK21 7.62 mm machine gun. In addition to that, they had two 5.56 mm H&K G36K assault rifles, one Steyr STM-556, one FN Herstal SCAR-L, and one Beretta ARX160.

They were all individually tough and outfitted with excellent European-made firearms. As the two with G36Ks used adapters, all five of the assault rifle members could share the same magazines.

Each one had his own type of fatigues and gear belt, but there were two features that the entire team shared.

One was a team logo attached to each member's arm. It was a skull with a knife in its teeth, printed in inconspicuous black and dark blue.

The other was a magazine pouch attached to the back of each member's vest. It wasn't in a place they could reach—this was for the sake of any teammates behind them. Sometimes when fighting indoors side by side, it was quicker to take an ammo refill from your teammate's back than from your own stock.

As evidenced by this level of preparation, the group took its teamwork very seriously, and they had breezed through the early stages of the Squad Jam. They'd started in the grass field on the western edge of the map and had taken down multiple teams on the way there.

They had approached the two teams camping out in the forest, split up, and defeated them both at the same time. The real difficulty had come from the team that had holed up at the downed spacecraft in the marsh.

The spaceship team had lookouts at the highest possible position and snipers in each direction, allowing them to easily take down any teams that traveled the few walkable paths through the marsh. Yes, it was a cheap strategy, but an effective one. It was their good fortune that they started SJ in such an advantageous position.

When the team gave up on them and turned toward the center of the map instead, they came across a little shack at the edge of the marsh with the hovercrafts inside. Strangely, they had looked in there just after the start of the event, and the shed had been empty then.

But it was a video game, after all. They concluded that the system automatically generated vehicles when the number of teams dwindled and movement time became a larger issue for the surviving teams to encounter one another. This was the key to their assault on the spacecraft.

They'd had practice with the vehicles in *GGO*, so it took little time for them to establish solid control of the hovercrafts and

speed across the marsh to their target. It was difficult for the snipers to hit the speedy vehicles, and seeing the bullet lines gave their pilots the ability to evade. Once they reached the ship, it was a close-quarters, indoor battle.

The spaceship team was undone by their choice to split up their members. One by one, they were picked off indoors, until only the leader at the top of the ship was left.

"Gentlemen! You have defeated the rest of my team! Well done! I don't stand a chance of winning! However! This does not mean I will surrender! And I will not stand still to wait for death! Instead, I will set an example for how to lose in battle!" the leader said, enjoying the moment. He strapped all his plasma grenades to his body, pressed the activation button on one, and jumped.

"Yaaaaaaaaaaaah!"

He exploded in a bright-blue blast that spread to the other grenades. His own red polygon shards sprinkled and glittered in the midst of it all, and the sight was so beautiful that one of the other team's members couldn't help but murmur, "It's like fireworks..."

It was a feature of the BoB and SJ that dead bodies stayed behind, which made the question of what would happen to this one rather interesting, after it had exploded into smithereens in midair. Right at the spot of the explosion, the little red shards silently reconfigured themselves.

They coalesced into a full body with a DEAD tag overhead, which promptly plummeted to earth. It flopped into the marsh and sank out of sight.

"That...was bizarre...," another one muttered.

Immediately afterward, the 2:50 Satellite Scan started. With just three teams left now, the closest was the one in the residential area—Llenn's team—and so they hopped onto their hovercrafts to close the gap.

Once they found them, the team descended on what they (mistakenly) thought were the two surviving members and ran two machine-gun strafes on them as a test of what to expect.

That was when they witnessed M's shield.

\*     \*     \*

"One of them spread out a fan-shaped shield that deflected the 7.62 bullets. His weapon's unclear, but the long barrel suggests a sniper rifle. The pink one's small and fast, with a P90," the machine gunner reported to the leader and his four other companions.

"It deflected them from that short distance? Crazy."

"That's gotta be a special order."

"I want one. Bet it costs a fortune."

They all had in-ear comms that carried their comments to one another over the noise.

The leader with the STM-556 was calling the shots from the back of his hovercraft. The other three controlled their hovercraft wheels with their right hands while holding their assault rifles in their left. This obviously didn't give them much of a chance for precision fire, so they had to get closer than usual to make a good shot.

The leader glanced at his watch: 2:56. He came to a decision after a moment.

"Let's finish 'em off before the next scan! Everyone prepare to charge. Watch out for bullet lines from the shield, and take evasive action if he aims at you. We'll rush the shore and get behind him. Spread out thirty feet back to front and sixty feet side to side. Jake, you guys are on the right edge, providing covering fire."

He got five affirmative responses—they all understood this was the best course of action.

It wouldn't do them any good to waste more time on the lake. The hovercrafts had fuel gauges that were under half of what they'd started with. Their speed gave them an overwhelming advantage. They needed to wrap up this team and conserve as much of that fuel as possible for the final battle to decide the winner.

That left the power play as the natural choice here. They'd use their mobility to charge and rush on land. Once there, they had the advantage of numbers to ensure their victory.

The sniper behind the shield was the scary part, but as long as they zigzagged and avoided his bullet line like with the snipers on the spaceship, they could handle him.

Jake, the guy with the HK21, piloted his hovercraft behind the others so it could take the rightmost position. Once they were all in a line, the leader smacked the shoulder of the driver in front of him and commanded, "Charge!"

The hovercrafts' high-pitched two-stroke engines whined, joined by the buzz of the propellers. The four crafts roared across the lake, as if blowing past any question of why a game set in the future would rely on ancient engines like these.

They took slightly offset positions and wove quickly back and forth in their own patterns as the charge took shape. The gusts from the propellers produced four separate trails of wake. On land, a small shape stood up and started running to the left.

"I see the squirt!" shouted the man with the ARX160 on the second craft from the right. He took aim at Llenn with only his left arm. A spasming bullet circle jumped into his view, thrown off by the shaking of the hovercraft and the lack of better support. He couldn't keep it focused on Llenn, with her speed. Shooting would only be a waste of ammo, so he didn't pull the trigger.

"Closer," said the leader. "We need to be closer first." They were about 250 yards from the shore.

M lurked behind his shield, flat on the ground, M14 EBR in his hands. Under the boonie hat, his right eye peered through the scope. Through that he saw black crosshairs with little dots at regular intervals.

A hovercraft racing across the red lake popped into the center of his view. Then it drifted off a bit.

"Two hundred yards. Begin covering fire, Jake!" the leader shouted.

"Roger that! Rock 'n' roll!" Jake replied.

HK21 gunfire started up from the rightmost hovercraft, as smooth as precision machinery, the bullets scattering as they hit the shoreline.

"Hyaaaa!"

Llenn dashed through bullet lines. The silent laser beams appeared and disappeared with the speed of the gunfire. She was surrounded by the whipping and screaming of bullets.

*At full speed, they can't hit me! I'm too tiny! If they do, it's because they got lucky! The likelihood is extremely low! I'm a lucky girl!* she tried to tell herself, but it was still scary. What if one hit her in the head, in the face, in the spine?

If it was this scary in a game where death was merely a mild inconvenience, how terrifying must actual warfare in real life be? *Thank God I live in peaceful modern Japan, where I can enjoy playing war like this!*

"HYAAAAAAaaaaaa!" she screamed, moving so fast that her voice underwent a Doppler effect.

Instantly, an idea popped into her mind. Maybe she could use the P90 in her hands to guard her head and neck. It would form its own little eight-by-eighteen inch shield. If there was one unlucky bullet out there with her name on it, the P90 could protect her from certain death.

But…she didn't. She would rather accept her death than subject her precious P-chan to such an ignoble fate.

Like M had told her to, she ran for a while, then flopped onto the ground and rolled over and over to keep her position moving. In the midst of that, she glanced toward the lake and saw the bullet lines, plus the much larger shapes of the approaching hovercrafts.

"Awww…"

For a moment, she thought, *Well, we had a good run.*

As Llenn groaned into his ear, M pulled his right index finger to the trigger, yanking it at the same time it made contact. For the first time in the Squad Jam, his freakish rifle spat fire.

Fire and exhaust shot from his low-lying muzzle, launching a 7.62 mm bullet at twice the speed of sound. The projectile shot across the water surface, barreling the air out of its way and sending up ripples.

It landed square in a person's face.

*"Gfhk!"*

The hovercraft pilot heard a strange noise from behind him, right as the HK21 abruptly stopped firing.

"Huh?"

He turned around to his left…

"Guhhh…"

…and saw Jake, with a bright-red bullet-wound effect in the middle of his face. The HP gauge to the right of his face dropped to yellow, then red, then zero.

He knew *what* had happened to Jake. It was an instant-kill headshot.

"Wha…? How?"

What he didn't understand was *why* it had happened.

Whenever an enemy in a known location fired, you would see a bullet line beforehand. Jake was close enough to him that the system should have shown him the line as a warning.

But he never saw anything. If he had, he would have yanked the steering handle. His every nerve was trained to do just that as he piloted the craft.

Then he turned back to face forward.

*"Gahk!"*

He felt an impact like someone poking him in the left breast with a pole and understood that he'd been shot. No bullet line again.

As his hit points plummeted, his body tilted sideways, pulling the handle to the left. The centrifugal force of the hovercraft caused it to lose balance now that it was sliding to its right, and the instant the side of the craft hit water, it violently capsized.

The bodies of Jake and his living partner were thrown overboard, skipped once off the water like stones, then sank.

*Shit!* the man went to scream, but he was already in the water and produced only the sound of escaping air bubbles. His body sank farther and farther. The G36K's sling was biting into his shoulder, and all the ammo and armor plating he had equipped added up to tremendous weight.

The lake water was pristine, and thanks to being in a video game, his sight through it was quite crisp. On the lake floor far below, the submerged houses of the neighborhood could be seen, as though he were looking down on them from the sky. Nearby, his teammate with the DEAD sign sank like a stone. All in all, he had to admit it was a remarkable experience.

The air from his lungs was gone, and he started entering drowning mode, which was clear from a sudden uptick in the loss of his HP. Within the game, he didn't have any trouble breathing, but it did inflict a kind of dull, general unease throughout his body. At this point, his drowning was inevitable. Even if he opened his window and unequipped all the gear weighing him down, he'd run out of HP before he could get back to the surface.

*Watch out for the shield, guys! You can't see his bullet line!*

But of course, he couldn't produce the voice needed to warn his friends. And even if he could, his communication device wouldn't work underwater.

As he sank, he wondered to himself how it was that a known enemy directly in front of him shot him without a visible bullet line of any kind...

*That's it!*

As the biggest gun fanatic on the team, he realized the trick's secret; it was something so simple, yet not simple at all to pull off.

But he didn't have the means to warn his team, so he sank and sank, until he reached the floor at a depth of seventy feet—where the man with the skull-logo patch ran out of hit points.

"That's two," M murmured into the scope, searching for his next prey.

"Two? You got 'em?" asked Llenn, who was still running around like a crazy person. She flopped onto the ground.

Out on the lake, the leftmost hovercraft had flipped over, and it sank beneath the surface right before her eyes. There had been two riding on that one.

"…Wow!"

When the hovercraft overturned and threw two of their teammates into the lake, the rest of the team knew there was no saving those two.

"What?"

"Whoa!"

"Huh?"

"Jake's down!" yelled the pilot of the other two-man craft.

Behind him, the leader spat, "Shit!"

*They were sloppy.* Jake had been so busy shooting that neither had noticed the bullet line.

"Be careful!" he ordered his squad. "Avoid the line!"

A man with a sharp look in his eyes, sitting in the back of a two-seater hovercraft, shouted something. M placed the center of the scope over his chest, then slid it off once again, just a bit downward. He held that lead with the sideways movement of the hovercraft.

There was no bullet circle.

He fired.

The shot had a significant jolt, but the weight of the M14 EBR and M's large frame held it still. A golden cartridge shot out to the right, bounced on the asphalt, and disappeared in a little tinkle of light.

Right as it vanished, the second shot rang out.

From the shore…

"I don't believe it…"

…Llenn watched what happened in shock.

There wasn't a single bullet line threatening her at this point. She didn't need to run around anymore.

She had seen it happen while on the move. M shot twice in succession, and this time it was the rightmost hovercraft that suddenly stopped.

Clearly, he'd taken out the two riders. Once there was no one left to hit the gas, the only force propelling the hovercraft was inertia. The other two crafts hurriedly spun into U-turns. After four of their squad went down in the span of a few moments, the remaining two were going to get the hell out of there.

Llenn pulled the monocular out of her pocket. Right as she caught a close-up glimpse of one of the turning hovercrafts, she heard the sound of M's M14 EBR and saw the right shoulder of the pilot light up red. Then another shot—this one hit him in the side of the head. He slumped forward, and a DEAD marker flashed above him.

This was the first time she'd seen M's sniping skill in action. It was a short-distance shot but on a fast-moving target. And he'd hit the man right in a critical spot without taking much time.

She pulled the zoom on the monocular out, looking for the last hovercraft.

"Ah!"

He'd stopped attempting his U-turn and gone the other way, heading straight for them. His last companion had been shot, so he wasn't going to bother running away anymore.

Through the scope, she could see clearly that the man in the hovercraft was totally prone. Only the fingers on his right hand holding the steering handle were visible.

"He's charging us, M!"

She lowered the monocular and grabbed the P90, which was hanging under her shoulder.

The hovercraft was coming in toward a spot about even between her location and M's, which was about thirty yards to her right

along the shore. It was at full throttle, faster than anything she'd seen from them yet.

It grew larger and larger as it closed the final stretch of water. The craft reached land within five seconds. Llenn wasn't sure whether or not she should shoot. It was close enough now that she was certain a few shots would hit the hovercraft, if not its pilot. But that didn't seem likely to stop the vehicle at all.

Just then, M warned her, "Get down."

She glanced in his direction and saw that he was standing behind the shield now. He hurled something with impressive form.

The projectile was a plasma grenade. And not just any plasma grenade, but the big ones that were about three times more powerful, colloquially known as *grand grenades*.

They were too big for Llenn's tiny hands, but M looked as comfortable tossing it as a quarterback would.

*No way! Is he actually going to hit that hovercraft?* Llenn wondered, but that did not happen. "Oh…"

The plasma grenade fell into the water about seventy feet out into the lake with an underwhelming little splash.

*Aw, darn!*

But in the next moment, the hovercraft shot through the space and was lit from beneath by a bulge of light. There was a muffled roar, then Llenn saw a sphere about thirty feet across erupt from the lake, right as the hovercraft passed over it.

The miraculous combination of high-speed vehicle and upward thrust of water pressure launched it into a massive jump.

"Byeeaaaaah!" the man shrieked, rather comically, as the hovercraft flew through the air.

From Llenn's left to her right, a screaming man in brown camo fatigues traveled by.

"AAAAaaaaah!"

The hovercraft flew a good thirty feet high and nearly a hundred feet long, and counting. She imagined it would keep flying

until it eventually landed with a heavy, padded thud, leading to the man's imminent counterattack.

But this scene did not play out like the movies.

The hovercraft turned upward and eventually flipped over entirely, unceremoniously dumping its passenger out. About seventy feet farther down the road from Llenn, the man landed directly on his back. "Aaaieeee— *Gulk!*"

A single beat later, the hovercraft landed farther away, the body of the craft crunching rather spectacularly. The water thrown up by the grenade explosion showered down in a heavy spray all over.

"Finish him off, Llenn!"

"Oh, right!"

She sped toward the upturned man with superhuman speed, then slid to a halt when she reached him.

"Wha—?" he said, dazed.

"I truly am sorry!" she said, with all the pity of a samurai, then unloaded the P90 directly into him. She had to overdo it to ensure he didn't strike back. He could switch on a plasma grenade and take them both out.

It took all of two seconds, but in the end, the man had thirty fresh bullet wounds glowing on him, limbs twitching, with red spots all over his face and torso. It was a rather grotesque sight.

The moment she stopped firing, the DEAD signal popped up.

"Ah!"

Llenn twitched, and she extended her index finger off the trigger. She shouldn't fire any more than that. Not only was it a waste of ammo; overkilling an already dead body was one of the biggest breaches of in-game decorum.

"Haaah... Phew..."

Llenn slung the P90 over her back and clapped her hands together remorsefully.

"I'm very sorry about that."

# CHAPTER 10
## Llenn and M

SECT.10

# CHAPTER 10
## Llenn and M

"M! I got him!" Llenn said, flashing a dazzling smile once she was done praying for her deceased opponent. You had to love video games—where you could kill someone, pray for them, then celebrate.

"Good job," M replied. He was folding up the shield that had kept him alive through the fight. The process was the reverse of when he opened it up—he reached wide and pressed his hands shut until the plates were stacked again and he could shove it into his backpack.

Llenn look around for her monocular and stashed it away. Then she trotted over to her partner, who had slung his pack on and was just getting to his feet with the M14 EBR in his hands.

"That was incredible, M! You just sniped those guys like it was nothing!" she gushed. "But...how come none of them tried to get out of the way of your bullet line?"

"They couldn't see it," he said, not a brag, but a flat statement of truth.

"Huh? Couldn't see it? How come?"

"Because I didn't create one."

"Huh? Huh? How'd you do that? They show up when you put your finger on the trigger."

"So I didn't put it there."

"Huh? What about the bullet circle?"

"No circle, either."

"Wha—? Then how did you aim?" she asked, the last of her rapid-fire questions.

"Directly," he said.


Llenn recalled something Pitohui had told her.

"Listen up, Llenn. *GGO* is a game, so they make certain things very convenient for you. Nowhere is this more true than when it comes to shooting."

They'd been in the ruins of a subway station, if she remembered correctly. They'd destroyed about three dozen cleaning robots whose AI had been corrupted to make them attack humans. Afterward, they sat in the midst of the leftover scrap under eerily colored LED lighting, sharing some tea from the thermos.

"Shooting is easier? How so?"

"Let's say that someone just gave you an actual P90 in real life, Llenn. Forget about the Japanese law against owning guns. You could pop in a clip, pull the cocking handle to load it, and point the gun pretty easily, couldn't you?"

"Yeah, probably."

"But could you shoot a human-sized target at a hundred yards like you can in *GGO*?"

"Huh? Um… I don't know…?"

"Outside of getting lucky, you probably can't. And that's because you don't have aim assist outside of the game."

"What's…that?"

"In *GGO*, as long as you point it in the right direction and get the target in the bullet circle, the game's system will decide, 'Okay, let's say that you hit it.'"

"So you're saying…we're not actually aiming that precisely?"

"Exactly. You might think you're just popping off headshots all the time in *GGO*, but truthfully, the game is giving you tons of help. And the higher your level gets and the more powerful and precise your in-game gun is, the more it will assist you. In other

words, the less careful you need to be about aiming in order to score a hit. It's like sword skills. *GGO* players get tougher and tougher in the game because the game gets easier for them."

"I see… So it's like my foot speed, huh?"

"I did a little test once. I lined up a nice, careful shot with a high-powered sniper rifle, waited until I had the bullet circle right over the heart of my target—then I jammed on the trigger in a violent way that you'd never expect would help your shot. Can you guess what happened to that bullet?"

"It…was accurate?"

"Right down the middle of the bullet circle. So that made it clear to me: The triggers on the guns in *GGO* might as well be buttons on a controller."

"I see… So that's what you mean by 'making it convenient' for us. So in that case, what would happen if *GGO* tried to model a true, completely fair simulation of shooting a gun?"

"Well, in that case, it'd be a ridiculously terrible game with such a Mount Everest–level learning curve that a new player would need dozens of hours of marksmanship training, like a soldier gets. Or it'd be a ridiculously terrible game where everyone faces off with assault rifles blazing and it turns into a comedy of errors where nobody can hit anyone else."

"Yikes."

"A game is a game. There's no point to getting too close to reality with it. This is the right choice for *GGO*."

"I see… In that case, I have a question, Pito."

"Your curiosity and willingness to proactively ask questions is to your credit. I expect you'll earn high marks, my pupil."

"Thank you, teacher! So…if you're already a pretty good shooter in real life, what happens if you play this game?"

"A very good question. You earn a hundred points."

"Thanks! So…what's the answer?"

"I had the same question on my mind, so I decided to test it out. I got an acquaintance of mine, who's a real gun freak and has gone to actual shooting ranges, to try out *GGO*."

"And what happened?"

"He was a bit bewildered at first, but once he got the sensation down, he was blasting everything in sight. He said, 'I can see the American sensibilities at work. It's quite realistic.'"

"Ooh! You're talking about what you said before! Where it's not the character's skill but the actual player's skill working!"

"Yes, exactly. But he also added, 'The bullet circle assistance system is a double-edged sword.'"

"What does that mean?"

"Because that tells you where the bullet will go before you shoot it. In other words, you can shoot at stuff without really trying to aim, so it makes for bad realistic shooting practice. In fact, it might even make you a worse shot. But it might be good training for knowing *when* to shoot, he said. It's kind of annoying how cocky that makes him sound."

"I see… But on the other hand, I can't play without it. So what did he say was the good part?"

"Well, he said, 'It makes long-range sniping incredibly easy.' It's super-duper hard to shoot an enemy that's leagues away. You do realize it's not as simple as getting the target in the middle of the scope and pulling the trigger, right?"

"I learned that from the NPC drill sergeant's tutorial. He said that gravity pulls the bullets in an arc, so the farther away a target is, the more you have to account for downward drift by aiming higher."

"And that's not all. When you're aiming for targets with a height differential, that will affect the level of drift, and the higher the temperature and altitude, the thinner the air and the better the bullet flies. If there's wind, that'll have an effect. The rotation of the bullet will cause its own drift. When you're firing ultra-long distances, you even have to factor in the Coriolis effect, which is the spinning of the planet."

"I can't keep up anymore, teacher."

"The point is, you need to make tons of calculations and have

plenty of experience to be good at long-range sniping. Real snipers practice firing hundreds of times, until they know exactly how the bullet is going to fly out of their guns. But—"

"I get it! The bullet circle is like having a computer that does all of that calculation automatically! I mean, it's literally telling you 'This is exactly where the bullet is going to hit.' That makes it so much easier."

"Exactly."


"Directly."

M's answer caused her to recall that conversation with Pitohui.

"Of course! So Pito's acquaintance who was good at shooting in real life was *you*, M!"

"Huh? …Yeah. That's right."

With this information in hand, everything else started falling into place.

"So when you say you aimed 'directly,' that meant you shot without using or needing the bullet circle in the first place? So you just looked through the scope and calculated where you would shoot inside your own mind!"

"That's right."

"So you didn't put your finger on the trigger until just before you knew you were going to fire! And that means you didn't create a bullet line until maybe the exact second you shot, when it was already too late to notice!"

"That's right," he said again, as if it was no big deal.

"This is incredible, M! That's…that's a huge advantage to have!" Llenn raved, unable to hide her excitement.

*GGO*'s bullet circles and bullet lines were designed to provide the same level of benefit to an attacker and a defender. But if M could shoot without needing a bullet circle, that meant he could remove the defender's handicap. And it wasn't even cheating—it was just an advantage based on player skill.

With his shield and his shooting accuracy, he could take any amount of fire and keep taking out targets all the while. As long as she used her size and speed to distract their enemies…

"We can win! We can beat that last team! Gold medal, here we come!"

"Let's hope so. The scan's nearly here."

"Huh?"

Llenn's wristwatch started vibrating. It was thirty seconds to three o'clock. They were reaching the one-hour mark.

"It's still only been an hour…"

Llenn felt like this had been the longest hour of her life. She'd been running and hiding and running and hiding, sheltering from hundreds and hundreds of bullets—experiences that she'd never had in real life.

She took the Satellite Scanner out of her left breast pocket. She'd smacked it against the asphalt multiple times with how often she hit the deck and rolled, but it was obviously a vital item to the Squad Jam event, so they'd made it indestructible. She hit the switch to bring up the map.

In twenty seconds, the scan would initiate. The team wandering around the desert and wasteland region to the south had to be alive still, because they hadn't heard a victory fanfare when they defeated the hovercraft team.

They'd been at the edge of the map ten minutes ago, so obviously they would be closer now, unless they were running away for some strange reason. Llenn glanced over at M, who was pulling something from the pocket on his left sleeve.

She figured it was some new kind of weapon. Instead, it turned out to be folded-up stationery. But before she could ask what it was, the scan started.

M glared at the device before he unfolded and read the paper. Whatever the paper was, the scan was obviously more important.

This scan was an extremely slow one, starting in the northwest. The first dots to appear were the gray dots of defeated and resigned teams in the field and marsh area.

"Hurry, hurry!" Llenn griped. It was teasingly slow. Eventually, their own dot appeared, next to a gray one that was almost perfectly in the same spot.

"Okay, here we go..."

She stared at the map. The only dot left to display would indicate the location of the last surviving team.

Where would it be? How far away? Given the speed of human legs and the ten-minute gap, they would have to still be in the desert, but where?

She was pumped up and ready to charge straight for the desert/wasteland area. Her pink camo would blend in there, so she could put on one of her famous ambushes. Or perhaps she'd do the full-speed attention-grabbing decoy thing so M could pull off his "no-line sniping" unimpeded.

The rush of competitive excitement welled up inside as she watched. "Where's it gonna be? How far away are they?"

The dot appeared.

"Huh?"

It was quite close by, within the same square-kilometer block on the map as they were. She gauged the distance at about six hundred meters.

"What?"

The bullet arrived before she could process what this meant.

She didn't hear it flying overhead.

Because it hit her.

"What?"

She felt a dull pain, like someone squeezing a handful of her right thigh, and the world flipped around her. The map flew to the edge of her sight, the red sky came into view, then cracked asphalt, then lake, then lastly, a type of grass whose name she didn't know.

*I got shot!*

*And knocked off my feet!*

Out of the corner of her eye, she could see her hit point gauge plummeting. It went frighteningly fast, first to yellow, and did not stop...

*Huh? Did I...get...one-shot..,?*

It turned red, then finally stopped with just a little sliver left. She was just barely alive, as if by the skin of her teeth.

"Wha—? Huh?"

The suddenness of it all kept her mind spinning. That was more due to the wild rotation of being blown off her feet than from the actual pain of being shot. Her head was floating like some kind of seasickness.

Then she was flying.

"Whaaa—?"

Her body rose up until the grass that had been an inch before her eyes was replaced by red sky.

"Don't struggle! We're getting outta here!" M said, and Llenn felt a sudden acceleration. He had picked her up and started running.

Bullets flew by, *byew-byew-byew*, both close by and farther away. In the distance, the sound of guns: *tak, tak, tak*. They were still under fire.

Then there was a very near sound of something being gouged, followed by a grunt. "Urgh!"

*M got shot. It was a sniper. We're in an open area—and there's not much room to hide. And if a single bullet brushes me, I'm dead.*

*That's it.*

*This is it.*

*We lose. We came so close.*

Just when she was ready to throw in the towel, M muttered, "Sorry."

Before she had time to wonder what he meant, he hurled her into the air. After a brief moment of free fall, she plopped butt-first onto rough ground.

In just about every VR game, fall damage was a thing. She briefly panicked that this impact would be enough to wipe out her remaining HP, but it turned out not to be the case.

"Pardon?"

All she saw was vivid-green camo pattern. Nothing else.

Where was she? What was happening?

*Byew. Byew. Byew.*

All she could tell was that she was right behind M, while they were still under fire.

*Byew, byew, bweeeeeeng.*

The last one was a high-pitched engine sound among the whizzing bullets. This was followed by the sensation of more backward acceleration and a gust of wind on the back of her head.

She tilted her head to the right to escape the camo pattern, and she saw red sky reflected in a water surface. It was rushing by from left to right.

"Oh!"

She finally understood.

They were on a hovercraft now. She'd been hurled into the rear seat, while M was piloting in the front seat. The camouflage pattern she'd been seeing was the material of his backpack.

"We're getting outta here!"

The hovercraft sped faster and faster, the engine noise and wind getting fiercer along with it.

"O...okay..."

"Shoot it now, while you can."

"G-got it..."

When he'd said "Shoot it," he was referring not to a gun but to her emergency med kit.

Llenn took the cylindrical object from its pouch and, not caring where she stuck it while they were on the shaking hovercraft, jammed it against her cheek and pressed the button on the other end. For a moment, a red healing effect infused her body.

The item would heal her from almost nothing up to about 30 percent of her full health, but the whole benefit would take three minutes to fully manifest.

*Byew-byew-byew-byew-byew-byew-byew-byew-byew-byew-byew.*

There was a sudden rush of more whizzing bullets, audible over

the roar of the engine. Bullet lines crisscrossed the lake surface like searchlights, sending up little water plumes several feet high as they went.

"That's a machine gun. They'll have to be lucky to hit us at this distance, though," M said, though it wasn't clear whether he was trying to put Llenn at ease, or himself.

For most of a minute, Llenn just sat in place, feeling the shaking of the hovercraft. Eventually, M said, "It's all right. We're at least half a mile away now," and lowered the vehicle's speed a bit. She didn't hear the bullets anymore.

She stared at the flowing water in a daze.

"…"

"Did you fall asleep, Llenn?"

"No, I'm okay… Thank you for saving me, sir."

"Are you sure you're not sleep talking? You're acting strange."

"Huh? Oh, whoops… I dunno. I'm sorry, though. I'm just… sorry. Sorry for being out of it…"

"You don't have to apologize. I wasn't paying attention to our surroundings, either. And even if I had been, six hundred meters away is a tough distance to spot someone. Especially if they were already hiding."

"Yeah…"

The hovercraft kept racing onward. Based on the position of the sun, she could tell they were moving southwest.

"What are we going to do, M?"

"Pull well away from them until the next scan. We'll get your HP full again."

Her eyes swiveled to check the upper left corner. Her hit points were recovering but were only a bit higher than 10 percent now. The bar was red.

M had lost a bit, down to about 80 percent—because either his body was tougher, the location of the shot wasn't as bad, or some combination of the two.

"I'll shoot you up, too, M."

"Thanks. It's stuck in the penholder on my left arm."

While he was busy squeezing the hovercraft accelerator, Llenn pulled out his med-kit item and stuck it into his neck. He thanked her for it.

"I had no idea they were so close…," she murmured, recalling the shock of the sudden sniping. "Brr…"

She shivered. It was amazing that a VR game could even simulate a nasty chill going down your back. "They were so far away ten minutes ago…"

"I wasn't careful enough. Same thing with these hovercrafts. They must've found some vehicles to ride."

"Oh! I see…"

"I'm guessing that when the game is nearing its end, they generate more vehicles on the map to facilitate faster movement for the remaining teams. Probably a 4x4 or a truck that can drive on the desert sand. And they must have a good driver on their squad."

"Darn… I wasn't paying enough attention…"

"Don't let it get you down. You're still our lucky girl, Llenn."

"Wh-why do you say that?"

"You got sniped, and you didn't die. If that had landed an inch or two higher, it would have damaged your heart or lungs and caused instant death."

"Oh…"

"It was probably about as far as that sniper could shoot. The farthest distance she could hit a still target."

"But you got shot, too."

"That was a fluke. I'm a big target. I saw the bullet line, but it was on my thigh, so I ignored it. The hovercraft with the two bodies had washed up onshore, so we were lucky there, too."

*Oh, right. The ones on the right edge that M sniped*, Llenn recalled.

"The sniper's gun was 7.62 mm, and the firing interval was short, so it was an automatic, with a magazine holding at least ten rounds. Be careful, because that one can tear you up quicker than a bolt action."

"Got it… I won't let my concentration lapse until the end of the game! I won't get cocky!"

"Good. I'm glad to hear it."

But really, it was Llenn who was glad to have *him*. She decided not to bother saying it, though. There was no end to the thanks she could shower upon him. Instead, she'd wait until the Squad Jam was over to express her gratitude.

She decided to ask, "Which way are we heading now?"

"Southwest. We'll get off in the wasteland; it's on our left now."

"Huh?"

She turned left to take in the sight. About a thousand feet away, the red lake gave way to a barren terrain of rocks and sand.

"How come? Shouldn't we go northeast and cut through the marshland instead? They've got cars, right? Won't they chase us down?"

"You're right, but we don't have another option. The fuel tank is low—no guarantee we could get through the lake and swamp."

"Oh…" Llenn tilted her head back in disappointment. Even this helpful tool was junk without the fuel to power it.

✳         ✳         ✳

Approximately four minutes earlier, at 2:59 PM, atop the spacious third-floor balcony of a mansion in the residential sector that stood out above its surroundings, a woman on her stomach, staring through binoculars, shouted, "Found 'em! Come on, Tohma!"

She was a good six feet tall, heavily muscled, with a burly chest and torso, like a pro wrestler. If not for the brown braids hanging down either side of her head, it might have been difficult to determine her gender entirely. Age-wise, she seemed a bit past her mid-thirties.

The woman wore a camouflage pattern riddled with green dots of various hues, and a gear vest with magazine pouches on it.

"Where, Boss?" a voice behind her said, as another woman

came crawling across the balcony. This one was a bit shorter but still nearly as tall. Her facial features looked a bit younger, too, but still fully adult. Her slender body was clad in the same camo and gear as the first. Atop her short black hair was a knit cap.

In Tohma's hands was a Dragunov, a Russian sniper rifle. It was very long and narrow, with an elegant, delicate profile—the signature rifle of the former Eastern Bloc. The bullets it used were 7.62 × 54 mm rimmed. It was semi-auto, firing with each pull of the trigger.

It didn't have the standard issue 4× scope, opting for a larger and bulkier one that could switch from 3× all the way to 9× magnification. She had a special bipod set up at the front of the magazine.

The first woman ("Boss") pointed through the balcony railing to the northwest. "Do you see where the water's edge meets the road up there? About the width of the downed spacecraft silhouette, left of its position."

Tohma quickly lowered the Dragunov bipod and took up a sniping position on the balcony floor. She put her right eye to the scope for two seconds, then said, "I see two. A little one in faded pink and a big guy in camo."

The boss glanced at the distance readout on the binoculars. "That's them. Six hundred and twenty-three meters to the little one. That's pretty far—can you do it?"

"I will! This is our shot!"

"Good! Start with the smaller target."

"Roger."

Tohma twisted the dial on the right side of the scope to maximize the zoom. Inside the circle, the enemy in that ridiculous pink color grew larger.

She heard the boss say, "Everyone, listen up. Tohma will take out the shrimp. Rosa and Sophie, ready machine guns. On my command, blast the northwest shoreline. Anna, you look for other members and shoot if possible. Tanya, watch the Satellite Scan."

Four other female voices chimed in through her earpiece. This team still had a full six members alive, and they were all women.

The clock struck three.

Through her binoculars, the boss saw the little pink one and the galoot in camo wander closer, then display the map on a projection from the scan terminal. If they were doing that rather than viewing it on the screen itself, it was evidence that they weren't worried about enemies being close.

Her smile widened, baring canines. "We're gonna blow their minds. Tohma?"

Tohma had her bullet circle trained right on the pink one. The circle expanded and contracted with the beat of her heart, but it moved slowly, and at its smallest point, it was just the size of the target's body.

"Ready."

"Do it."

Before her heart could jackhammer with excitement, right when the circle was at its smallest, Tohma squeezed the trigger. The Dragunov roared, and its elongated body jerked like a whip. The empty cartridge shot to the right.

As for the bullet, it tore through the length of air in front of it—and knocked the little pink target ten feet backward.

"Hit! Nice work, Tohma! That's gonna be an extra pudding for you after the game!" the boss exclaimed happily.

"Make it two, if you can!" Tohma answered, right as the second shot went off. This one was headed for the large man. The bullet circle was directly over his body, but the shot missed. He'd darted over the little teammate and left the bullet's path.

"Damn!"

Tohma placed the circle over the man and fired again. This time, her heart was racing, making the circle larger, and so again she missed.

The man hauled the shrimp up with one hand, slung the teammate over his shoulder, and headed for the lake. A beached hovercraft lay at the water's edge.

"I don't think so!" Tohma kept firing. One hit his left thigh, producing a visible effect.

But the man didn't stop moving. He unceremoniously dumped out the two bodies in the hovercraft, hurled the shrimp into the rear seat, and took the controls.

Tohma's tenth shot sent up a jet of water to the side of the hovercraft. The bolt's repetition stopped and left it in the downward position, indicating no ammunition left to feed.

At that point, Tanya said, "Boss, their location is on the shore there. One of them is the leader."

"Use the machine guns," the boss ordered. Two of the windows on the mansion's third story erupted into noise.

They were inside a child's bedroom and a storage room. Each window had a woman stationed with a PKM machine gun propped on a bipod, their menacing muzzles spitting fire toward the lake.

Like the Dragunov, these machine guns were Russian. PK stood for *Kalashnikov machine gun*, for its designer, the legendary Mikhail Kalashnikov, who created the classic AK series. The *M* at the end was for *modernized*.

The PKM emitted bursts of a few bullets at a time in a steady rhythm. A box attached to the underside of the gun fed an ammo belt through from right to left. The bullets shot out the front of the gun, and the cartridges and empty belt were ejected to the left.

Their shots flew toward the escaping hovercraft. From what the boss could see through her binoculars, plumes of water shot up here and there, but none struck home.

"Cease fire! Looks like they got away."

The dual machine guns stopped roaring, and the world abruptly fell silent.

"Boss, their location on the scan is moving over the lake," Tanya said.

Without taking the binoculars off, the boss said, "Did you see anyone else, Anna?"

"No, Boss. I couldn't find anyone."

"Neither could I. Which means it's quite possible they only have two left."

She followed the hovercraft, wake trailing behind it, until it was no longer in sight. It shrank until it was just a black dot, even with the binoculars, and vanished.

"They escaped to the southwest. Could be a trick, but I suspect it has more to do with remaining fuel," she said, placing the binoculars back in a waist pouch. "We'll be heading to the northwest part of the wasteland. Everyone into the truck."

The team, once designated *Foxtrot* by one of their enemies, loaded into a large truck parked behind the mansion—to finish off their final prey.

✳　　　✳　　　✳

At 3:06, Llenn and M finished an otherwise leisurely lake cruise by disembarking into the wasteland of rocks and sand in the southwest part of the map.

The ground at the lakeside was red and soon turned rough and rocky. Obviously, this was not hovercraft terrain, besides which, they were nearly out of fuel.

Llenn had administered a second med kit to herself while they were on the water, and the HP recovery from that one was nearly finished now. Even this left her with only about 60 percent of her actual total. She'd need another one to get back to full.

M and Llenn abandoned the hovercraft at the shore and cautiously surveyed the area. It was mostly flat. Ugly rocks and boulders in a variety of sizes dotted the landscape, from about three feet to a side, to huge ones closer to twenty. That meant there was plenty of cover, at least.

There wasn't much in the way of elevation, but thanks to the boulders, it was fairly easy to climb up to a spot with good visibility. Depending on the height of the rock you climbed and the ones surrounding it, you could probably see a good thousand feet. The ground was packed gravel, not exactly as firm as asphalt, but good footing nonetheless.

"It's not a bad place to fight," M noted. "We can defend ourselves and snipe from atop the rocks. The same thing goes for the other team, but we've got your speed."

"And they can't get their car through here," Llenn added. She had been scanning the horizon with her monocular but hadn't seen the other squad yet.

Her second med-kit dose finished healing, so she shot the last one into her neck. She didn't have any left after this, but their final foe wasn't going to let her sit around and heal more anyway.

"We head west. That way we're not right next to the hovercraft, but we can still keep our back to the water and wait for the next scan," M said.

Llenn started walking. She was cautious, due to the possibility that the enemy would take one of the other hovercrafts and chase them that way, but nobody appeared on the water.

Then it was 3:08. They crouched behind rocks to wait out the last two minutes. Her hit points were almost completely recovered now. She scolded herself: *I won't get sloppy this time!* The seconds ticked down, agonizingly slow.

"Oh! That reminds me…," she said. M had been about to read from something just before the three o'clock scan, and it was all forgotten when she got shot. "Hey, M," she said, turning toward her partner, who was crouched about ten yards away. "Weren't you going to read from a letter or something? What happened to that?"

"Oh!" He looked completely shocked. He'd totally forgotten. "Thanks for reminding me. I was supposed to read it right at three o'clock."

He took the letter out of his arm pocket, opened it, and began to read. While he did so, Llenn looked away so she could watch for enemies. She had to be the one keeping watch while he was busy reading.

She was curious who the letter was from and what it said, but even in virtual reality, snooping on someone else's private correspondence was not cool. She was just surprised and pleased to

learn that you could actually write and hand over letters in a VR game.

The only things in sight were rocks, gravel, and sand. The P90 was in her hands and ready to fire at a moment's notice.

She'd taken two fresh clips of ammo out of her inventory, meaning that including the one loaded into the gun, she had seven on her person at the moment. She'd even brought out the two plasma grenades, just in case, and hung them from her left side.

When the next fight started, she was going to shoot her enemies. If she died, she'd at least be taking one or two—preferably more—down with her. If all seemed lost, she'd pop the switch on a grenade and charge into their midst.

As she sat there, competitive juices surging through her veins, all senses on a razor's edge as the seconds until the scan ticked away, she heard M fold up the piece of paper. Then he got to his feet.

She noted that with the gravel below, his footsteps were very clear, audible even at a distance of several yards. It was a reminder to take as few foot movements as possible when she tried an ambush here.

*Shuk, shuk* went the footsteps. He was getting closer to her. The time on her wristwatch was 3:09.

*Is he going to bring up the map for a strategy session? Or will he show me the letter?* She turned toward him.

"Huh?"

M was standing about six feet in front of her, HK45 in his hand, pointed directly at her face.

"Sorry."

He fired.

Llenn clearly saw the flash of the HK45's wide muzzle.

# CHAPTER 11
Death Game

**SECT.11**

# CHAPTER 11
## Death Game

Llenn clearly saw the flash of the HK45's wide muzzle.

She heard the sound of the .45-caliber bullet passing by her right ear, loud and clear.

If she hadn't moved before her mind could think—if she hadn't made full use of her considerable agility stat—the bullet would have hit her right eye, wiping out all the hit points she'd just healed, killing her instantly.

M's hand moved, keeping his aim trained on her head.

She saw the world in slow motion. The bullet line extending to her face was vivid. She twisted farther left to avoid it.

There was another shot. Again the bullet whizzed past her, nicking her favorite cap and yanking it off her head. If her reaction had been any less violent, it would have hit her.

She didn't know *why*, but she did know *what*.

M was shooting at her. He was trying to kill her. Without explanation.

As he prepared for a third shot, his grim face betrayed no emotion. But she didn't need to sense that.

Only one thought was on Llenn's mind: *I'm not going down.*

Her left foot caught the gravel ground, which gave her a surface to push against. When the third bullet line approached, trying to lock onto her right there, she leaped in the other direction. "Tah!"

If she kept moving to her left, his aim would overtake her. That gave her only one solution.

*Do the reverse!*

She made a dangerous wager, one that would put her directly in the line of fire if her timing was off—and Llenn's agility won out.

Her body hurtled to the right, and the bullet shot by her left side, missing by inches, erasing the bullet line as it went. It was less than an inch from the P90 slung under her shoulder.

Llenn's right foot hit ground, finishing a very wide side step. She was now barely a yard from M, with his HK45 even closer, perhaps a foot away. Certainly close enough that she could reach it with her hand.

"Yah!"

She made an open-hand slapping motion at the HK45. M moved his right hand outward to avoid losing his grip on the gun. Her tiny hand brushed the side of the HK45 and M's broad thumb, then slid upward and onward.

Having kept control of the gun, M stared down at the little person before him and pointed the barrel at Llenn's forehead.

"Ah-ha-ha," she laughed.

His eyes met hers, and he promptly pulled the trigger.

Except that he couldn't.

The HK45's trigger refused to move. If the trigger didn't move, the gun couldn't fire.

M's eyes bulged, and then he realized: That faithful, familiar gun of his, right there in his hand, had the tiny safety lever raised.

Llenn's slap hadn't been meant to knock it out of his grasp.

She had turned the safety on.

As this realization sank in, M's right hand suddenly began to hurt.

In the space between the large body and the small one, the P90 spat automatic fire.

It was only for an instant, just a brief *bu-du-duh* trio of bullets.

They left red hit marks on M's right wrist, passing out the other side and vanishing into the air.

"Agh!"

The HK45, safety still deployed, fell out of M's weakened grip and sank halfway into the sand.

"Don't move."

The muzzle of the P90, an extension of Llenn's upraised arm, pressed into the base of M's neck.

"If you try to move a muscle, I'll pull the trigger, M!" she shouted.

It was probably the fiercest vocalization she'd ever produced in her life. The watch on her left wrist was vibrating, but she wasn't going to be bothered with it now.

If any part of M's considerable body budged a fraction of an inch, she was going to yank the trigger, emptying the remaining forty-seven bullets of her magazine into him from neck to face. M was a tough, thick guy, but even he would still die.

"…"

M looked down at her, gun pressed just to the left of his Adam's apple. His stern eyes and mouth were open wide, as stiff as if time itself were frozen.

"You just listen to me," Llenn said, grinning. "First of all, thanks for teaching me the location of the safety switch, just in case I needed to use it. That advice came in handy!"

"…"

"Now, I have a simple question for you: Why?"

"…"

"Why did you try to kill me? If there's a good reason, I'm all ears."

"…"

"We've been fighting side by side all this time, helping each other out, and made it to the final two teams. Why? I'm not saying I demand to win at all costs, but I'm not going to sit back and die without a good reason. If we can't keep going in the event,

you could at least tell me why and let me give my opinion! Am I wrong?"

"..."

"If you can't answer that, fine. Either way, I'll fight on my own and—"

Llenn pushed the P90 harder against his throat.

"Nooooooooooooo! I don't wanna die! P-p-p-p-p-please... please just wait! I'm asking you... Don't do it! Don't—don't shoot me... Oh my God, oh my God, please, *please*!"

It took a few moments for Llenn to understand that the pathetic begging and blubbering was coming from M.

She withdrew the P90 and took a large step backward. It was such an abrupt and hard shift that she practically warped away from him. Then she steadied the P90 against her shoulder and took aim right at M's face.

Her finger was still on the trigger, so the bullet circle was displaying over his face, rapidly shifting in size with the pounding of her pulse. No doubt he would be seeing the blinding bullet line, too. His entire vision might as well be red.

"Aah...aaaah..."

He fell to his knees, moaning. Llenn kept her aim focused squarely on his head. She heard his broad knees digging into the sandy gravel, and then he slumped to the ground. Without being ordered to, he wound up in a formal sitting position, kneeling with his feet pointed behind him. Sitting this way, he was still about as tall as Llenn standing up. They faced each other at a distance of about ten feet.

"Please...don't shoot me...," he squeaked. His head tilted down as he said it, so that the wide brim of his boonie hat covered his expression.

Llenn kept her circle pointed at his hat and said, "I won't shoot you until you explain why, but if you don't tell me, I'll shoot."

"I'm going to die..."

"Well, yeah."

"I'm…I'm gonna diiie…"

Llenn felt a shiver down her back at the eerie change in his attitude. "Stop acting like that! It's creeping me out!"

He'd been like an adult family member, an uncle perhaps, and now he was suddenly more of a wimpy cousin in elementary school. The shift was so bizarre and drastic that it made her skin crawl.

It was like the person playing his character suddenly changed. Llenn had never done this, of course, but theoretically, if she borrowed his AmuSphere, she could be M as well. "You didn't change players, did you?"

He blubbered, "No, I didn't… This is what I'm usually like… and if…if you shoot me now…I'll die… I'm going to die…"

*What is he talking about?* Questions bounced around Llenn's mind. "Yeah, I know your character will die. But that's only in *GGO*—in the Squad Jam. There's no penalty for death in this event, and you don't have to worry about losing your gear…"

"No, not like that!" he yelped, raising his head.

"Eugh!"

She saw something she really didn't want to see: burly, menacing M with tears streaming down his red face. The more macho the character model, the stranger it looked.

"What do you mean, 'not like that'? Like *what*?"

"If I die in the Squad Jam…I'm going to die—the real me—in real life!!"

"…Are you…feeling okay?" Llenn asked him, thinking back to the old *Sword Art Online*, which had truly turned deadly.

That one had involved a device called a NerveGear that was designed to fry the player's brain cells when their in-game character died. It was like wearing a deadly microwave on your head—she remembered being quite frightened by the news stories.

Naturally, the AmuSphere they used now had nothing like that in it.

"This isn't *Sword Art Online*, so that's not going to happen. How did you get so mixed up about this, M?"

"..."

"Plus, you were tearing it up in battle just minutes ago. You even got shot..."

It was at this point that Llenn realized there was only one thing that could explain his sudden change in demeanor.

"M...I don't mean to pry, but can you tell me what that letter said?"

He flinched, causing tears to drip off his face. He even had a tremendous rope of snot coming from his nose. *It doesn't seem like the game really needs to re-create the effects of crying to that extent*, she thought.

"..."

M silently reached over to his sleeve pocket and pulled out the envelope. He hung his head and reached out his hand toward Llenn.

"So can I read it?"

He nodded.

"Then I'll take it now, but any funny movements, and I'll shoot." She approached carefully, not letting her aim drift, reached out and snatched the envelope, then jumped backward again to keep her distance.

"I'm going to read it. Okay?"

"Yes..."

She opened the envelope with her free hand. It was upside down, and in the process of trying to turn it over, she nearly dropped it. At last she had it right and brought the letter up toward her face with the P90 still pointed at him.

"Here goes."

She took a look at the Japanese written on the paper. In hand-writing that looked like an example from a calligraphy teacher, it said:

*Hey, M. Is the battle blazing around you? I told you to read this after one hour on the dot. You didn't rip it up, did you? If you did, I'll kill you. Now put this away.*

This was a rather violent opening statement. It also explained

why M was so insistent upon reading it exactly at three o'clock. She continued.

*You're playing in my place, so enjoy it all for me! This is all a game, and it's all for fun! If you die some pathetic death within an hour, I'll slaughter you. But if you survive over an hour as just a duo, that's incredible. I'll rub your head in praise.*

Well, in that case, if he died before he read it, he'd still be dead. There was one final part.

*If you die after that, I'll still kill you. No suicide, either. You have to survive through it. There's no fun in doing battle unless there's a little tension to it! Now go out there and have fun! Savor your life! Over and out.*

Llenn flipped over the paper, just in case, but that was it.

She folded it deftly with her left hand, then stuck it into her belt. With her free hand back on the P90, she took close aim again. "Who wrote this message? Wait, why bother asking... It was Pito, wasn't it?"

"Th-that's right..."

"I guess that makes sense. This sounds like something she'd write," Llenn admitted, envisioning Pitohui's breezy smile with those tattoos on her face. "But all this stuff about dying and killing—she's just talking about the game, right?"

It was a perfectly sensible question. Within *GGO*, everyone regularly used terms like *shoot* and *kill* and *die*, but it was only in reference to the game. Nobody would be foolish enough to consider those things happening to the person in real life. And nobody was dumb enough to get mad by mixing up reality and a video game and lecture people like, *Do you really understand what it means to die, you guys?*

M's grizzly-bear head rose, again revealing a face smeared with tears and snot.

He smiled. "Ha-ha-ha-ha! You don't understand a thing."

"Wowww." She was so taken aback by the unexpected change in expression that she couldn't think of anything else to say. All

of a sudden, the bullet circle resting over M's face pulsed faster. "What exactly...don't I understand?"

"How crazy Pitohui is."

"..."

"If she says she'll kill you, she'll actually do it. In real life. Kill you in-game? Ha-ha-ha-ha-ha! No way would she be that soft! I know she's talking about killing me for real! And she knows I'll know that, and it's why she wrote the letter this way! First she says to have fun for an hour, then she says this! She's obsessed with the death game! That game still has its hooks in her heart! She's crazy! Ha-ha-ha-ha! This is exactly what she'd do! Ah-ha-ha-ha-ha-ha-ha!"

"..."

Llenn was feeling dizzy now.

Pitohui and M knew each other in real life—*that* she knew. But what in the world kind of relationship did they have?

Before, she'd considered this information the kind of stuff she "didn't need to know." Now it was something she *definitely* didn't want to know. And Pitohui's real life, which she had once been quite curious about, was also something she *definitely* didn't want to understand.

But the conversation had to go on.

"M...do I have this right? Are you saying that the letter is literal, and that if you die in battle during the Squad Jam, Pito is going to kill you in real life?"

"That's what I've been saying this whole time!" he whined.

"..."

There was still the possibility that M was a master actor in real life and was putting on a performance now. But for the moment, Llenn took her finger off the P90's trigger. The bullet circle disappeared.

"Th-thank you... I was so scared... I don't want to die," M said, now that the bullet line wasn't in his face.

"Then why did you have to kill *me*?" she asked.

"I thought...I should be the leader...," he said vaguely.

She thought this over for two seconds. "What would you do as the leader?"

"I can surrender. It didn't say anything about surrendering in the letter. It'll be an excuse."

"But that's so stupid...," she said, stunned.

"But I was going to explain the situation to you after I surrendered..."

"Ha! And you didn't count on my agility, did you?" she said, teasing him.

"That's right. I should've just tossed a plasma grenade without any warning. I really regret that now," he said, completely serious.

"...Well. Now that that's out of the way," she said, grabbing the envelope with her left hand. "Sorry for not handing this back properly."

She hurled it toward M. Then she checked her watch. It was now three and a half minutes after the 3:10 scan.

"I'm sure the scan is long over by now..." She pulled the scan device out of her left breast pocket and turned it on, just in case. "Yep. Knew it."

It displayed only an empty map. As of three minutes ago, the other team knew where they were and was on the way to them. If they'd been in a more open location, they probably would've gotten sniped at already, like before.

There was no time for squabbling anymore. After a moment's thought, Llenn muttered, "Oh well."

She put the terminal back in her pocket and said, "All right, M! Enough of this! I'll go and fight on my own now! You go hide somewhere so that you won't die! If the other team beats me, you'll become the team leader, and then you can surrender! Thanks for all the help! Bye!"

And she turned on her heel and started trotting. She moved behind a nearby boulder, mindful of being shot from behind, then took off in a sprint.

He didn't shoot her. Llenn thought over where she wanted to go,

then said, "Okay! I'm gonna go tear it up!" and ran east—directly toward the oncoming foes.

She raced at full speed, weaving through the rocks, and touched the communication device in her left ear.

Then she did something she never expected she'd do. She turned off the device.


Back where they'd been hiding, M sat alone.

"Okay! I'm gonna go tear it up!" said Llenn's voice into his ear.

\*       \*       \*

Back around 3:01 PM.

A small shipping truck stopped at the border between asphalt-paved neighborhood and gravelly wasteland. It had reinforced armor plates along the body and cab that had obviously been tacked on afterward.

A group of six women wearing the same fatigues were standing next to it.

First was the boss, a massive lady standing six feet tall. At her feet lay a huge backpack. A gun barrel stuck out of the top opening, as it was too long to fit inside. The type of gun was unclear.

On her right hip was a black automatic pistol in a plastic holster. She turned to the line of her teammates, braids swaying. "Our final target is two kilometers to the west! Let's finish the job, everyone!" she bellowed.

"Let's do it, Boss!" Tohma, the sniper who'd shot Llenn with the Dragunov, said. She was tall, slender, and black-haired, with a number of magazines for the Dragunov on her belt and a protective plate covering just the front of her torso. Her gear was arranged to make it easier to go into the optimal prone sniping position.

"It's the last battle! I'm all pumped up!"

That was Sophie, who had a PKM hanging in front from a wide

sling. She was the shortest of the six but made up for it in width. Combined with her stern features, her size made her look like a dwarf from a fantasy game. Her long brown hair was pulled into one rough bunch behind her head.

She'd probably look good hauling a battle-ax around, but that was not the case here. Strapped to her back was a large pack with spare ammo boxes, as well as replacement muzzles for the PKM.

"It's too bad that once we beat them, there's no more fun to be had!"

That voice belonged to the other PKM machine gunner, Rosa. She looked like the oldest of them all and was tall and well built. Her short red hair and freckles made her look like a badass mom. She had the same bag slung over her back with spare barrels, and three plasma grenades dangled from either side.

"We can think about that after we've won, my sisters."

That sultry voice was Anna's. Physically, she looked like the youngest of the team, in her early twenties. A green knit cap sat atop her wavy, medium-length blond hair. She hid her eyes behind sunglasses. She, too, was a sniper with a 4× scope Dragunov, and a pair of binoculars hanging around her neck.

"I hope I get the last shot."

The final member was Tanya. She was short—but still over five feet—with close-cropped silver hair. Her sharp glare and features made her look like a fox. She had the same pistol holster as the boss. They were the only ones equipped with handguns.

Tanya held a Russian submachine gun in both hands: the PP-19 Bizon. It looked like a miniature version of the AK series, with a striking cylindrical "helical magazine" that sat just below the barrel.

It was designed to hold bullets in a spiral formation, which enabled it to store more ammo. Tanya's 9 × 19 mm Parabellum Bizon held fifty-three bullets in a single magazine. That allowed her to fire consecutive shots longer than Llenn could with her P90.

There was another cylinder on the end of the muzzle itself. This was a silencer that worked to cut down on the sound of the gunfire.

\*   \*   \*

All of them used Russian guns, and in *GGO*, there was a common feature of all Russian weapons: For their quality, they were extremely cheap.

In terms of pure craftsmanship, American and European guns were better, but when price was factored in, the Russian weapons were much more advantageous. You could save quite a lot on the weapons and their ammo.

Depending on who you asked, you'd get many different reasons why.

"Because Russian-made guns are cheap to begin with."

"It's an American game, so they stereotype the Russians by saying they're cheap and crappy."

Perhaps most convincing of all was "The Russian gun manufacturers set the licensing fees to be cheap."

Even in a game, using real brands and products, whether cars or airplanes or guns, required the approval of the companies that made them.

*GGO* was very picky about re-creating guns, from the look to the sound to the capabilities, and they had all the requisite licenses for it. Even though their actual existence in the game was rationalized as "past weapons, excavated and re-created in the future."

Most people seemed to believe the gun manufacturers sold the license to the developers very cheaply, ensuring that Russian weapons were affordable and easily available in *GGO*, and thus popular and widely recognized among anyone who played the game.

But ultimately, the developing company, Zaskar, did not reveal the answer to any of these questions, so the truth was a mystery.

And even then, the most popular guns in *GGO* were still the American- and European-made kinds.

"All right! We're all pumped up!" the boss declared, pleased with her teammates' enthusiastic replies. She turned to them with a smile, braids swaying. "Let's go hunt rabbits!"

All of a sudden, Anna burst into a classic traditional children's song. "I go a-chasing rabbits / on that distant hill..."

The rest of the team burst into laughter, except for Tohma, who asked seriously, "Wait...isn't the lyric 'I got a tasty rabbit'?"

Sophie the dwarfish machine gunner snapped, "No! It's 'chasing,' not 'tasty'! The fact that the rabbit is tasty is *why* you're chasing it! Who's gonna bother chasing something that isn't tasty?"

"Oh, I see!" Tohma said, breaking into a belated smile. "So you still eat it!"

The boss said, "Don't eat *this* rabbit if we catch it. I doubt it'll taste good."

They roared with laughter.

"But give your all to the hunt! This rabbit has survived a long time. Don't get careless now!" she ordered, and they snapped to attention. "Beware its fangs! Let's go!"

Five voices echoed across the wasteland.

"Rrraaaaaaaaaahh!"

＊　　　＊　　　＊

As she ran, the pink rabbit muttered, "What do I do, what do I do, what do I do? What can I do on my own? No, really, what do I do?"

She checked her watch, which said it was 3:16. Even on foot, if they were running at full speed, they should have been making contact right about then.

Llenn stopped running and hid behind a large boulder. As she crouched, her short brown hair brushed her cheek. "Oh, right..."

That was when she realized M had knocked her cap off. *That was my favorite!* she fumed, then decided it was better that than her head. She removed the bandanna tied around her neck and covered her head with it.

While her hands were busy, she thought about what had just happened. She felt relieved that she'd escaped yet terrified at how much danger she'd been in.

But she was also proud of herself.

She'd been face-to-face with gunfire and avoided it. This body and its phenomenal agility were fantastic. And she had stared right down the barrel of that gun, bullet line between her eyes, and pulled off the maneuver without losing concentration.

She tied the bandanna behind her head and pumped herself up by shouting, "Yes! Last battle! Let's do this!"

From this point on, the only things she could rely on were herself and her weapon.

Her tools: First, the trusty P90, P-chan. Seven magazines ready to use, one more in her inventory. 397 rounds remaining. Two plasma grenades attached to her left hip. Behind her back, one combat knife that had been foisted upon her. No emergency med kits.

Her opponents were almost entirely a mystery. All she knew was that they had a sniper and a machine gunner, and multiple members. They'd survived all the way to the end, which proved their formidable skill.

"Okay, last battle! I'm gonna do this! Well...as much as I can, at least," she clarified. "But what can I do to maximize my strengths...?"

How had she fought so far? How did she survive to this point? How did she defeat her five victims? What did her opponents know about her? How would they attack?

"..."

Llenn paused and glanced at her watch.

3:17.

"Three minutes until the Satellite Scan..." She clenched her P90. "All right... Time to run!"

She sped over the gravel, leaving footprints behind, racing like the wind.

The live replay camera watched her go from overhead.


"It's n-not my fault! I'm r-right about this!" a man shouted from the rocks, all alone. "Nobody knows how scary she is! That's

why they say what they do about me! But I'm not wrong! It's not wrong to be scared of death!"

M continued to plead his case, but there was no one around to hear him out.

There were no cameras floating nearby; they'd determined there was nothing worth showing there.

The only noteworthy feature was a set of tiny footprints that led away from him.

# CHAPTER 12

Save the Last Battle for Me

## SECT.12

# CHAPTER 12
## Save the Last Battle for Me

Six women marched through the wasteland of rocks and gravel.

The three o'clock sun shone over their left shoulders, which meant they were heading west.

A preponderance of rocks all around blocked the sight lines, reducing visibility to about forty yards at best.

Petite Tanya took point, her Bizon with suppressor held at the ready. Her finger was on the trigger at all times, meaning that there was always a bullet circle where the gun was pointed. She treated it like a laser sight, so she could point and shoot as soon as she saw something.

She leaned around a boulder, silver hair hardly moving, and turned back to her squad mates to announce, "All clear ahead."

The job of the point man was to stand at the lead and report when you spotted enemies. It was the most dangerous position, naturally—the first to get blasted by an ambush.

Elsewhere, Sophie the machine gunner and Tohma the sniper were a two-woman cell, as were Rosa and Anna. These pairs were placed to the right and left of the point, about thirty yards back, meaning that the team occupied a wide space stretching forward and to the sides.

"Good. Move forward twenty," ordered the boss, who stuck to the rear and occasionally climbed a rock to peer forward through binoculars.

Nobody took independent action. They all waited for orders and moved through the map with the minimum of conversation.

The clock read 3:19:20.

"Forty seconds to scan," Tanya heard the boss say. Last time she'd been the one checking the scan in the back, but the places were switched now. It was the boss who was bringing up the rear and would be staring at her scanner.

During the scan, they'd stop moving and keep an eye out for danger. Tanya paused beside the closest boulder and crouched a bit.

Just then, a pink rabbit jumped around the rock right in front of her. Unfortunately for Tanya, the sound of the boss's voice in her ear drowned out the faint sounds of the approaching footsteps.

Llenn rocketed like a bullet out from behind one of the rocks and spotted an enemy to the right of another boulder about twenty yards away. "Ah—"

Green camo, an unfamiliar black gun, and short silver hair. "Aaaah!"

She was startled, but judging by the look on the other girl's face, so was she.

*Don't stop!*

Llenn didn't let her pace slow. If she stopped, she'd just get shot. If the battle thus far had taught her anything, it was that quick movement was her greatest source of defense.

A bullet line traced behind Llenn's path. There was a dampened sound of gunfire: *shko-ko-ko-ko-ko-ko-ko*. The Bizon rattled mildly, spitting out empty cartridges to the right.

"Tah!" The bullets tried catching up to speedy Llenn, but she hid behind the rock first. The 9 mm rounds gouged the surface of the boulder instead.

"En—"

Before she could say *Enemy spotted!* Tanya leaped out around

the rock. At almost the exact moment the bullet line appeared, automatic P90 fire hit her precise location. The bullets scored the rock and sent sand flying.

As Llenn shot out from her rocky hiding spot, she sprayed gunfire at the fleeing figure on her left. *How did she dodge that?!*

She swung the P90 left to chase her target, completely reversing the original situation: Now she was the one firing on her fleeing prey.

When her opponent pointed a gun back at her, she started a furious sprint. It was like she was using the bullet line as an elaborately long katana to slice at the enemy. Red lines blazed from both muzzles, like level swords swiped toward strafing opponents. Or perhaps like a fight between two dogs, each racing to snap at the other's tail.

The raucous fire of the P90 and the quiet thump of the Bizon intersected across a sandy arena twenty yards across—until two shots glowed on Tanya's back and shoulder. All of her own shots passed Llenn.

Both guns ran out of ammo at the same time and fell silent.

"Ack!" said Llenn.

"Ugh!" said Tanya.

They each took cover behind the nearest boulder. With nearly robotic precision, they pulled magazines from their ammo pouches and switched them out, racing for their lives.

With a larger magazine and gun itself, Tanya was just a bit slower. Once she'd jammed in the magazine and pulled the cocking lever that loaded the first bullet into the gun, there was already a red bullet line chasing her from the far rock like a searchlight.

"—!"

Tanya realized she didn't even have the fraction of a second necessary to point her gun in that direction.

She hurled her beloved weapon into the air.

The Bizon shot out into the open, intersecting with the bullet line and taking fire in her place, orange sparks flying from its black metallic body.

In the brief moment that her gun getting blasted through the air bought her, Tanya was able to report, "One hostile! P90! Very fast!"

Her hand reached for her holster, but by the time her message was done and her fingers squeezed the grip of her gun, the little pink shape was darting right in front of her, slicing through her torso with a red line.

All told, it took less than ten seconds from start to finish.

The 3:20 Satellite Scan had not yet begun.

"I did it…"

In that short time, she'd sprinted quite a lot, shot nearly a hundred bullets, and taken down one member of the enemy team. But in the next moment, she felt a dull pain in her left shoulder and saw the glimmering hit indicator focused there.

*Run!*

It was pure instinct that jolted her into motion. She never saw the bullet line, but she certainly heard the sand kicking up behind her and the noisy rattle of a machine gun.

She raced back the way she came and hid behind a rock, which promptly rattled and chipped with the gunfire. It was so furious that her previous opponent's attack felt like child's play.

"Eeeek! Eeeek!"

She had no time to cheer her brief victory nor exchange her empty clip. Llenn could only flee.

"Take that!"

"Yaaah!"

Sophie's and Rosa's machine guns blazed. They had climbed atop small boulders, stocks under their right arms, left hands on the carrying handles, spitting automatic fire in a crouch.

The hit point bar visible in the upper left corner made it clear that their squad mate who had made contact with the enemy had died in less than ten seconds, before anyone could provide backup.

In her dying message, she'd revealed the number of enemies and type of weapon.

They had good visibility from atop the rocks. The little pink shadow flitted from cover to cover, putting distance between them.

Anna the sniper crawled atop a higher boulder to get into position. She set up her Dragunov, peered through the scope, and fired at the back of the pink shape. "Die."

But the sheer speed of her prey threw her timing off, just barely causing her to miss.

"Shit!"

"Aaaaaaaaaaaaaaaaaaaaaaaah!!" Llenn screamed.

*How many times has this been todaaaaaaaaaaay?!*

She wove her way through a storm of bullets. Red lines gleamed all around her, like laser pointers at a concert. The gunfire just kept coming, bullets kicking up sand that landed on her face and in her mouth.

*"Pteh!"*

If she was going to survive, she needed to put distance between them. She'd beaten the first one with coincidence and sheer good luck, but if she got stuck in the midst of this kind of firepower again, she would not survive.

"Eeeeeeep!" she shrieked, practically sobbing, as she ran and ran, for however many dozens of seconds she did not know, until eventually the world was quiet again.

At the foot of a rock was Tanya's body, floating DEAD sign above it.

In the BoB and the SJ, a dead character—when a player lost all their hit points—wore the expression they had when they died. Tanya was smiling with her eyes closed. It was the face of contentment, of a job well done.

Boss crouched down and patted her little shoulder. "We'll avenge you."

Then she removed the pistol holster from Tanya's waist and tossed it to Tohma behind her. "You or Sophie take this. You might get the chance to put a few shots in 'em."

"Got it." Tohma took the gun.

Boss put down her huge backpack on the gravel and pulled a black gun barrel out of it.

"But I'm going to get the kill shot."

She'd been sprinting at full speed for so long, in such desperation, that she had no idea how far away she was now.

"Haaah…"

At last, Llenn stopped for a breath. Not because she was winded—she was just mentally exhausted. She hid behind a large boulder for a little break.

First thing was to check her HP level, which she'd been too panicked to glance at while running. Not to mention that going full speed was like riding a bike; if she didn't look ahead, she'd slam right into a rock.

The shot to her shoulder had only grazed her. She still had 70 percent of her health left. But that was enough damage that just two or three ordinary shots would kill her now. And she didn't have any healing items left.

She checked her Satellite Scanner, though it had to be long over by now. To no surprise, she found that there was no scan info left, and she put it back away.

Next, she switched out her depleted P90 magazine. For as sudden as the encounter had been, she'd gone a bit haywire with the ammo and used up two whole clips. She went into her inventory and materialized the last one so she could stash it in a pouch.

"Six magazines left. Only three hundred bullets…"

She had to last the rest of the Squad Jam with that. If it was going to take her a hundred shots for each person, she was way

short. Given how much fire she'd been under, there was no way there were only three enemies left.

"If there are five, that's sixty per person…"

Any more than that, and she'd just have to surrender. Yes, she had two plasma grenades and that combat knife, but she was thinking of them for more negative uses. "I guess I could go down with them…"

Just then, a distant burst of machine-gun fire raised her hackles.

"Eeek!" She flinched and got to her feet on instinct, then dropped to the ground.

This time, it wasn't a continuous spray. The shots came in bursts—*ta-ta-ta-tak, ta-ta-ta-tak*—of about four or five at a time, one second apart.

"That's about two hundred yards in that direction," Llenn murmured, recalling M's training. Just knowing whether they were close or far made a big difference in how she felt—it was a very good thing she'd practiced that, indeed.

She didn't hear any bullets actually landing, so she carefully lifted her head and body. "Hmm?"

Bullet lines were visible high in the air.

They were many feet above her height. The bullets whizzed overhead, erasing the lines as they went. She could see two bundles to the right and left, suggesting there were two machine guns firing in alternate bursts.

It didn't take long for her to realize that they weren't shooting at *her*. Was it M, then? Probably not that, either.

They were just shooting into empty space where they figured an enemy would be. She recalled something that Pitohui had once told her.

*If you're losing a fight against another player, no matter how scared you get, the one thing you should never do is just fire wildly. It's like a drug that makes you forget your fear while you're shooting. But it's wasting valuable ammo. It tells them where you are and that you're scared. It's the worst decision in a bad situation.*

With the constant patter of gunfire in the distance and the faint sound of bullets passing harmlessly overhead as background music, Llenn grinned and murmured, "Maybe I can still win…"

*I was scared earlier, but so are they! They're rattled because they lost one of their teammates! That's why they're shooting wildly without knowing where I am!*

And just as she realized she still stood a chance, her optimism went into overdrive.

*I've still got three hundred rounds! At ten bullets a target, I could kill thirty people!*

Llenn got to her feet and raised the P90. "Okay…start with the right."

She started to trot toward the bullet lines of the machine gun to her right. It was a much easier forward advance than the last time. The unhinged shooting and visible bullet lines were like a lighthouse, a North Star guiding her to her destination.

Carefully, she wove her way between the large rocks, darting and hiding, peering out, then zipping across again. She even had the presence of mind to *enjoy* the tension.

*I'll beat them all on my own, and then I'll be the hero of the Squad Jam. No, the heroine! That'll really show M for deserting his post and Pitohui for giving him those bizarre orders! If they give me an on-mic interview right after I win, I'll tell them, "Actually, it was easy winning on my own at the end."*

Her mind was filled with visions of triumph when the silent shots hit her from the left.

The first one hit her arm, causing it to go numb and lose strength.

The second one hit her side immediately after. Luckily, this one struck her P90 magazine pouch, ruining that stash of ammunition.

The third one, which came after the shot to her side knocked her off-balance, merely grazed her neck.

"Agk!" she squawked at the sudden pain, picking up her pace. She waited for the sound to see whether she could tell where the shots came from—and didn't hear anything.

She was stunned. The hits had come in the brief moment of silence between machine-gun bursts. She could even hear her own footsteps during the lull. And yet, she'd failed to pick up any sound from three quick shots in succession.

It was almost like someone very close by had stuck her with some invisible spear, but that was silly. She could see the bullet-wound effect on her upper left arm. Furthermore, her HP bar had suffered quite a bit, down into the yellow zone at about 40 percent.

"Ugh." There was a large diagonal rip in the pouch on her left thigh, through which she could see the ruined clip. That was fifty bullets she wouldn't get back.

But if the bullets had landed in even slightly different spots, her leg pain and damage would have been far worse than what she was dealing with now. She would've fallen to the ground, made for a stationary target, and almost certainly been dead by then.

"I...I'm...," she muttered, scrunching up her face, "still a l-lucky girl..."

"Damn lucky bastard," Boss grunted as the pink target vanished from sight.

She was the one who'd shot at Llenn, from a distance of about a hundred yards. It had been a quick sequence as soon as the enemy came into view.

The first shot had hit her swinging arm, blocking the bullet from hitting her heart. The second should have hit her side, but there had been no visible effect, probably because it hit some gear and didn't cause damage. The third shot had grazed her neck.

She told her squad, "I didn't finish the job. The small one's going farther south. I'll pursue as we planned. She shouldn't have much HP left, but don't be lazy. Also, the pink color doesn't stand out as much as I thought it would."

Her teammates replied in the affirmative. The boss turned the mode selector behind her gun trigger to set it to automatic.

Her gun was like a squat, compact version of a Dragunov, a weapon no one would ever call beautiful. It was about three feet long, and it looked like an assault rifle with a scope and a long twenty-round magazine. What made it strange was the barrel, which was surrounded by a fat cylinder.

This was the Russian silenced sniper rifle, the VSS, aka Vintorez. This weapon was designed for special forces to snipe middle distances (around four hundred yards) without making any sound.

It had two major features. First was a large sound suppressor at the end of the short barrel by default, which absorbed the sound of the gunfire explosion. The actual barrel was very short—the fat cylinder on the end of the gun was actually the suppressor.

The other feature was its use of special 9 × 39 mm rounds designed to be subsonic, meaning slower than the speed of sound. Normal supersonic bullets create a shock wave cracking sound. The bang of a gun is a combination of the gunpowder explosion and the supersonic boom.

A suppressor can cover the combustion sound but not the boom. Therefore, even guns with standard suppressors create a cracking noise to some degree. That makes it easier to notice when you are under fire, but the Vintorez and its subsonic bullet speed ensures that even sound will not escape. It's just a large and very quiet bullet.

When under attack by a Vintorez, you won't know where your friend got shot from, or perhaps that they got shot at all.

It was useful for situations just like this one, where machine guns drew attention with intentionally wild fire, making Llenn think, "Heh-heh! They're shooting scared!"

And when the enemy came out of their position to get closer, two Dragunovs were ready to aim from far away. In a place with lots of cover and poor visibility, speedy Tanya was good at SMG runs.

Or, as Llenn had just suffered, the boss could sneak around

and pick the target off with silent precision. Sometimes she and Tanya worked together—either as a two-woman cell or in a pincer maneuver.

This tactic was how they'd carved their way through the Squad Jam: working as a team, acting on the boss's orders.

When they were fortified in the advantageous ruins, they were so formidable that they actually had three teams tackle them at once in a kind of loose alliance. Ultimately, the lack of teamwork between those groups showed them to be inferior to this squad.

None of their opponents realized, until the moment of their defeat, that the firepower of those machine gunners was nothing more than an empty lure.

"Let's finish up! Sophie cell, move west-southwest. Rosa cell, back them up."

Five soldiers moved in for the kill. The machine gunner and sniper pair ordered to provide backup started firing intermittently in the direction of their target. By spraying a healthy range of bullet lines and projectiles, they could limit the target's range of movement.

In the meantime, the other cell made its move, finding the most advantageous terrain—in this case, the top of a rock with particularly good sight lines.

Tohma climbed a large boulder first and spotted a little pink shape darting between the rocks about a hundred yards away.

"Visual! Under the sun, one hundred!" she told her comrades. She aimed the Dragunov and started shooting. The glimpse of pink dived behind a rock. It was a smaller one, maybe seven feet across, so she aimed through the scope and shot twice, *tak-tak*, once on either side of the rock. That would ensure that the target didn't try to run.

A few seconds later, Sophie ascended a different rock with her PKM on her back. "That one?" she asked, gesturing toward where Tohma had shot the Dragunov.

"*Da!*" Tohma replied.

"Give me your shoulder!" Sophie insisted, lifting the muzzle of the PKM high. Tohma had stopped shooting the Dragunov, which was running low on ammo, and let it hang from her sling in front. With her free hands, she grabbed the legs of the PKM's bipod, rested it on her own shoulder, and crouched.

In cases where the gun has nothing to rest upon and a prone position with the bipod is too low, sometimes another person can suffice. With a steady surface now, the dwarf lady began a furious hail of gunfire.

"Diiiiie!"

It was just a bit over a hundred yards to the rock where the tiny enemy was hiding. The bullet circle captured the rock such that at its widest, it was only two times the size of it. The rumbling hail of bullets had turned into supersonic blades that fell without mercy.

"Hyaaaaaaaaaaaa!" Llenn screamed.

*I can't, I can't, it's all over, I'm gonna die, this is it, I'm gonna die, I'm gonna die, I'm gonna die!*

She'd been shot at by machine guns many times today, but none were as terrifying as this.

The boulder she was resting against, which had to be many, many hundreds of pounds, was rocking with the impact. She could hear hideous scraping and chipping sounds on the other side of it. On top of that, lines and bullets kept appearing steadily on either side, sending up little splashes of sand.

The gunfire was louder than anything she'd heard so far, a sign that they were close. Bullets cracked to her left, her right, and directly overhead.

*Can I get out of this...?*

The next rock in the direction away from the shooters was about twenty yards off. After that, the rocks were clustered closer together, which would make it easier to find cover.

*But I caaaaan't!*

Bullets were landing all over the stretch of ground. Forget

actually reaching it; she'd take a hit as soon as she moved out from cover. And given that she had only 40 percent of her HP at best, one hit would be all it took.

*What happens if I just stay hidden here?*

That was an easy one. The other members of their squad would be approaching from elsewhere, ready to lob a grenade toward her position from the side. *Boom,* game over.

She imagined a plasma grenade rolling at her feet, then exploding in a vicious blast, and shivered. "Brrrr…"

*Plasma…grenade?*

Then she remembered that she had her own. Her hand went to her left hip and found two orbs there. They were barely inches from the hole in her pouch where she'd been shot.

Plasma grenades were cheap and powerful, but as a counterbalancing measure, they were designed to be very sensitive and would go off under gunfire. That was why everyone hung them from the back of their waists: It was considered the best trade-off between convenience and safety. And if you got blown up by a stray shot from the flank, well, that was the cost of using plasma grenades.

If those shots had hit her grenades, she would have died instantly, even at full health. Yet again, her good luck had saved her. On the other hand, her survival meant that now she was faced with this terror…

Llenn pulled a grenade loose while the bullets whizzed all around her, and she stared at the black ball. By twisting the knob on the top, she could set a countdown, but the default usage was pressing the button to activate a three-and-a-half-second timer.

If she just pressed it to try it out, the countdown plus the time for her HP bar to empty would total only five more seconds of hell she had to endure in the Squad Jam before she could relax.

"…"

She squinted hard at it, strong enough to bore a hole in the grenade shell.

"Here we go."

She pressed the button.

*One...*

Bullets kicked up gravel and dust. The boulder rocked.

*Two...*

Llenn hurled it backward over her head.

*Three...*

She crouched against the rock, preparing to sprint.

"Yah!"

She darted into motion at the same moment that the plasma grenade exploded on the other side of the boulder.

The fifteen-foot blast rattled the heavy boulder but didn't destroy it. However, the shock of the explosion did affect all the bullets passing through it. They deflected and curved, upward and to the sides—so the blast worked as a shield to protect Llenn's back as she ran.

"Whaaat?!"

Sophie was so shocked, she stopped firing. Even Tohma, who was acting as the machine gun's base, saw it clearly.

A pale explosion right in front of the rock was altering the course of their tracer rounds—and a little pink shape darted away. Sophie pulled her aim a bit higher as she resumed firing, but the bullets fell short just as her aim was about to catch up to the target's legs.

"Damn! Too fast!"

She got to the other side of the rock that was twenty yards farther away. Sophie immediately held up and said, "She used the grenade as a shield! Moving farther west! The rocks are thicker there! Be careful, everyone!"

"Got it!" replied the boss. "I saw the spot by the blast. That's about forty yards to the northeast. In pursuit."

"Copy that! We'll chase after reloading!" Sophie got the PKM down off Tohma's shoulder and removed the dwindling ammo box from the underside of the machine gun. Tohma opened Sophie's backpack and pulled out a fresh box.

"That's a tough one."

The lady dwarf had to agree. She reloaded as she said, "Ugh... I'll be damned if they didn't save the toughest one for last."

*It worked, it worked, it wooooorked!*

Llenn had no idea that the plasma grenade blast would physically shield her from the incoming bullets. She'd just been hoping that it would help her *somehow*. Now that her gamble had worked out and given her an escape route, she kept on the move. But the density of the rock placement around her meant she had to slow down quite a bit so that she didn't run into them.

*Run, run, run.*

*What now?* she wondered with a gasp. *What will running away get me?*

"..."

Her feet slowed. Once she was walking through the maze of boulders, she thought it over.

There were still at least three enemies, and realistically, probably more. They had two machine guns that delivered a hail of 7.62 mm bullets and at least one automatic sniper rifle that could hit a target at six hundred yards. There was also the mystery gun that shot her in total silence.

On her side, she had a P90 that could maybe shoot two hundred yards at best, one plasma grenade, and a knife.

*Wait a second... Is taking extra distance just putting me at more of a disadvantage? When I beat that one person earlier, how did I do it? How was I able to win? In fact, I've beaten five people, and what were the circumstances in all those cases?*

"..."

Her pace slowed to a stop.

*I was close. Every time I beat another player, they were extremely close to me. That's it...*

"I shouldn't run away..."

She looked down at P-chan, which was nestled in her right hand.

The odd pink gun seemed to be saying, *That's right, Llenn! You finally figured it out! C'mon, no more running away from the enemy! We've got to take the fight to them! Use your speed and agility, and fight the way you do best! I'll be here for you! Whether we live or die, the important thing is that we'll do it together!*

But Llenn didn't want to be the kind of crazy girl who imagined her gun could talk to her, so she decided she hadn't heard this.

"No way."

"Let's make this the last fight!" the boss said, revving up her squad. "Come on!"

She stood at the lead and charged toward where the little pink enemy would be hiding. A leader had to brave danger, or her subordinates would not trust her—a fact she understood well.

There were clear footprints in the gravel leading away from the rock where the explosion had happened. The boss trotted along with the utmost caution and nerves, Vintorez held at waist level. At intervals of about fifteen feet behind her were Rosa, the lady hauling the PKM, and Anna, the Dragunov sniper with the blond hair and shades.

Only one of the three was in a hurry at a time. The other two stayed on guard with their guns at the ready. After enough distance, they would switch roles. This formation was designed so that if one person got shot, the other two could easily take out the enemy. The boss was at the helm, of course. They were familiar enough with the process that they did it naturally; no conversation was needed.

*Where are you? Come on out!* the boss thought, her predatory gleam turning positively feral. At this point, the braids just looked out of place.

Just as she was moving from one rock to the next, she spotted something.

"Ah!"

Just ten yards ahead, a little figure in pink, from her bandanna to every other part of her outfit, sat atop a rock about as tall as a dinner table. She was watching the boss, but the P90 in her hand wasn't aimed in her direction. In fact, it wasn't really *aimed* at anything.

The shrimp was smiling, her face alight, as though she'd just spotted a friend she'd been waiting for. When the boss pointed her gun at her, the little girl said, "Were you looking for me?"

The length of this statement, which was barely a second and a half, was enough to delay her pulling the trigger.

"Yeah!" she said, shooting the Vintorez.

"Ah-ha-ha-ha!" The little one rolled backward at the same moment. The bullet passed silently through the space between her legs, where her chest had just been.

"Dammit!"

That was Rosa, who had caught up to the boss and now charged past her. She unleashed the PKM, which she held at waist level. Heavy, thudding gunfire drowned out everything else. With a hundred bullets to a belt, she could fire continuously while chasing a target for a good ten seconds.

"Raaaaaah!" she screamed, almost as loud as the gun, and sprayed lead as if she were holding a water hose as she plodded toward the rock.

Behind her was Anna with the Dragunov. "Take the left, Boss!" she called out, spreading to the right.

That put Rosa in the middle, Anna on the right, and Boss on the left. They'd circle and descend upon the rock all at once to finish off their target.

There was nothing wrong with that strategy for this situation—except that the boss shouted, "Stop!"

"Here we go!"

Llenn rolled backward off the rock, landed smack on her feet, then hopped up straight. She didn't speed away.

She understood now. Turning and showing her back was just making herself into a target.

*So if I don't show my back, what do I do? I close the distance to them!*

Llenn jumped back onto the rock she'd been sitting on. Then she pounced with all her strength—a massive leap, making use of all her agility. As she soared through the air, she saw the three enemies below her.

A middle-aged woman firing a machine gun as she advanced.

A blond woman with sunglasses on the left, carrying a long sniper rifle.

And on the right, a burly woman shouting. The one she'd just made eye contact with.

Llenn began to choose her prey.

*Which do I shoot first?*

The boss and Anna saw it happen.

A wreath of red lines around their busy machine gunner, coming from above. Then there was sand flying up all over, with the glimmer of bullet-hit effects in the middle.

"Gah!"

The PKM stopped firing, and its carrier toppled to the ground.

The little pink person descended to Rosa's side from the air.

"Damn you!"

"Shit!"

Anna and the boss pointed their guns at the little freak together—and they both very nearly pulled the trigger. If they had started shooting, they'd have suffered friendly fire. The pink target had landed directly between them and in the next moment rolled into a somersault.

*Just die already!*

Anna swung the long Dragunov to her left, following the little pink blur as it got up from its roll, and she fired in succession. The shots passed over the head of the target, which started speeding away.

*It's too fast! It's too small!*

She couldn't hit the enemy, despite being less than thirty feet away.

*I'm going to take her out here!*

Anna continued firing, but her concentration was so focused that she failed to notice the left arm of the target swinging wildly. Or the black sphere that landed at her feet.

"Run!"

Boss's voice was the last thing she heard.

Llenn sprinted away, the force of the blast pressing her back, as she pulled a fresh P90 clip from her thigh pouch and swapped it in. The outgoing magazine still had a good twenty bullets in it, but she didn't have time to stick it back in the pouch. They would have to get tossed aside. That left her with just two hundred rounds.

She didn't have time to check the status behind her. The grenade landed at the feet of the sniper, so that had probably been fatal, but the machine gunner was likely still alive. She'd noticed that many of the shots she'd fired from midair hadn't hit the target below her.

As if to prove the point, a swarm of bullet lines started chasing, then caught up to her. She didn't have time to hide. A dull pain shot through her left ankle, and she sprawled out. At full speed, this was quite an impressive spill.

"Aaaaaaaahh!!"

She spun and rolled, shooting up waves of sand and grit, like an airplane in a crash landing, until her back and head slammed into a rock.

*"Guhf!"*

She finally came to a stop, her legs splayed in front of her. The sand gradually cleared.

"Uh-oh…"

First, she saw her own hit points. They were under 30 percent now, down into the red.

Then her empty hands. Her gun, which had been in its own

sling, was not in her hands. The physical sensation told her where it was: her back. It had gotten flipped around her body in the fall and was now wedged behind her.

Lastly, the enemy. Standing atop a rock about thirty yards away, body glowing with bullet hits, was the glowering older lady. Her machine gun was propped onto her shoulder, and the bullet lines it created were pointed at her face, head, arms, and legs.

*Yeah, I bet she's mad.*

Anyone would be mad when two of their friends were killed and they got punched full of holes, too.

Llenn didn't have time to swing the P90 forward from behind her back. She didn't have the opportunity to bend her legs, pop up to her feet, and run.

She simply watched in a daze, certain that the bullets would be coming momentarily. This would be her death—the last thing she saw in the Squad Jam.

Then she noticed six plasma grenades, three on either side, hanging from the lady's backpack. *If only my earlier burst of fire had hit one!* she thought, lamenting her bad luck. *Oh, but then the chain explosion would have taken me out, too.*

So in fact, she had been lucky after all. It was ironic that this was what she was choosing to think about in her last moment of competition.

But the next moment brought not bullets but words.

"Well done, little one!" boomed the machine-gun woman, who seemed to be in the mood to give a victory speech.

*Okay? I'm all ears.*

So she was going to last a few seconds longer—perhaps as much as a minute. Maybe she'd have a bit of time to pull the P90 loose.

"Now die!"

*Well, that was three seconds. She could have gone on a bit longer. She could have gotten all of her thoughts off her chest,* Llenn grumbled in her mind. She stared out dully at the face of the person who was going to kill her.

Then the woman exploded.

*   *   *

Everyone saw it happen.

Multiple overlapping explosions engulfed the woman with the machine gun.

Llenn saw it happen, and so did the boss, who was not far removed from her.

So did Tohma, who had her Dragunov aimed to provide cover from atop a rock about forty yards away, as did Sophie with her PKM.

And there was one more, farthest away of all.

In the midst of the cavalcade of explosions, Llenn was the first to understand exactly what had happened.

One of her plasma grenades had gone off, starting a chain reaction. And there was only one possible reason why.

She put her hand to her left ear and reactivated the device there.

"*Now* you're back in, M?"

His reply was immediate.

"For the last battle, at least."

# CHAPTER 13

Battle to the Death

**SECT.13**

# CHAPTER 13
## Battle to the Death

When her teammate went up in the massive explosion, the boss was knocked off her feet by the force of the blast, too. There were six plasma grenades on Rosa's waist, and unluckily for the boss, one of the grenades that got jostled loose in the original blast exploded in her direction. There was nothing she could do to escape damage. Her large body flew about ten feet, and she came to a stop on her bottom amid the gravel.

"Dammit! Who uses their team leader as bait?!" she swore, realizing they'd been tricked, and got up to view the damage.

She had 60 percent of her HP left. That was fine.

"Ugh!" But the worse damage was to her precious Vintorez. It wasn't in her hands any longer.

Tanya and the boss were in lots of close-range battles, so they didn't use slings, in order to give themselves more freedom of movement with the guns.

In this case, that had backfired—the force of the blast knocked the gun out of her hands. It was somewhere nearby, obviously, but she didn't have time to go around looking for it. Instead, the boss pulled the black handgun from her leg holster.

It was an automatic pistol with a flat design, another Russian gun. This was the Strizh, a 9 mm pistol from Arsenal Firearms. Strizh was Russian for *swift bird*, and the export title was Strike One.

The boss held it in her right hand, loaded with a seventeen-round magazine, and gave orders to her two surviving squad mates.

"There's a sniper to the northwest! Don't climb up the rocks!"

Sophie said, "Roger that! Heading there now!"

Tohma the sniper replied, "I got him to shoot me, too!"

That meant she had intentionally leaned out atop the rock, even after the explosion, hoping to draw sniper fire. She'd taken a hit, but for now, she was still alive.

"The line was from the north side! The distance is at least two hundred yards off!" Tohma continued, making use of her sniper expertise to put together some kind of useful information.

"Good! Let's finish off the little one! Surround her!"

"Sorry, Llenn. I didn't take out the sniper."

"It's fine!" she said, getting to her feet. She yanked the sling around so that the P90 was in front again.

They didn't have time to chat. There was still another enemy behind the rock just a hundred feet ahead of her, and approaching every second. She knew that because it was what she would have done, too.

Llenn ignored the two on the sides and ran straight forward. She made a beeline, expecting to come face-to-face with the enemy. Any rock that loomed into view practically jumped off the side of her eyesight as she passed it. Suddenly, a woman leaped out from one of them with a pistol pointed at her. "Yaaaaaaah!"

Llenn charged, tightening her grip on the P90's trigger. By rushing closer, she could duck beneath the enemy's shots. She saw her own bullets hit the large woman's leg, but the enemy was tough enough that this wasn't going to knock her over.

*I'll just have to keep charging, then!* Llenn thought, weaving through bullets as she continued.

"Don't mess with me!" the woman bellowed, lifting a long, burly leg. It swung toward her like a log.

*"Gu-hya!"*

The foot kicked Llenn. While she was airborne, she put all of

her mental and physical strength into holding the P90. *Don't let this slip away!*

"Bwuh!"

She landed flat on her back, atop a flat and wide rock about seven feet high. How far had she flown?

"Ugh…" It wasn't piercing, but she did feel an ugly throb that left her helpless for about two seconds, like someone shoving her in the back, hard.

*Crunch.*

Just when she was getting up, a heavy leg stepped on her right arm—the leg of the large woman, bullet wound still glowing, standing atop the boulder with her. She had Llenn's whole arm pinned, including the P90, right against her stomach, as immovable as a vise. Llenn's arm was trapped, and her stomach hurt, like she had overeaten.

"You've really done it now!"

Llenn couldn't see the woman's face, because it was framed against the light—but she had enough presence of mind to be glad she couldn't. It must have looked demonic.

"You're finished!" The woman's arm pointed at her. There was a black pistol at the end of it. A red line extended downward, straight at her left breast, the location of her heart.

*Da-da-dam.*

Three merciless shots.

*You didn't need to overdo it. One would have killed me. You're just wasting bullets,* Llenn thought, her body shaking with the impact. *Hmm. It's not as painful as I thought it would be.*

For a series of shots to her heart, the most it felt like was just someone tapping at her chest. Maybe the first shot killed her, so there was no point in sending the signals for the subsequent shots?

But that wasn't true.

Her hit point bar was red, but it was still in the same position as before. It hadn't dropped a bit, despite taking three shots. Actually, she couldn't see the bullet-hit effect, either.

*Why?*

"What?!"

Her enemy seemed even more shocked than she was.

*Dam, dam, dam, dam.*

This time it was four shots to the chest, patient and deliberate. The pistol's slide moved back and forth, and Llenn clearly saw the empty cartridge that ejected with each repetition.

But she didn't die.

"Is she immortal? Is she cheating?"

*Um, of course not?* Llenn wanted to reply—but then she realized something. She remembered something. She remembered what she had in the left chest pocket of her fatigues.

The Satellite Scanner—an unbreakable object.

"Shit! A protector!"

*Actually, no—but, in a way, yes.*

"All right, then…"

The bullet line moved up from her chest. It caught her right eye, turning the world red.

"Yeek!" Llenn twisted her head left. The 9 mm bullet clipped her right ear and gouged a hole in the rock below her.

The line came for her again. This time she craned to the right. She heard the bullet land just next to her left ear.

Then the large woman pushed the pistol closer. It hung less than a foot away from her forehead. The first two shots had missed, but this one wouldn't. Once again, Llenn steeled herself for death.

"Wha—?! Shit!"

And yet again, she realized it would not happen, due to the woman's curses and the disappearance of the bullet line.

The slide of the pistol pointed at her head was locked in the rear position. This phenomenon was a reproduction of what happened to automatic pistols in the real world; it indicated a failure to reload or a lack of ammo.

In this case, it was the latter. The woman had shot too many times. Against the light of the sky, Llenn saw the woman, leg still in pinning position, drop the empty magazine from her pistol and reach to her left thigh for a pouch. She was clearly going to reload

with a fresh clip, and if she succeeded, there would surely be a hail of a dozen bullets upon Llenn's head soon.

*Yeah, I can't let that happen. But how do I do that? What can I do?*

Llenn used the one weapon she had. She reached for her thigh pouch with her free left hand, pulled out the long P90 magazine, and threw it as hard as she could. "Taaa!"

The heavy magazine, laden with bullets, struck the woman's hand.

"Wha—?!" Her pistol magazine was knocked loose, and it fell off the rock to the ground.

"Try one more!" Llenn pulled out her second magazine and chucked it at the woman's face this time. The elongated container struck her eye from the side.

"Eeek!" she screamed, a rather cute outburst that accentuated the fact that the player was a girl. That succeeded at loosening the pressure of her foot. Llenn shoved with her arm as hard as she could. The large woman's leg buckled, and she started falling backward. "Urgh!"

But she merely teetered, then regained her balance. Llenn rolled to her left and leaped to her feet immediately, pointing the P90 with her freed arm at the woman about six feet away.

"Taaa!" she yelled, holding the trigger to blast every last bullet into her.

*Brrrrrrrrrrrrrrrr.* The dozen-plus remaining bullets burst forward all at once.

Only the first five shots landed, hitting the woman's left arm and hand.

"Huh?" Llenn was stunned.

She couldn't have imagined that anyone would do what the woman just did.

Realizing that there was no escape from that distance, she had plunged forward instead, reaching out with her left arm for the P90's muzzle. She grabbed the end of the gun as it was still firing and shoved it away from her body, forcing all the remaining shots down to the ground below.

And then they paused, a dramatic pose atop the boulder: Llenn with her P90 outstretched, and the large woman with the end of the gun squeezed in her hand.

"D-doesn't it hurt?" Llenn asked. The game was nowhere near as painful as real life, but all those holes in her arm should've made the physical sensation rather unpleasant.

The large woman, arm and hand glowing red with damage indicators, said rather pleasantly, "When you're amped up enough, you barely notice it. I just can't grip that hard... What's your name, little one?"

"Llenn. How about you?"

"Eva. But everyone else just calls me Boss."

Llenn pulled, trying to yank the P90 out of the large woman's hand. Boss held strong, despite the numbness in her arm. If she hadn't been hit there by those bullets, she'd have pried the P90 out long ago.

They rocked and trembled in the anguish of a battle of strength. Their legs worked, almost in a kind of dance, as they turned around on top of the boulder, trying to seize a better position and leverage.

Llenn tried to reach for her right leg pouch with her left arm but didn't have the freedom of movement. If she could have pulled out the magazine there, she might've been able to stick it into the P90.

"You're out of ammo," Boss said, wearing a demonic smile.

Llenn wondered what her own expression was. "So are you."

Her opponent still held the empty pistol in her right hand and was unable to load it again with her left hand holding the SMG. But if time kept passing, Boss's left hand would eventually regain its strength, putting Llenn at a disadvantage.

Then an even more significant disadvantage arose.

"Boss!"

Out of the corner of her right eye, Llenn saw a woman with a machine gun standing atop a rock about twenty yards away. But

though the stout woman had her PKM pointed right at Llenn, she couldn't fire. "Shit!"

It was clear that if she opened fire, she would hit her boss, too.

"Just fire!" Boss yelled back. That gave the woman the determination to blast both enemy and ally—but she still needed to lift the machine gun higher so that she could get a better aim.

The span of less than two seconds—the time it took her to haul it up from her waist to her shoulder—was all it took to expose her.

Llenn clearly saw the sparks explode from the right side of the machine gun that was pointed at them. There was a *gwang* sound of metal scraping, and the direction of the gun jolted to the left.

It had to be M's lineless sniping.

A second shot hit the faltering woman in her right side, creating a bright splash on her body.

"Urgh!" She fell to her knee, unable to stand, and reached for her right holster while she was a sitting duck for a potential third shot. It was originally Tanya's gun, a Strizh like Boss's. She pulled the magazine out of the gun and, with all the strength she had left, hurled it.

"Use this!"

The magazine left her hand right at the moment M's shot pierced her head.

Her lifeless body and the machine gun toppled onto the rock. A DEAD marker appeared over her.

The magazine hurtled through the air, rotating slowly, as it proceeded toward the two with admirable precision.

As she watched it, Llenn thought, *If she grabs that with her free hand, sticks it in the pistol, and shoots me, how many seconds will that take? How many tenths of a second?* It was obvious that this was what Boss would try to do.

But it was also an opportunity. Once she took her left hand off, Llenn could switch hands on the P90, reach into her right pocket for the magazine, and switch it out. At that point, it would simply be a battle of speed.

But Llenn felt confident. She had top-level agility, dexterity—and so much practice with exchanging clips.

*I can do it! I can win!*

She kept the tension in her right arm, increasing her chances of pulling it free from Boss's left.

"That's not going to work, little one," said the other woman with a grin, flexing harder with the arm that was now regaining strength.

*Can it be?*

When she imagined what Boss was trying to do, she doubted the woman's sanity. It was impossible.

The magazine flew closer. Boss held the base of the pistol in the direction of the oncoming clip, then turned it just a bit.

*Can it be? Is she really?*

She tilted the pistol to match the rotation of the hurtling magazine—

*No way!*

And it clicked neatly into the base.

Boss lowered the switch on the slide stop, allowing the slide to return to its original position with a fresh bullet loaded.

Llenn couldn't help but wonder who these people were in real life. After that tremendous juggling demonstration, the only thing she could think of was some kind of street performer. The extremely beside-the-point adage "An audience is obliged to give a little money to the performer once they've seen the act" passed through her brain.

At last, Boss took her hand off the P90. Llenn's constant tugging caused her to topple backward without the counterbalancing force. Boss's right hand swung the pistol down toward her stomach.

"Eat..."

Boss's mouth, and everything else—

"...this..."

—seemed to move—

"...hot..."

—in slow motion.

"...lead!"

*Well, that's that. I'm really dying now—can't remember how many times it's been today, but this is the end, for good.*

But then she thought she heard a voice say, "Don't give up, Llenn! I'll keep you safe!"

Scratch that—she definitely heard it.

Boss pulled the Strizh's trigger with abandon, aiming at the stomach of the small target before her.

She was merciless—all sixteen bullets shot into the stomach rather than the chest. The pistol let out a staccato burst like a submachine gun, the cartridges discharging in a brief arc all at once.

"How do you like me now?!" shouted Boss, assured of her triumph.

The little pink target disappeared into the haze of gun smoke. Boss didn't assume anything—she dropped that clip, reached for the backup she'd been unable to grab earlier, and prepared to jam it into the Strizh.

"Huh?"

The silhouette stopped her in her tracks.

"How could you—?"

The shrimp dressed in pink was alive. After all the shots she'd taken to the gut.

"How could you—?"

And she was roaring like from the depths of Hell.

"How could youuuuuu—?"

Then the smoke cleared, and Boss saw her opponent, still alive, holding the tattered, mutilated remains of the pink-dyed P90.

"My P-chaaaaaaaaaaaan!"

She didn't understand what that meant.

Llenn had to wonder why she'd used P-chan as a shield.

She thought that since you couldn't randomly drop your weapon

upon death in the Squad Jam, there was no chance of losing your favorite weapon. But as in all things, there were exceptions.

For one, and it was truly a long shot, it was possible for a gun to take enough direct damage in combat to surpass its durability rating, rendering it irreparable—in other words, lost forever.

*I knew that. I understood it—and yet, I used it as a shield.*

*To not die. To win the game.*

*And I didn't die.*

*But P-chan did.*

"How could you, how could you, how could youuuu?!"

*Yeah, I'm definitely going to kill her.*

"My P-chaaaaaaaaan!"

Taken aback by the furious little girl with the bloodshot eyes, Boss paused in the act of reloading her Strizh. The pieces of the P90 crumbled apart and fell onto the boulder.

"I see... So you guarded yourself with that. Incredible!" she raved. Then she finished inserting the fresh clip and closed the slide.

*Compliments don't make me feel any better, so yeah, I'm still gonna kill her.*

The day a while back when Karen had run across those cute little high schoolers, she'd had to stifle the desire to shoot them all. But now there was no need to hide that urge. Now was the time to give in to it.

Llenn watched Boss preparing to fire again and thought, *I don't have any weapons left, but I can still bite her. I wonder, which part of her should I bite that will actually damage her health?*

As a matter of fact, M had mentioned something about that. When had that been? On Friday?

No. It was today. In fact, it had been less than *two hours* ago.

And then she remembered what he'd handed her.

The moment Boss pointed the pistol at her head, Llenn stared the bullet line down and leaped.

*        *        *

"You little—!"

Boss fired the Strizh at Llenn when she came charging. But the tiny, speedy target evaded her shot, slid through her legs, and vanished. She spun around, holding the Strizh close to keep it from being stripped away. "Don't even think about it! You can't escape from—"

Then the world tilted a bit. She couldn't tense her left foot the way she wanted.

"Wha…?"

She noticed her hit point gauge was dropping precipitously. When she looked down at her left thigh, she understood. There was a very long bullet effect—no, not a bullet effect. That was a long, long slash.

*I got sliced?*

Then she looked up and again saw her opponent charging at her.

"Shaaa!"

This time, she brandished a wicked black knife pointed downward.


"Shit!"

Tohma had been watching the two fight atop the rock for quite a while now. She was lying prone on top of a boulder just fifty yards away, Dragunov aimed and ready. But this rifle didn't have a scope. It had broken off and fallen next to the rock, shattering its lens. She'd climbed the rock to find the enemy sniper's location, and for just an instant, she'd caught sight of the target aiming back at her as he fired. She had seen the rifle's muzzle flare, even though there had been no bullet line.

The next moment, she'd seen nothing through the scope. Only when she had fallen off the rock, as though pushed by the gun itself, had she understood. The bullet had hit the scope rather than her, rendering it useless.

His accuracy and speed had given her chills, but on the other hand, she was still alive. She'd quickly taken off the scope and

the cheek pad used when peering through it and cried, "I'm not done yet!"

Instead, she had poked her head low around a different, small rock and used the ordinary metallic sights attached to the Dragunov to aim as she tried to help Boss. When the pink shrimp had gotten kicked onto the rock, Tohma had immediately taken aim but had to call it off when Boss leaped up immediately after.

"Ugh!"

With a scope, she could pick an individual finger off a target at fifty yards, but normal sights weren't nearly as easy to use. Instead, Tohma just had to lie in wait and watch as the two fought their battle to the death. If she fired, it was likely she'd hit Boss, who was a much larger target. Even if she hit the shrimp, it could certainly pierce her and hurt Boss anyway.

Tohma didn't want the bullet line to be a distraction, so she'd kept her finger off the trigger, removing her bullet circle. Her period of passive observation had dragged on and on—until Boss caught the clip from their teammate and started firing. Then she knew the battle was won.

Surely she couldn't have enough HP to survive a barrage of point-blank bullets like that. And yet…

"H-how? Is she a zombieee?!"

The sight of the little pink combatant moving again had caused Tohma's heart to leap into her throat with terror.

"Taaaa!" Llenn plunged forward.

"I don't think so!" Boss fired but missed again.

Llenn slipped past it like evading a punch, charging straight for her legs and slipping through them, slashing the femoral artery along the way.

"Rrgh!" This one hit Boss's right thigh, causing another drop in HP. That put her in the yellow zone.

*This is a swordfight now!* Boss finally realized. She had a gun, but this was no longer a gun battle. She recalled the footage of

the third Bullet of Bullets. For whatever reason, there had been a battle right at the end between swords in that event, too.

Her pink foe with the knife could see the bullet line coming from the Strizh. Once she knew where the bullet was going to be, it was a simple matter of evading the line, as though it were a sword of its own. On top of that, her opponent was far more agile.

She was a big target swinging a long sword, while the other combatant was a small target with a short-reach knife that could strike from any direction without warning.

*In that case...*

Boss swung her arm, changing tactics.

After her second swoop through the legs, Llenn thought, *Just once more! Or as many times as it takes!*

She spun around, watching for the bullet line coming from the pistol in Boss's hand. *I just have to dodge that. As long as it doesn't touch my body, I can't get shot.*

Llenn had been through so many battles up to this point that there was no second-guessing anymore. The only drive in her mind was to avenge P-chan. But when she started her third charge with the knife...

*Huh?*

Boss was switching her grip on the pistol. She gripped the front of the gun with her left hand and let go with the right.

"Yaaaah!" She pulled back to swing. Using the pistol like a hammer.

There was no stopping Llenn's charge once she started it. And without the bullet line as an indicator, she didn't know where the pistol-whipping would come from until just before it happened. And by the time she saw that it was coming for her hand, it was already too late to lower her arm or pull it back.

*If it hits my knife, it's all over.*

She opened her right hand as far as it could go. The butt of the pistol smashed her wrist, making an ugly bone-crunching sound.

The impact smacked her right arm outward. The system recognized this as bone-breaking damage and set her wrist glowing as the hit point bar dropped again. It was down to 10 percent.

*I knocked the knife away!* Boss thought.

But then she saw it floating in the space between her and Llenn—followed by Llenn's left hand reaching for it and grabbing the handle.

*Oh! She let go of the knife before I hit her!* she realized, impressed. She couldn't help it. "Ha-ha!"

Spontaneous laughter leaked out of her.

With the knife held backhand with a firm grip, Llenn hopped off the ground.

"Taaa!"

She swiped from left to right, across the thick neck of the smiling head.

Llenn's feet hit the ground as the large woman fell, DEAD tag above Boss's body.

"Damn you!" Tohma no longer had any reason to hesitate. She raised herself up off the rock and placed her finger on the Dragunov's trigger, summoning the bullet circle. When it was entirely contained with the little target's body, she pulled.

"Die."

"Get down!" screamed a voice in Llenn's left ear. Her body reacted before her brain could.

She flattened herself against the rock just as the Dragunov bullet screamed, barely inches over her head.

"Eeeep!" she shrieked.

The roar of the Dragunov sounded, and then she heard a voice say, "Over here, bad guy!" and a trio of loud shots. She tilted her head to look in the direction of these shots.

"Uh…M?"

There was M, standing proud against the sky atop a rock about 150 meters away. The figure was small at that distance, but the proportions and camo color couldn't be anyone else.

"Watch out, M! Get down! If you die, you're dead, remember?" But M didn't respond.

"Very bold of you!"

Tohma got to her feet. She bared her teeth; pointed the Dragunov at the man who stood, challenging her to hit him; and placed the bullet circle on his wide torso.

The two snipers stared each other down at a distance of just 200 meters, guns at the ready.

They fired simultaneously.

The bullets sped toward each other and then past.

Each landed in the midriff of its target.

Two bodies fell onto rock.

Llenn clearly saw the larger one collapse.

There was a loud, flashy musical fanfare, and a huge message appeared in the sky, reading:

CONGRATULATIONS!!! WINNER: LM!

Llenn raced toward the area where M had been, looking for his body after he'd been shot.

"Aaaah!"

She spotted him lying facedown on the ground.

"M— Aaaaaaaaaagh!" she screamed, noticing that his head was turned around 180 degrees. M's face was on the same side of his body as his backpack was. His eyes turned and glared at her.

"Eeegyaaaaaaaaaa!"

She was so shocked, she almost thought it was going to knock out her last HP and kill her.

"You don't have to freak out like that. What's the big idea?"

"Aaaaah! He talked! He's a ghoooooooooost!"

"Who is?"

"You're a ghoooooooooost!"

"What are you talking about?"

Then M raised himself up off his stomach.

"Gyaaaaaa— Huh?"

In the middle of her scream, Llenn finally noticed that there was actually nothing wrong with the direction of M's face or his limbs. It wasn't his head that was backward; it was his backpack. He had it over his stomach rather than his back, and there was a little bullet hole right in the middle of it.

"O-oh… You used it to guard yourself," Llenn murmured as the triumphant background music continued blaring.

"Yeah, well… I really didn't want to die," M mumbled.


The total game time was 1:28.

The first Squad Jam was over.

Winning team: LM.

Total number of bullets fired: 49,810.

# CHAPTER 14
## Postgame Review

SECT.14

# CHAPTER 14
## Postgame Review

Light surrounded Llenn and M, and they appeared back in the original waiting area.

A glowing CHAMPIONS! sign hung overhead in the cramped room. Under it were the full team results, including the time stamp when each team was wiped out or had surrendered.

At the top was their team: LM.

Below that was SHINC. Llenn didn't know what that was supposed to mean, but they were certainly a formidable opponent.

After that point, Llenn stopped reading. She glanced at herself instead. The fatigues that had been coated in gravel and sand just a moment ago were fresh and new again. The knit cap that had fallen off in battle was placed at her feet.

"P-chan…"

But the gun that had been destroyed was nowhere to be seen. Not even a piece—nothing usable was left.

"Bye-bye…," she mumbled.

"Yeah," her partner sighed, sitting down with a thump. It felt like the earth itself shook, though that obviously wasn't the case.

"Good job, M. We survived."

"Y-yeah…"

M took off his boonie hat and raised his head. When she first met him, Llenn had thought he was like a real-life grizzly bear, but at this point he was more of a teddy bear to her.

He swung his left hand to call up the menu and unequipped nearly all his gear. The M14 EBR he'd used to take down so many foes, the backpack that had saved him from many bullets, and the HK45 he'd shot at Llenn with all disappeared, one after the other.

When it was done, he was just another big tough guy, wearing camo pants and a T-shirt.

Following his lead, Llenn brought out her robe and then undid her equipment once she was covered, so that she emerged in her usual inconspicuous green outfit.

An enormous numerical countdown appeared in the space before her, starting at 110. Below that was a message: THE SQUAD JAM HAS CONCLUDED. WILL YOU LOG OUT, OR RETURN TO THE PUB? IF NO ACTION IS TAKEN, PLAYER WILL BE SENT TO THE PUB.

Back at the pub, Llenn would be the champion. No doubt she would be the focus of attention and questions from all the people who'd been watching the event live.

"I think…I've played enough. I'm really tired," Llenn said, selecting the log-out option, which brought up a confirmation prompt.

"I'm tired…too…and I'm not good with cheers and applause, so I'll log off," M said.

"You're a lot more reserved in real life, aren't you, M?"

"Huh? Oh…yeah. To be honest, it's hard to act tough and gruff like this… I prefer just being myself."

"Well, either way, you survived, right?"

"Y-yeah… Um…so…well…," he stammered, looking bashful.

"And why did you save me at the end?" she asked, almost teasingly.

"Because I was safe," he answered. It was so straightforward and shallow that she couldn't help but roll her eyes.

"Well, if Pito's so scary in real life, this result should satisfy her!" Llenn encouraged him. "All's well that ends well!"

"I—I sure hope so…"

Llenn didn't know how the two were related, and she had no idea what to make of this letter about killing him in real life. But whatever the answer might be, Pitohui couldn't complain about him surviving and winning the event. That was a huge prize. And speaking of prizes…

"Oh yeah. We won the event…so what did we get?"

She recalled what the rule book for the Squad Jam tournament had said: The top three teams got some kind of prize. It just didn't say what.

Since this wasn't a huge thing like the BoB, just a personally sponsored event, she assumed it probably wasn't worth getting excited about—and Llenn never thought they'd wind up in the top three anyway, so she hadn't given it much thought.

"Huh? Oh…the prize…," M said, without much enthusiasm, either. "Since I survived…I don't really need anything else."

Choosing to be magnanimous, Llenn agreed, "Yes, there's no greater prize than life."

"If I had to guess…it's probably like the BoB, where they'll send you a catalog afterward."

"Kind of like a wedding gift bag, I suppose. Speaking of which, I wonder if Pito's getting anything at her event."

"Maybe."

"Do you suppose one of the options in that catalog is a P90…?" Llenn wondered, knowing the answer already.

"Probably not. Not in either one," M replied.

"Yeah…"

Several seconds of silence passed.

"Well, I'm going to log off. We'll have to reconvene for a post-event meeting later."

"Y-yeah."

"Say hi to Pito for me!"

Llenn hit the YES button on the confirmation prompt.

\* \* \*

Karen saw the ceiling of her room through the clear visor of the AmuSphere. The next sensation she felt was the smell of abundant sweat. Then her weight against the bed, followed by the sticky cling of damp pajamas.

"Euuugh," she groaned as she got up and took off the AmuSphere.

"..."

The room was empty. The color of the sunset sky over Tokyo was just as red as in *GGO*. It cast a dim, dying light through the curtains. Karen got up slowly and took a few steps, then saw the black P90 on display in the corner of the living room.

"..."

She picked it up and held it in front of her stomach. Then she looked in the mirror. The black gun wasn't big enough to cover her whole stomach, leaving the pale-yellow fabric visible around it.

"..."

Karen lifted the P90.

"..."

She propped it against her shoulder.

"..."

She took aim at the tall girl with the long black hair in the mirror.

Then she took a breath and exclaimed, "Bang!"

She turned on her heel and walked to the bed, crouched down to where her smartphone was placed on its charging stand, and turned it on, gun still in hand. She brought up one of the numbers in her contact list and called it immediately.

When someone picked up the phone on the other end, she said, "Hello, my name is Kohiruimaki. Do you have room for an appointment tomorrow?"

\*　　　\*　　　\*

"I wonder what we did wrong."

"Yeah. What did we do wrong?"

"Stop repeating yourselves. And obviously *something* was wrong."

"Don't be idiots, you guys! Let's be constructive. Also, we lost, and that's that. Let's accept it for what it is."

"Yeah. Man, I shot so many bullets, though."

"Yeah, so did I. God, it feels good to shoot so much with a machine gun."

"You wanna enter the next Squad Jam, if they do one?"

"Yeah!"

"No shit!"

"Of course we will. But I'd rather last longer next time. I mean, the longer you go, the more you get to shoot."

"Agreed."

"No objections here."

"Good! Then we train until that point!"

"Training…? Yeah, I guess that makes sense. I'm in."

"So what's the plan?"

"You don't know? We all raise our strength, obviously."

"And then?"

"We get it to the max value, and then hold two guns at the same time! Forget dual-wielding pistols—dual-wield some frickin' machine guns, man! That's double the firepower! *Double!*"

\*       \*       \*

It was just after nine AM on Monday, February 2nd, 2026.

In a room at Hyakuri Air Base in Ibaraki Prefecture, two men were holding a meeting.

One was a man in his forties with an easygoing face and the insignia of a major on his Air Self-Defense Force uniform. He was seated with his elbows on a table.

"So that's what I can report today, broad as it might be," said the other man, who stood before him. "I'll have a full report with all members' experiences within two days."

The lower officer was a man in his twenties with sharp features and a first lieutenant's badge.

The major nodded a number of times and said, "Understood. I'll be looking forward to that. So let's speak frankly now. What did you think?"

The first lieutenant replied, "Sir, I would say that for better and for worse, it was a game."

"All right. Let's hear the bad part first."

"There were a number of points where the enemies and their movements were very specific to the game, and unlikely to give useful real-life feedback. And in particular, it makes aiming and shooting easier than it really is, which could lead to sloppiness."

"I see. And the good points?"

"Well, sir, I lost four subordinates due to my own mistake, but right now, they're all laughing about it."

After the first lieutenant left the room with cap in hand, the major reached for the phone on his desk. Once the person on the other end of the line picked up, he said, "Some of my boys took part, as we planned."

Then he briefly went over what the first lieutenant had told him, adding at the end, "Does that help you at all, Mr. Kikuoka?"

✳     ✳     ✳

Tuesday, February 3rd, just before four o'clock.

"Whaaat?!"

On the grounds of the women's college, one of the high schoolers passing by Karen shouted at her. Screamed, in fact.

She didn't know their names, but she knew their faces. It was the group of six cute, tiny teenagers she always passed on campus with their sports bags, one being Caucasian.

After the first one screamed, the other five each exclaimed in their own way.

"Huh?" Karen was taken aback by the sudden attention.

Before she could figure out what it was they were alarmed by, the smallest of the six, with her hair done in black braids, trotted over and asked, "Um, e-excuse me! Y-you're the older girl we always pass by, right?"

Still confused as to why they were talking to her, Karen said, "Uh, yes, that's right…"

"Did you cut your hair?"

"Uh…"

Now she understood. She tilted her head, and the black hair that she'd shorn off to be as short as Llenn's swayed and bounced. "Yeah. I got a haircut yesterday."

The other five girls crowded around her as the first one positively exploded, "It's beautiful! You look so cool!"

"I…I do…?" Karen mumbled, overwhelmed by the tiny girls.

"We always talk about how tall and cool you look, just like a model, every time we pass by you! We're so jealous—you always look good in whatever you wear! I mean, we're all so short, you know? I liked your long hair, but this way looks so much better on you!"

"Uh…uh, th-thanks…"

"I wish I was taller like you! But I just haven't grown any more!"

"Oh really? I've always hated being tall. But about two days ago, I just decided it didn't matter anymore."

"H-how'd you just get over it like that?"

"W-well…I guess I was tackling something that day that was so tough, I felt like I was going to die multiple times. I realized that if you just refuse to give up, people can do some pretty extraordinary things."

"Wow, that's just… Wow!"

One of the girls in the back reached forward to pat the braided girl on the back. "Doesn't this feel good, Boss? You got to talk to her!"

"Boss...?" Karen repeated.

The teenager with the braided hair grinned back at her. "It's a weird nickname, right? It's because I'm the captain of the team." She bowed and continued, "I'm Saki Nitobe! I'm in my second year at the high school here! I'm the captain of the gymnastics team, and these are all team members. Two are in the same year as me, and three are first-years. This one is Russian, and her name is Milana Sidorova."

The five girls gave her very sporty introductions, and Karen bowed back. "Hello. I'm Karen Kohiruimaki, freshman in college."

"Karen? What a beautiful name."

"Thanks. It's nice to meet you, Saki."

"Thank you so much! Well, we have to go to practice now, but if you don't mind, is it all right if we say hello when we see you again?"

"Of course. We always pass by each other, don't we?"

"Thank you. Well, good-bye!"

All the girls bowed together with the force of athletes and the grace of gymnasts, and Karen waved a hand.

"So long."

As they happily passed by, Karen murmured, "There's no way..." to herself. Then she turned back in the direction she'd been going. The miniature pink P90 charm, now attached to her bag, smacked against it. When she had taken about ten steps, short hair bouncing, she heard quiet footsteps approaching.

"Um...Karen?"

She turned around and looked down to see Saki Nitobe staring up at her, eyes full of intent.

"Do you mind if I shake your hand?"

"Huh? Of course not."

Saki held out her right hand, and Karen clasped it. Instantly, the little hand squeezed hard.

"Congrats on your victory. But we'll win the next time, little one."

And upon hearing the pleasure in Saki's voice, Karen realized that her hunch from a moment ago was correct, and she grinned back.

"I'll take you on anytime, giantess."

They let go, then slapped their open palms.

It made a crisp, pleasing sound under the wintry Tokyo sky.

The same day, after ten PM, somewhere in Tokyo, the city skyline shone through the window of a pitch-black room.

Inside, a young woman's voice said, "Awww! This sucks, this sucks, this sucks! I wanted to take part in a hard-boiled battle to the death!"

A young man tried to console her. "You don't have to be that upset. It's not like *GGO* itself is over…"

"But you had so much fun fighting in there, darling, and you survived the ordeal, too… Why couldn't I participate? Why, why, why, why?!"

Between each outburst, there was a sound like a person being hit, combined with a brief shriek from the man.

"Because…you already had plans…"

"Why?"

*"Guhg!"*

Another loud impact, and the man had clearly doubled over.

"The little one sure was incredible, though," the girl said rapturously. "I could tell she was special from the absolutely stable core she had from the first time we met, but I didn't expect *this* kind of mobility… I guess there really are people who are born with an innate genius for VR games. I'm so jealous."

The man said nothing. She continued, "And now she's developed a talent for combat. So tough, so tough. I wonder what sort of body she's got in real life? What kind of girl is she? I'm so curious. Aren't you curious?"

"…"

He didn't answer and got socked a few more times.

*"Gahk! Guh! Gnf!"*

"Ugh, this sucks! This sucks, this sucks! Next time! They just have to hold another one! Squad Jam Number Two! I mean, you guys turned it into quite a finish! I bet that insane writer earned a lot of cred after this time! Surely they'll consider holding a second one!"

"M-maybe…"

"And then—"

Another blow. *"Hrng!"*

"I don't care what's on my schedule—I'll tear through them to participate! You too, darling! Orders from the top! And once we're in there, we'll go crazy and fight and fight and fight and fight and fight and fight and fight—"

"And…what's the plan?"

"Isn't it obvious? To die!"

*To be continued…*

# AFTERWORD

Hello to all 900 million residents of Japan! I am your author, Keiichi Sigsawa.

What's that? There aren't that many people in Japan? I've got my numbers wrong?

Listen, I was a liberal arts major.

Now, I would like to thank you for picking up this book, titled *Sword Art Online Alternative Gun Gale Online, Vol. 1: Squad Jam*.

The title isn't as long as my current original series, *I'm a High School Student and Popular Light Novel Author, but I'm Being Strangled by My Younger Voice Actress Classmate: Time to Play*, but it's still a pretty long title.

We don't have an official abbreviated version of that yet, so feel free to call it *Sword Art Online Alternative Gun Gale Online, Vol. 1: Squad J*, or *SAOAGGO1SJ*, or *SwArOnAlGuGaOn1SqJa*, or *Squid Jam*, or *Keiichi Sigsawa's Latest Hobby Project*, or whatever you like.

This is where the afterword of the book starts.

As you all surely know, it is a rule in the Sigsawa dynasty that there shall be no spoilers here. Read ahead without fear of ruining the story.

Incidentally, I am the first and last generation of the Sigsawa dynasty.

As the title suggests, this is a spin-off of the *Sword Art Online* series. *SAO* is one of the most popular and successful light novel series published by Dengeki Bunko in Japan.

It's a story set in the near future, where virtual reality games can simulate all the senses directly to the brain, and our hero, Kirito; heroine, Asuna; and a cast of wonderful characters have adventures together.

It's written by Reki Kawahara and illustrated by abec.

For more information, you can check out the (Japanese) official site at http://www.swordart-online.net/ if you're interested.

I get the sense that if I describe it any further, I'll get something wrong. Also, someone's probably going to yell at me for padding out my afterword.

As for this book, it uses the background of the *SAO* series and the game environment within it as the setting for an entirely original Keiichi Sigsawa story and cast of characters.

In other words, this is not a book where you'll see Kirito or any other *SAO* series regular. This is very important to me. I wanted to make it very clear, even if that's technically a kind of spoiler, so I'm letting you know here.

Furthermore, the setting for this story is the VR online game *Gun Gale Online* (*GGO*), which appears in the Phantom Bullet arc (Volumes 5 and 6) of the main *SAO* series. It's not a fantasy game with swords and magic spells but a science-fiction shooter RPG full of guns.

As a gun fanatic myself, I remember reading the Phantom Bullet arc in August of 2010 and writhing with frustrated agony. *Aaah, that was so good! And...why didn't I think of this setting?! I could have used this to write any number of stories featuring*

*gun action without having to kill off characters! And I can actu-*
*ally make a modern Japanese person the protagonist!*

Once I was done flopping my limbs in frustration, I came to
a realization: *I want to write a novel set in the world of SAO, in*
*the game of GGO! I want to take it seriously! And then I want*
*to publish it! I could do it on my own, of course, but I'd prefer to*
*get official permission and have Kouhaku Kuroboshi illustrate it*
*and have Dengeki Bunko publish it!*

It was a nice idea, but I had no clue if it was feasible. There was
no precedent for this sort of thing.

*Probably not gonna work out, is it?* I thought, practically giving up before I even tried. Can you blame me? No, nobody could.

But eventually I figured, since I had the idea, I might as well
float it by the appropriate people. A little while later, I suggested
the idea of a spin-off to my novel editor. To my shock, after
contacting Kawahara, abec, and the various people in charge, I
received word that it was very much on the table.

"Okay, I'll write one someday!" I swore, but then it didn't happen. I got busy writing other books, and time flew by.

Just when it seemed likely that no idea would ever materialize,
the push that my ambitions needed came from the second season
of the *SAO* anime.

The second season showed the *GGO* arc. I ran into an anime
producer, Oosawa, at an event, and I was asked about some
gun-related research for the second season. Oosawa wanted the
anime staff to have the chance to shoot some guns and asked if
I knew a place that would help with that. (As a matter of fact,
Oosawa was also a producer on the 2003 *Kino's Journey* TV
series. Who could have guessed that the old *Kino* anime would
play a part in all this?)

I told them about a good shooting range to visit in Guam and
accompanied them on the trip. Eventually, they asked me whether
I should just officially join the production in exchange for proper
compensation.

And that's how I became the supervisor of firearm material on the second season of *Sword Art Online*. So what did that actually entail?

In this case, they asked me questions about the guns and situations in the story, and I gave my thoughts and suggestions. I also snuck some model guns into the studio that I thought might be useful for the animators.

Once they had the script, storyboards, and animation stages done, I would look over each one and check for any major errors, aside from scenes where a specific and intentional gun effect was desired.

It was a very fun job. It was the first time I ever had my name in an anime's ending credits where it wasn't listed as "based on the novels by…"

While supervising that project, I got myself in a tizzy and went to beg my series editor, Kawahara, and Kawahara's editor, "If I'm going to do that *GGO* spin-off I've always been mulling over, now's the time, while I'm involved in the *SAO* series! This is it! I'll write it, so please let me do it!"

And now you're reading the afterword of the result!

That was the grand, sweeping historical context for the creation of this series. Gosh, we've been through so much.

I suspect this is the first time Dengeki Bunko has ever published a spin-off of another Dengeki Bunko series. I must take this opportunity to express my heartfelt thanks to Reki Kawahara for the blessing and supervision of the end result.

Thank you so much!

After this book was first announced, there were many people on Twitter and such asking, "Do I need to understand *SAO* to get this book?" so I'd like to give them a serious answer here.

Essentially, I wrote this in such a way that you can enjoy this book without having read any of the original *SAO* novels or even seen the anime series.

However! I believe that if you read up through Volume 6 of *SAO* (the Phantom Bullet arc) or watch the entire first season of the anime and up through Episode 14 of season 2, you will enjoy this book much more! *SAO* is great, and I recommend you check it out!

So that's how you came to hold this VR-game gun action novel with every last ounce of Sigsawa's firearm obsession contained within it.

I'd like to thank my longtime illustration partner Kouhaku Kuroboshi for yet another adorable protagonist design!

I hope you enjoy the world's first "Dengeki Bunko spin-off Dengeki Bunko"!

That's it from me.

Keiichi Sigsawa—December 10th, 2014

Hello! This is Kouhaku Kuroboshi. I tried my best so that nobody says something like, "Mr. Sigsawa supervised the firearms on the *Sword Art Online II* anime, and yet Kouhaku Kuroboshi can't draw guns at all."
Basically, I tried to hide them behind bodies as much as possible...